LOVE POTION NUMBER 99

A TOUCH OF MAGIC
BOOK 1

DAPHNE JAMES HUFF

PROLOGUE

The dog was happy, but he was the only one. The two humans were both yelling.

He knew one of the humans. There was his human, who fed him and played with him, and taught him tricks. His human was a happy guy, most of the time. Sometimes he got sad, and the dog would lick his hand or his face and get a few cuddles and then the man didn't seem so sad.

Right now, though, his human was mad. Even madder than the time the dog had peed inside the house.

The man's red face was turned toward a woman standing on the stairs of the big house. She was holding the delicious leaves in her hands the dog had been digging up a few minutes ago. "He's a puppy. These kinds of things happen."

"They don't when there's a fence." Her face was red too, but the dog could sense that underneath the anger, she was sad. Really sad. The dog whined and wanted to go lick her hand, but he'd learned that if he stayed by his human's side, he'd get a treat.

"It's been a busy few weeks. I haven't had time for—"

"What you don't have time for is taking care of this dog." She shook the delicious flowers, and the dog whined again, this time loud enough for both humans to look at him. "See? He's clearly miserable and mistreated. No wonder he ran over here."

"That's not what happened. He snuck out and . . ."

The two humans kept yelling. The dog lay down, then put his head on his paws. The little sigh he let out didn't seem to get any attention.

He liked the man. He took great care of him. It wasn't the man's fault he'd run over here. The dog liked sneaking out the back door. It was fun. Digging was fun. Listening to humans yell wasn't very fun.

What might be more fun than this? The dog raised his head, an idea storming into his brain the way they always did. If he ran back to the man's house, they could play! This was the best idea ever, just like all of his ideas.

"Lucky! Come back!"

The man was following! This was great.

Lucky turned back to make sure his human continued to follow, then stopped. The woman standing on the porch looked so sad. She wasn't yelling anymore, just staring at the flowers with tears running down her cheeks. Sometimes when his human did that, Lucky would lick them off. They tasted funny, but it always made the man smile.

When he tried to run to her, however, the man had his hand on his collar.

"That's enough, Lucky. You're supposed to be on a leash whenever we go outside." The man tugged on the collar and Lucky struggled for a minute, trying to get to the woman.

"No, we're going home. Leave the angry woman's yard alone."

Lucky barked. *She's not angry*, he wanted to say.

Lucky knew he was an important dog. He was supposed to help people. This woman needed help. Couldn't his human see that?

Maybe Lucky would have another chance soon, he hoped, as the man led him back into the house.

ONE

BROOKE

Eleven months later

Just follow your plan and everything will be fine.

A familiar knot twisted around Brooke's heart as the earthy smoothie coated her tongue. Her nose wrinkled. The recipe still wasn't right.

Looking around the room for ideas, her eyes landed on the window overlooking the backyard her grandmother had spent decades filling with plants. Brooke's long-simmering anger rose in a wave. She pulled her gaze away and set her glass on the pristine counter before she was tempted to throw it out the window.

Today's plan was simple. Make her smoothie, get dressed, meet with the board. None of that should be difficult.

Except she was already stalled on step one. The mixture lacked the zing that made Gran's smoothies special. It needed something, but the turmeric that would have made the drink perfect had been decimated by her neighbor's dog a year ago. Two replacement plants hadn't grown at all, like the ground was now cursed

Brooke double checked the notebook laid out on the counter, her knotted heart pinching even tighter at the familiar scrawl of Gran's handwriting, then she lined up the possible substitute ingredients. None of them would give her exactly what she needed right now, but she might as well try a few.

Mint would help settle her stomach.

Lemon balm would improve her mood.

Garlic would intensify the potion.

Her bitter chuckle echoed in the empty kitchen. Curses and magic potions. Gran would be thrilled.

"It's a smoothie, not a magic potion." Her words echoed in the immaculate, sun-dappled kitchen, as if daring Gran to come back from the dead to smile and wag her finger at Brooke's stubborn disbelief.

As a girl, Brooke had been willing to accept her grandmother's smoothies were magic. As an adult, the painful truth was that magic didn't exist.

But just in case, she added some lemon balm to the smoothie. The last thing she needed today was for her rotten mood to leave a bad impression on the animal shelter's board of directors. The vote this morning was legally required, but there was no risk of it ending any other way than officially making Brooke the executive director. It was the last thing she wanted, but after everything that had happened over the past year, this was her chance to start making it right.

To make her grandmother proud.

The doorbell rang, barely audible over the whirring of the blender, but Brooke was expecting it. Next, the door opened without her needing to answer, and a chipper voice called out, "Brookie! I brought bagels!"

A moment later, her best friend Krista appeared in the doorway of her grandmother's kitchen.

No, my kitchen.

It had been almost a year, but it still didn't feel real. Nothing did about this new life, including what Brooke was preparing for today.

"Ooh, what's this potion?" Krista peered at the bright-green mixture in the blender, then set the bagels onto the pale marble island in between the neat rows of ingredients Brooke had lined up. The rest of the kitchen was spotless, the way it always had been when her grandmother had been alive.

"They're not potions. They're—"

"Smoothies," Krista finished for her with an eye roll, just like she had the eight thousand other times they'd had this same exchange. Not quite as powerful as Gran's finger wag, but warmth still flooded Brooke's chest at her friend's familiar words. "What's today's blend? Something good?"

The routine was soothing, in the same way the smoothies were. Before any big event, her grandmother would make her "something special." Today's meeting would have gotten her "something *extra* special."

"Spinach, apples, carrots, and lemon balm."

Just like she always did, Krista made a face and pretended to gag. Brooke laughed and filled three glasses. "It's to feel powerful and in control. Isn't that how lawyers like to feel?"

"I don't need a magic potion for that." Krista shook back her mane of blond curls, like a preening lioness.

"Well, then drink it for the vitamin C so you don't get sick before the Halloween party."

"Fine, fine."

The warmth in Brooke's chest spread to her whole body, like slipping under the covers on a stormy night. Almost word for word, it was the same routine every weekday since Brooke's grandmother had died. Krista came by on her way to work, they bickered like the sisters they always wished they were, and they waited for the third of their trio to rush in, a ball of chaos dressed in fluorescent clothing.

Two minutes later, right on time—or rather, late as usual—the front door banged open and Aisha burst into the kitchen, out of breath and resplendent in a bright-green top that clashed horribly with her faded orange pants. Somehow it all still worked though, the cut of the clothes fitting her to perfection, her tawny skin glowing instead of overpowered the way Brooke or Krista's pale complexions would have been in the same outfit.

"Brooke, your neighbor is out there doing pull-ups again . . . " Aisha lifted an eyebrow, and Brooke braced herself for what she knew was coming next. "Shirtless."

Just like she did every time this happened, Krista let out a shriek of delight, grabbed Aisha's arm, and they both hurried to the living room, where a side window gave a clear view of his backyard. With a resigned sigh, Brooke pulled out a serving tray from the cabinet, placed the glasses and a stack of napkins on it, along with the bagels, and followed them.

The tray went into the center of the low coffee table, just like Gran would have done. Pride warmed her chest, thick and sweet as the honey she should have put in this smoothie to make it slightly more palatable. She smoothed down her hair and set a napkin next to each glass. A sharp stab of anxiety about what was coming today overwhelmed whatever meager satisfaction she had from living up to her grandmother's expectations around hostess responsibilities.

"Brooke, get over here. Stop worrying."

Of course Krista knew what she was thinking. With a groan that she only kind of meant, Brooke made her way over to the window. It was small but tall, set into one of the fifty-seven nooks and crannies the Victorian home contained. This one, thanks to the trees in her yard, was the perfect spot to observe the neighbors without them seeing her. As a kid, she'd sit there all day, watching Mrs. Mercer feed the birds in the backyard.

When Mrs. Mercer had moved away, there'd been only one reason to linger at this particular window. Ever since her neighbor installed a fence just a few days after "the turmeric incident," this was how she kept tabs on his dog.

Though Brooke only seemed to venture to the spot whenever Krista and Aisha were there, and he was working out.

"This is creepy," Brooke said. "The dog's not even out there."

"This is a distraction from your meeting today." Krista grabbed her arm and pulled her closer. "Enjoy it."

Her skin heated under Krista's firm hand, and she wriggled out of her grasp.

"I don't need a distraction." She needed to focus. To feel powerful. To be in control. "And there's nothing I enjoy about the destroyer of Gran's turmeric plants."

Krista turned away from the window long enough to give Brooke an "oh really" look. Brooke shot a "yes, really" look back, and barely stopped herself from sticking out her tongue. Despite everything, she knew she couldn't lie to her best friend.

Because maybe there'd been a few times she'd glanced out and stopped in her tracks to watch her incredibly fit neighbor do push-ups and lift weights bigger than a tree trunk. It wasn't like she knew his schedule or planned her meals around it.

Not lately, at least. She'd been much too busy.

"Technically, it was his dog who ate the plants," Aisha said, her eyes never leaving the slow movements of the guy's arms as they lifted a dumbbell the size of a small child over his head. The sun glinted off the sheen of sweat that covered his body, and it was almost possible for Brooke to forget why they hated each other.

Almost.

"Actually, I haven't seen his dog in a few weeks." Krista glanced back at Brooke. "What happened to it?"

"How am I supposed to know?" Brooke ran her hands through her hair, flat-ironed smooth and straight less than an hour ago, yet she could feel the frizz already returning. Krista's wild and curly mane suited her leonine bearing, but Brooke's natural waves gave her more of an evil, woodland fairy vibe, which was the last thing she wanted today.

Beneath the curtain of her hair, Brooke's fingers rubbed her temples, though it did little to soothe the headache simmering under the surface. The pain would rise any second now if they kept staring at him and talking about him, reminding Brooke of the worst things about herself.

The first few weeks after the turmeric incident, Brooke had seen the dog a few times in the backyard, always on a leash. Then the fence had gone up, and it was harder to see anything if you weren't at this particular window. Whenever he put the dog into the car, it was on a leash. In fact, she'd never seen the dog without a leash since that day she'd yelled like a maniac at her new neighbor and his puppy.

Then, about a month ago, there was no more dog.

The guilt of thinking he'd gotten so strict with it, then gotten rid of it all because of her wasn't the highest on her list of things she lost sleep over, but it was certainly in the top ten.

Realizing if he *had* gotten rid of his dog, and there was still no animal shelter in town where he could have left the dog—also because of her—was in the top three.

"You haven't talked to him?" Aisha's eyes were wide, though still directed toward the guy. He'd moved on to push-ups, his long lean body moving up and down with military precision.

Maybe he was in the military. Or had been.

Not that Brooke cared.

"I see you every day. Don't you think I would have mentioned 'oh hey I finally talked to the jerk whose dog ate an irreplaceable plant, and I didn't scream at him this time'?"

"Are you really still mad?" Aisha shook her head. "It's been almost a year."

"Actually, it's been exactly a year."

There'd been no deadline in Gran's will for fulfilling her biggest request, but Brooke had felt every single passing day like a personal failure. Once she was officially the executive director, then she could sign off on everything that had been put on hold, and the shelter could finally open. It would mean giving up her voting spot on the board, not to mention abandoning her own career, but this was the only way to ensure Gran's vision became a reality.

"That seems like long enough to forgive and forget." Aisha's breath fogged against the window.

Unfortunately, none of Gran's smoothies were for forgetting. They were all for power, energy, and intelligence. The extra special ones were for keeping nerves at bay, falling in love, or mending a broken heart.

Brooke had tried that last one at least once a week after losing Gran, but it hadn't worked. Even if she'd gotten over the anger and frustration and—yes, guilt—that her neighbor's dog had ruined one of the oldest perennials on the property just a few days after her grandmother had passed away, the pain of her loss had lingered. It was like the dog had dug the heart out of her chest when she'd caught it digging up the plant.

Brooke knew that it was just a puppy and getting mad was pointless. That the pain had been so raw, so fresh, she'd been lashing out at whoever had been around her. Unlike Krista and Aisha, however, the poor dog and his owner didn't know that. They'd just seen the worst of her, the imperfect, angry, hopeless side of her that she never let herself show in public.

Up until then, Brooke had been handling things how Gran would have wanted her to. With poise and politeness and decorum. That single slip was like a giant black spot on Brooke's record, and she made sure to keep extra tight control over everything since that day she'd let it all out.

She took a sip from her smoothie, turning away from the window and the reminder of her failure. Maybe she should have added a double dose of lemon balm just to be safe.

If word got around town about how she'd overreacted to a dog doing perfectly normal dog things, that she'd been the reason someone had given up their puppy, it could wreak havoc on her reputation. In this town, Gran's name meant something. It was

Brooke's responsibility to make sure that legacy continued, after her mother had almost ruined it forever. The thought that one moment of unrestrained emotion from Brooke could bring the Adams' name back to the edge of infamy was enough to douse her in grief all over again.

Was she making a big deal out of nothing? That's what her friends would tell her. What they had told her many times over the past year. All three of them had to deal with the fallout of the choices their mothers had made. But Krista and Aisha weren't the ones with the Adams' name.

Her two friends let out a collective sigh and Brooke glanced over, struggling to hold back her own. He'd moved on to lunges now.

Of course she'd thought about going over to apologize once she'd calmed down. But there'd been so much to do in the days and weeks following Gran's death, the funeral to prepare, the house to sort out, and then the biggest news of all:

Gran had saved several million dollars to start an animal shelter.

The establishment of the nonprofit had taken some time, then there'd been the building to buy and renovate. Things had been looking good for it to open months ago, until the original executive director they'd hired—at Brooke's suggestion—had turned out to be a complete fraud.

Brooke leaned back against the edge of the couch, hands clenched around her glass. *Definitely should have added another dose of lemon balm.*

Now it was all up to Brooke to make sure the shelter would open. After the board meeting this morning, officially giving her control she'd never wanted over countless details, she'd spend the rest of the day at the shelter, getting organized.

Just follow your plan and everything will be fine.

The plan did not involve spending an hour gawking at her neighbor and wallowing in her past mistakes.

Almost as if he'd heard her thoughts, he stacked his weights on their stand and went inside.

"At last." Brooke reached for the smoothies on the table and held them out to her friends. "You're here to help me pick out an outfit for the board meeting, not ogle my neighbor."

"I can only do one of those things well." Aisha gestured at herself, managing to spill some of her smoothie on her bright-green shirt. "I don't think it's the outfit advice."

Brooke handed her a napkin while Krista took a sip from her glass. "This isn't actually as bad as I thought it would be."

"My smoothies are never bad." Though they weren't the same as when Gran made them.

Krista took another sip. "I think you'll be fine today. What's on the agenda after the vote?"

"All of the inspections that Jason lied about doing need to be done this week. Then I need to order the rest of the supplies so the kennels can be set up."

"Decorating!" Aisha beamed and clapped her hands excitedly. "You probably don't need help with that, do you?"

The ground shifted a little under Brooke's feet at the reference to the apartment staging job she'd just quit last week. In the middle of three huge projects. If the shelter didn't work out, then there was no way her old boss would take her back.

"No, but I do need help decorating for the Halloween party."

"Of course." Krista reached over and rubbed her arm, her tone shifting to something softer and gentler. "I'm glad you're having it this year. I know Gran would be happy to see the tradition continuing."

There hadn't been a party the previous year, only a small memorial ceremony for those closest to her. Every holiday would be harder now without Gran, but the giant Halloween parties she used to throw were something everyone in town looked forward to.

That's what Brooke wanted. To keep the legacy going. That was her job, and she was already close to failing with the shelter.

The party, at least, shouldn't be too hard to manage, especially with Krista and Aisha helping.

They polished off their smoothies, and Brooke realized she did feel a little calmer, a little more powerful, and her mood was slightly better.

She looked at her two best friends and warmth filled her chest. It had nothing to do with the drink, and everything to do with these two women.

There was no such thing as magic potions. Just the magic of best friends.

TWO

ETHAN

Just follow the universe's plan, and everything will be fine.

Ethan pulled into the parking spot closest to the station that was always open whenever he got here. He tugged at his collar, still not used to the crisp, tan button-up that was his uniform now. Did he miss the familiar flame-retardant, dark-blue tee shirt and pants that he'd worn for ten years? Of course. Was there any point in wishing things were different?

Nope.

He made his way into the station, his feet, at least, used to turning right toward the offices rather than left toward the engines. One had passed him on his way to work that morning, lights flashing and siren blaring. While the tug in his chest was much lighter than it had been a few months ago, it was still there. Maybe it always would be.

I'm still fighting fires. His eyes landed on the arrow labeled "Fire Inspector" on the wall, and he turned in that direction. *Just in a different way.*

All of this was happening the way it was supposed to. Just like his parking spot, the opportunity had presented itself at the right time, so he didn't question it too much, just pulled in to whatever the universe was offering him.

"Ready for today?" Jerry, his mentor, suddenly appeared beside him, and Ethan choked back his startled reaction. Had he not seen Jerry, or had he just been lost in thought?

The older man slapped him on the shoulder. "It's okay if you want to wait."

"Course I'm ready." Doubt coiled in Ethan's stomach, hot and twisty. "Thanks to you."

The past six months of ride-alongs with Jerry, observing the fire inspections, had been slowly heading toward this. It would be Ethan leading the inspections today, which got him one step closer to getting the job officially. When the guy who'd been the assistant fire inspector for years had moved out of state, Ethan's name was the one put forward to take his place. It hadn't been on Ethan's radar, but he was just happy to still be in the fire station at all.

"I've kept it simple for you. Let you ease into things." Jerry waved him into his office when they got there, and he bent to rifle through a stack of papers set on a chair. "There's a new housing development that just finished construction, a restaurant, and the reinspection of that animal shelter that we did a month ago."

"They finished up the repairs?" Ethan remembered that one, since the manager had been such a jerk about all the code violations, first blaming the contractors who'd done the renovations, then the nonprofit's board for being stingy with the budget. It had been the biggest test of his patience since the incident with Lucky and his neighbor last year. At least he hadn't yelled at anybody, though Jerry had had some choice words about the guy on the ride back to the station afterward.

"Sounds like it." Jerry checked something in his notes. "Someone called a few days ago, asked if we could come early so they can open next week."

Ethan's eyebrows shot up. "They had a lot to fix."

"Well, hopefully they got it all done." Jerry gave him an appraising look. "It'd be nice to finally have an animal shelter in town. Maybe you could get another dog now that Lucky is gone."

"Maybe."

It wasn't the reminder Ethan needed today of his dog-free life. He'd known he wouldn't have Lucky forever, but the transition was harder than he'd expected. The house had felt so empty for weeks, so he spent as much time as he could outside, continuing his habit of working out in the backyard that he'd started after bringing Lucky home, since the puppy was always a little too distracted when he did it inside.

Once he'd realized his neighbor and her friends were watching him workout from a window shaded by trees they must think kept them hidden, he kept doing it. Their eyes on him were a reminder that even though so much had changed recently, at least one thing hadn't. The body he'd gotten from his ten years as a firefighter was still drawing just as much attention as it always had, even if that body was no longer fighting fires in the way he used to. His neighbor hated him after what Lucky had done to her plants, but at least she didn't seem to hate his body.

There'd been no hint of that when they'd first met, however. The look on her face when she'd come storming out of the house to scream at Lucky . . . the memory of it set his nerve endings tingling, even here in the middle of Jerry's office. She'd been like some beautiful, raging goddess, her dark hair in messy waves around her face and blue eyes sparking with anger. Even in Ethan's outrage, he'd noticed how spectacular she was.

Did he work out in his yard now just to taunt her?

Maybe.

Definitely.

"Ready to go?"

Ethan blinked away thoughts of his petty grudge against his beautiful neighbor to find Jerry looking down meaningfully at the stack of papers. With a slow inhale, Ethan stuffed them into his bag. Leading things apparently didn't get him out of being the note taker and filer.

It took a few minutes to gather his things, double and triple checking he hadn't forgotten anything, then they were on the road with Jerry behind the wheel.

The sun glared through the windshield, promising a good day. A great day. He'd show Jerry everything he'd learned, and the job he'd been training for all these months would be his. When he trusted the universe's plan, there was nothing to worry about. Things would work out, just like they always did.

Fifteen minutes later, Ethan looked up at the restaurant's facade and tried to remember everything he'd been learning over the past six months. It was a jumble in his mind, the endless regulations and calculations, the different kinds of risks dependent on the type of building and business.

He took a deep breath and closed his eyes, then popped them open almost immediately. The lack of visual noise didn't calm him the way it used to. The eyesight he'd taken for granted his entire life wouldn't always be there, and he should use it as much as possible while he still had it. He let his gaze soften, not fixing on any one thing, and let his brain take a break so it could find the information he needed.

Jerry stood silently next to him, waiting for Ethan to get started.

Having only lived in Adamsville for a little over a year with little to no social life for the large majority of that time, most of the places he'd watched Jerry inspect had been new to him. This particular restaurant Ethan had actually been to once before, which felt like a good sign. A tiny slice of familiarity to help calm his nerves.

"A fire code inspection starts outside." How many times had Ethan heard Jerry say that? It seemed fitting to start with the older man's words. He got a nod in response, so he kept going, trying to see the building through Jerry's eyes. "The address is visible. Nothing blocking the hydrants."

"Good. Let's head inside."

Ethan waited for Jerry to step forward, but the older man held out an arm, indicating Ethan should go first. Hope fluttered deep in Ethan's belly.

It went ever better than he'd expected. The owner was friendly and had all the paperwork needed in a stack on a table in the front. They were in and out in less than half an hour, and Ethan was practically floating.

"Not everyone is that easygoing," Jerry said as they headed back to the truck, and Ethan's positive mood dipped. "This job is ninety percent convincing people to do what needs to be done and ten percent bringing out the big guns when someone won't budge. Knowing the difference will be key. Most people want to follow the rules, but when things get expensive, they'll always try to cut corners."

"Gotcha." There was so much more to this than Ethan could have ever thought when he'd first started. The paperwork Jerry had him doing was repetitive and boring. The courses and tests and certifications, though easy enough, were all just numbers and words. Shadowing Jerry as he carried out the inspections was the best part. To see it in action, how it could actually help people, felt amazing. Like he wasn't giving up the life-saving part of the job he loved so much.

But that was only a tiny part of the job, and he didn't even officially have it yet. This extended trial period had been Jerry's idea, and Ethan had to trust that's what was best. Questioning things too much, or hoping for different outcomes, had only ever led to disappointment and heartbreak for Ethan.

"Let's head to the new animal shelter, since it's on this side of town." The older man opened the driver-side door to his truck, and Ethan mirrored him on the passenger side, sliding into the seat with barely controlled excitement at his second shot of the day to prove himself.

Just follow the universe's plan, and everything will be fine.

On the way there, Jerry ran him through the things they'd be looking out for after the first failed inspection months ago. The code for animal housing facilities had been updated just a few years ago, and while each case was individual, depending on the kind of animals there, the most important thing would be to make sure there was an evacuation plan for both the humans and animals.

A few minutes later, Jerry turned onto a street not far from Ethan's house. They pulled up next to the only car in front of a small building with a fresh coat of paint and a bright-red door. There were pet-friendly flowers in window boxes, and there was a large, fenced-in yard behind the building.

"Oh wow. It looks way better than when we first came out here."

"Don't let the outside fool you." Jerry shook his head. "I've seen all sorts of things. Keep an eye out for what we talked about."

Ethan nodded, eager to keep learning, to keep soaking it all in. The more he knew, the sooner he'd officially have the job.

And he needed this job.

Nothing else had presented itself when his whole life had turned upside down almost a year ago, so this must be what he was supposed to do. The universe took care of him, looked out for him. All signs pointed to Ethan's future as assistant fire inspector. He'd passed the last of his courses and exams last week, so if he did well today, the offer must be coming soon.

The two men walked up to the door, and Ethan knocked. There was no answer. Jerry frowned and looked at his watch. "I thought someone would be here."

Ethan knocked again, and this time there was a muffled "coming!" from somewhere inside the building. A moment later, the door opened, and all Ethan saw was the flash of blue and smooth, sleek black hair.

Vision blurring, he sucked in a breath. His neighbor was standing right in front of him. The eyes that just hours before had been peeking out of her window while he did his workout were now wide in shock that, after a few breathless moments, transformed into pure hatred.

THREE
ETHAN

Silence stretched between them as Ethan's heart beat a steady rhythm in his eardrums. Though desperate for something to say, he bit his tongue to keep from blurting out the colorful mix of swears that popped into his brain. At his side, Jerry waited for a few wordless beats, then sighed and held out his hand.

"Good morning. I'm Jerry Fulbright. This is my colleague Ethan Mercer. We're here for the final fire inspection."

"Already?" She blinked her wide, blue eyes, and Ethan felt a little unsteady to see her so flustered. Where was the vengeful yet nosy supernatural being who lived next door to him?

"Somebody called to say we could come by this week to reinspect. Was it the manager? Is he here?" Jerry looked around, as if more cars might have appeared in the past two minutes. But no, it was still just Jerry's truck and—now that Ethan knew it was his neighbor—a very familiar white SUV. "The message said you wanted to open as soon as possible, so here we are."

The color on her cheeks rose, and her eyes narrowed. Ethan's spirits lifted despite his stomach dropping to the ground in alarm. He knew that look and braced himself for the tirade that he was sure was heading their way.

"I called you. I simply wasn't expecting you until later in the week." Her voice was strong and clear, with just a hint of haughtiness. "I'm Brooke Adams, the new executive director of the shelter."

When her eyes flicked to Ethan's, something in her posture shifted. She tucked her long, dark hair back from her face and lifted her chin slightly. "Come on in."

Brooke Adams. Finally, a name for the face, for the eyes that were staring right at him instead of peeking through curtains. It had been a year of living next to her, wondering what her name might be, and now he had it.

She stepped aside and they walked past, Ethan catching the faintest hint of lavender. It was too light to be perfume. Her shampoo, maybe.

He gave her a tight smile, but there was no recognition in the cold stare he got back. He swallowed, his mind still drawing a complete blank on words that weren't mildly to excessively vulgar. What could he say, what could he do, to make sure the woman who must hate him didn't mess anything up for him today?

Then, in a flash like a spark hitting a pile of dry leaves, he realized he could actually mess things up for her. If he spotted anything during the inspection, if something wasn't up to code, her shelter wouldn't be able to open. Nerves gone, he lifted his gaze to meet hers. There was a slight tightening of her eyes as she pursed her lips in response to his silent challenge.

Thankfully, Jerry didn't seem to notice anything as they walked into the reception area.

"Adams? Are you related to Michele Adams?" asked Jerry, his voice echoing in the large, empty space. A built-in desk separated the reception from an area in the back that was filled with boxes and a half-assembled dog kennel.

Brooke's eyes focused on Ethan's boss, her expression as steely as ever. "She was my grandmother."

"I was so sorry to hear she passed." Jerry looked around and nodded a few times. "I didn't know her granddaughter was involved with animals."

"It was in her will." Brooke smoothed a hand along her hair, though it was already sleek and perfect. The wild waves that had haunted his dreams for months were gone, as if they'd never existed. "She wanted a shelter opened in her name. The sign won't be here until Friday."

"Nice to see you doing something she'd be proud to have her name attached to." Jerry flicked his eyes to Ethan and lowered his voice. "Unlike that daughter of hers."

Ethan's heart shot into his throat. What on earth did that mean? Jerry was still looking around the room and didn't see the twitch of Brooke's eye. But Ethan caught it, along with the way her hands clenched at her sides.

"Your grandmother liked animals?" The words burst out of Ethan before he could think of anything else. It was clearly a painful topic for Brooke, but he had to say something, anything, to cover up the comment Jerry intended for only Ethan to hear.

At least, that's what he assumed. Jerry had never been outwardly rude to anybody during inspections, saving his comments for afterward in the truck.

Brooke's eyes slid to Ethan's. "She loved them."

Something niggled at the back of Ethan's brain, and he narrowed his gaze on her. Given how she'd acted around Lucky, an animal shelter was the last place he'd expect to find her. It sounded like she was only doing this because she had to.

"Do you?"

It was like a thundercloud had descended. The room grew as chilly as her expression, her eyebrows drawing together and her eyes sparking, just like they had that day in her yard.

"I love them too. I'd never mistreat an animal."

Oh yeah, she definitely hates me.

Pulse pounding in his ears again, Ethan knew it wasn't worth his time to argue that Lucky had been spoiled rotten the year he'd had him. So he said nothing, only dimly aware of the fact that Jerry was looking between the two of them with a curious expression. Turning his head a little to look at his boss, Ethan looked away from Brooke's heated glare. The spell between them broke, all the tension evaporating like water in a heated pipe.

"Alrighty." Jerry clapped and rubbed his hands together, a frown tugging at his mouth. "Ethan, where should we get started?"

Maybe by restarting completely.

Furious with himself for messing things up so quickly with less than a dozen words, Ethan shuffled through the endless checklists in his head to find the one Jerry had talked about on the way over. "Let's take a look at the electrical panel first."

Brooke nodded once, her face a cold mask. "This way."

They followed her, Ethan sweeping his eyes back and forth, turning his head to make sure he didn't miss anything. This was his chance to show Jerry that he was the right person to be the assistant inspector. Even though they were focused on rechecking a few things, Jerry would want to hear his thoughts on everything.

Ethan noticed at least two minor violations of the fire code already, which didn't fill him with the surge of victory he thought it would. Bringing uptight, frosty Brooke down a peg or two was a satisfying idea, but the town desperately needed this shelter.

When they got to the electric panel, Ethan talked his way through the inspection, and Jerry nodded along, while Brooke's laser gaze made him stutter on a few words. He swallowed and went slower, making sure each word was clear, and her gaze heated even more.

Once he'd established everything was fine there, they moved on to other areas of the building that they needed to check.

Brooke stayed by their side the entire time. At one point, Jerry mentioned that she could leave them if she had work to do, and her reply was simple.

"This shelter is my responsibility. I need to know everything about it."

Jerry seemed to like this response, and Ethan thought about what the older man had said at the restaurant. The battle was usually getting business owners to care.

That certainly wasn't a problem with Brooke.

It was with this thought in mind that Ethan decided to speak up as they passed from the reception area back into the kennel. If she really cared, then she'd want everything perfect.

"How wide are these doors?" He stopped in the middle and held out his arms. "They don't look to be much wider than the standard."

"Thirty-six inches. Four inches more than typical interior doors."

Goosebumps shivered up his arms. The irritation was so clear in her voice, he didn't even have to turn around to see the spark in her eyes he knew must be there.

"How large will your biggest dog be?"

"I don't know yet."

He turned and held back a satisfied smile to see the steely glint in her eyes. It shouldn't have made him so happy to see it, but the challenge was irresistible. "You won't be able to take anything bigger than thirty inches. Not with these doors."

She put her hand on her hips. "I'll take whatever dog needs me."

"And put them in danger by not providing a safe way out of the building in case of an emergency?"

"So you'd rather have me abandon dogs in need?"

"If you can't ensure their safety, then no, you shouldn't take them."

"I'm not the one who gives up on dogs."

"That's not what happened, it was—"

"The doors are fine." Jerry shot Ethan a look, and he closed his mouth, biting back the colorful response he wished he could give. "There are two other exits out of the building, all clearly marked. Things look really good, Brooke. Your builders did a good job."

"Yes, *they* did." Brooke sent a pointed look Ethan's way.

Irritation flared, but he kept his mouth shut. He could tell Jerry wasn't happy with him, and it was more important that he keep his boss happy than continue to irritate Brooke.

Tomorrow's outdoor workout might be twice as long though. In the little spandex shorts he normally only wore as part of a costume.

"Hello? I have a delivery for you."

All three of them turned to the uniformed driver who'd just walked in carrying a giant box. "Where can I put this?"

"What is it?" Brooke left Ethan standing there, his pulse still racing and face flaring with heat. Not even a backward glance to acknowledge the simmering tension she'd just turned up to eleven.

Ethan had handled a lot of fires, but nothing that had sparked like this.

It took several long, slow breaths before his brain was able to focus on the task at hand. The goal was compliance and safety, not alienating the business owners. From the look on Jerry's face, however, Ethan had just blown it with Brooke.

Keeping a desperately needed animal shelter from opening wasn't the way to get back at her for yelling at his dog. He didn't even want to get back at her, not really. He just wanted to show Jerry how much he cared, how much he knew. Instead, he'd shown a complete lack of control over his emotions. Which never happened to Ethan. Well, except the last time he'd yelled at Brooke.

While she finished up with the delivery, Jerry and Ethan walked through the rest of the building, the older man taking over and pointing out everything they were there to double-check. Ethan remained silent as his boss did a picture-perfect job. When Brooke finally came over, Jerry was the one to smile and tell her everything looked good.

"So I'm all set to open next week?" she asked Jerry, avoiding looking at Ethan entirely.

The mounting pressure of failure sucked away all of Ethan's air.

"I don't know what other inspections you still have left, but everything on our side looks good."

The relief on her face was like a sunbeam peeking out from behind a cloud. Guilt licked up Ethan's chest. He'd been the one to make her doubt herself, all because of his own insecurities.

Jerry held out his hand for her to shake. "The paperwork should be ready tomorrow, if you want to come pick it up."

"Thank you." She smiled at Jerry the way people used to smile at Ethan when he'd show up in his firefighter uniform.

A different feeling settled itself in Ethan's chest. Not guilt, but something just as uncomfortable. It might have been jealousy, if he looked at it closely enough.

"Have a nice day, ma'am." He put on his cheekiest smile and held out his hand too. She eyed it warily, like he was going to pull away at the last second and yell *psych*!

Okay, maybe the ma'am had been uncalled for.

Still, she shook it. For a fraction of a second.

Then she turned to say goodbye to Jerry. A zing of electricity prickled along Ethan's palm where their skin had touched. It stayed with him through the silent walk back to the truck and only disappeared when the older man finally burst out with the angry commentary he'd been holding back the entire visit.

"What the blazes was that?" Jerry didn't even look at him as they pulled out of the parking lot and onto the street. "That's not how you get people on your side, Ethan."

Heaviness solidified like a rock in his stomach, and he ran a hand over his mouth. It wasn't the right time to bring up what Jerry had said about Brooke's mother, to ask what it had meant. Clearly what Ethan had said was much worse in the man's eyes.

"I'm sorry, I didn't mean to say anything, I just wanted—"

"Let me guess. You wanted to show off in front of the pretty girl?"

Like he'd ever admit to that. If that's what he'd been doing. Which it wasn't.

"She's not a girl. She's a woman."

Jerry rolled his eyes at this, the way Ethan knew he could. Ethan hated this kind of talk, had put up with it for his entire career, but this wasn't the moment to get into it, he knew that, not when Jerry was already irritated.

"That's not why I acted that way. I just wanted to do a good job."

"You can't let your temper get to you, especially with an Adams." Jerry shook his head, like somehow Ethan should have realized upon hearing the name that Brooke was important. "Her mother might have been a total hellion, but the Adams name still means something here. In *Adams*ville."

Great. So his neighbor who he'd pissed off from the second he'd met her was a big deal, and she'd gotten an even worse second impression of him. Ethan rubbed his hands over his face, wishing he could disappear.

"I know this is what you want to do, but it's a lot to learn, and you haven't been doing it that long."

"I can do it." Sweet Saint Florian, he needed to be able to do it. To be able to do something, anything, that would keep him from feeling the way he had for the past year.

Powerless.

There was a rhythm to Ethan's life. A flow that he was happy to go along with. Things worked out for him, as long as he didn't worry too much about it.

Getting his retinitis pigmentosa diagnosis a few weeks before this inspector role opened up was a sign. What were the chances of learning he had a life-changing condition that would eventually end his firefighting career just as another job appeared literally right down the hall? It must be what he was supposed to be doing. There was no other way to explain it.

So why was he doing so badly?

Jerry turned onto the main road in the direction of the fire station. "You were a great firefighter, Ethan, but not everyone's cut out for this job. You know the code and the laws. But that's only part of the job. It's really about dealing with people. Being out in the community. Getting to know them and getting them to trust you."

This wasn't quite the same thing as he'd said earlier that morning after the restaurant inspection, but it did fit with what he'd seen Jerry do over the past few months. Making small talk and joking around with people was how Jerry liked to start inspections. Ethan could do that part, even if he was a little—okay fine, a lot—awkward about it.

Knowing all the gossip and who was who in town was something else entirely. Ethan had no idea how to even begin learning that.

This wasn't the time to argue about the job description, however. All that mattered was if Jerry thought Ethan could do it.

"Trust. Community. Got it." All of it was code for something else, something a firefighter didn't have to deal with.

But he wasn't a firefighter anymore.

"Hmm." Jerry grunted. "Well, you'll either learn or you won't."

Heart pounding, Ethan let his gaze settle on the houses passing by out the window. "I'll watch what I say. I promise."

They were on the road to the station, though they'd be going into the administration building. Ethan would never ride in an engine again.

He turned back to Jerry, and the lines around the older man's eyes softened. "You've got a good eye and are smart as hell. You've already been watching me for a while, but you might want to start doing more around town."

"You mean like doing the school visits and scout talks?" Ethan had liked doing those as a firefighter. It would be nice if he could start participating again, maybe even with his former crew. He'd only been with them for a few months before his diagnosis and had only just started getting to know them. Reaching out to talk about teaching kids fire safety didn't feel as burdensome as asking one of them for a ride when they went out at night.

"Not exactly." Jerry pulled into the fire station, turned off the truck, and looked at Ethan. "The chief wants to see someone with a lot of experience in this position. You know you're at a disadvantage moving here not that long ago and not spending much time on a crew. You've gotta be more visible."

Visible. The word was a tricky one for Ethan. It was something he was slowly losing, the entire reason he was sitting in Jerry's truck right now instead of a fire engine where he felt at home.

"You know your stuff. Now you just gotta figure out how to talk to people, so you can integrate yourself into the community better."

"Right."

Jerry slapped him on the shoulder, then got out of the truck, leaving Ethan alone with his thoughts.

It wasn't how he'd pictured the role, even after observing Jerry for all these months. He knew what it really meant when he said talk to people and integrate. Figure out who was important, who really ran things in town. If it was that important, why hadn't Jerry brought it up before now?

Because until he saw you today with Brooke, he assumed you knew what you were doing.

The reality of just how badly he'd messed up sank in. There were other options, of course. Fire inspector wasn't the only thing he could do, but there was no way to know how much time Ethan had before things got really bad, before he wouldn't be able to work at all. There might not be time for him to learn anything else. Fighting fires, helping people, saving lives . . . that's all he knew. He'd be nothing without it. The universe had led him here, so this was where he was supposed to be.

He took a deep breath and closed his eyes.

Whatever's going to happen will happen.

It was what he'd been repeating to himself since he was twenty and he'd gotten the call that had changed his life. Losing his parents hadn't made any sense until he'd let go of hoping for things or trying to control his life. Everything worked out the way it was supposed to.

Like Jerry said, he'd either learn how to do this job, or he wouldn't. Then fate would decide what happened next.

FOUR

BROOKE

Brooke spent the rest of the day in a blur of activity. The only good thing about Ethan's unexpected visit to the animal shelter was that it had been short. There was still plenty of time left in the day to check off items on her to-do list.

It was almost possible to forget just how irritated she was at her neighbor when she was busy ordering supplies, making sure the other inspections were happening this week, and calling local vets to set up partnerships.

It was almost possible to forget just how intensely beautiful his gray eyes were when she spent the better part of her afternoon building animal crates that seemed to be missing half their pieces.

Almost.

She only came up for air when Krista texted her to let her know she was at her house with Aisha, waiting to start decorating.

The Halloween party had its own separate to-do list she hadn't even looked at today. It was just as important as everything at the shelter, but at least it was something she didn't have to do on her own. She rushed home to find her two friends waiting on her porch, bags of supplies in hand, including a few that looked like they were from her favorite burrito place.

Tears prickled at Brooke's eyes as she dragged herself up the stairs. "You two are the best."

"Rough day?" Aisha dropped her bags, then swung her arms over Brooke's shoulders and squeezed. "You wanna go see if your neighbor is doing an evening workout?"

"He's the absolute last person I want to see right now." Shaking her head, Brooke avoided even looking in the direction of his house as she unlocked her door. Her friends followed her inside. "He was already at the shelter today for the fire safety inspection."

"Shut the forking front door!" Krista's voice echoed in the foyer.

Aisha giggled and did just that. "If he's an inspector, does that mean he's a firefighter?"

Krista gave an exaggerated shiver. "You know I don't like firefighters, but I knew all those muscles had to be for something."

Rolling her eyes, Brooke turned back and grabbed the bags from where Krista had let them fall on the floor in her shocked excitement. Like most of Krista's quirks, her aversion to firefighters had appeared one day without explanation and no amount of pestering would get them any information from the tight-lipped lawyer.

"Yeah, for making my life miserable." As she led the way into the living room, Brooke rummaged through the bags, looking for the garlands of purple skulls that she'd had to special order weeks ago.

"Oh, stop." Krista reached into another bag and pulled out a purple cloth that she spread over the mantle while Brooke untangled the garlands. "It couldn't have been that bad."

"Well, it wasn't good." Brooke tossed Krista one end of a garland, and they stretched it across the cloth-covered mantle. Every year Gran chose a color and a symbol, using a few Twister spinners she'd doctored for the purpose of "letting the Halloween spirits" choose for her. This year, purple skulls had come up, so the house would be covered in them.

"But it passed inspection, right?" Aisha asked, her voice a bit muffled from where she'd set herself up by the window.

Decked out in purple coveralls and her chocolate waves swept up into a messy bun, Aisha was painting an intricate design on the glass, like she had every year since she was eleven and Gran had discovered this talent of hers. That was another thing Brooke missed about Gran—always seeing the potential in people.

What would Gran think of her neighbor, Ethan? What potential was hiding under his muscled surface? Other than showing up at exactly the wrong moments in her life to somehow make things even worse.

"It passed, but he made me feel like an idiot. Like I shouldn't be running the shelter." Not to mention that whispered comment from the other inspector about her mother. After thirty years, she should have been used to it, but they always caught her off guard.

Brooke secured the garland and stepped back to take in the effect. A frown tugged at her mouth. Should they add candles too? Gran's parties were always so over-the-top. There needed to be more. It's what people would expect. "He was probably just getting back at me for yelling at his dog last year."

"Did you ask him what happened to his dog?" Another muffled question from Aisha, her head only inches away from the window. In just a matter of minutes, a landscape of dancing skulls and boiling cauldrons like something out of a children's horror movie had started to take shape. It was perfect. Her friends were incredible.

And way too obsessed with Ethan and his dog.

"This wasn't a polite social call. He was there to shut down the shelter."

Krista pulled another garland from the bag and dragged a chair over to the wide doorway to the room. "Was that really a possibility? You have a checklist a mile long, and this inspection wasn't even the one you were most worried about."

Brooke knew her friends were right. The mess Jason had left

her included a mountain of unfinished business, ranging from unpaid bills for the contractor and landscaper, all the way to using an unlicensed plumber who had installed all the water taps backward. The fire inspection wasn't even in the top five of her biggest worries.

It wasn't just that she had huge shoes to fill. It was knowing that any mistake Brooke made, no matter how small, would bring comparisons to her mom. Was failing a safety inspection the same as leaving a baby behind to run off to who knows where? Of course not. But being an Adams in Adamsville had always meant something good until her mother, and Brooke wasn't going to be the one to remind everyone of that.

The shelter wasn't just Gran's legacy. Yes, she'd loved animals. She would have had dozens if not for her asthma, and she'd donated thousands to different charities over the years. But the shelter was more than that.

It was proof that she'd raised Brooke right. That Brooke was more like her grandmother than her mother.

Even if it had only been for a moment, Ethan had put all of that at risk.

"I still haven't gotten everything signed and approved for it to open." The garland wouldn't fit over the doorway like Krista wanted, so Brooke grabbed a chair to help her. "I may need to do some sweet-talking at this party. Ethan's probably already told everyone who works for the town what a monster I am."

There was a snort from the window painter. "I thought I was supposed to be the dramatic one."

"If you run into him again, maybe you can talk about it. Clear the air." Krista shrugged, like this was the most logical thing in the world. "Apologize."

"Me? Apologize? Why?" The anger flared out of nowhere, as if it had just been waiting for an opportunity to show its ugly head. Suddenly unsteady on her feet, Brooke stepped off the chair. "He's the one who questioned my motives for the shelter and made the inspection way more stressful than it had to be. His dog ruined Gran's garden. Not just the turmeric that refuses to grow back but dozens of perennial flowers and herbs. I haven't even replanted half of them because some were hybrids Gran had grown herself. Five decades of work and care gone in less than five minutes. What do I have to apologize for?"

There were plenty of other things she was sorry for, but none of them had anything to do with Ethan.

Hiring that crook, Jason, even though the board wasn't sure? Brooke's choice, now her problem to fix.

Quitting her apartment staging job of ten years that she absolutely adored to run the animal shelter, even though she had no idea what she was doing? Brooke would figure it out.

Throwing Gran's annual Halloween party the same week the shelter opened despite being absolutely exhausted? Eat some extra protein and avoid alcohol to stay alert.

Apologizing to Ethan would mean admitting she was wrong, and in both of their interactions, Ethan had been the one to endanger something that was important to her.

Gran had never wasted any breath apologizing for her wayward daughter. She'd chosen to raise Brooke in her place and gotten on with life. Now it was up to Brooke to make sure that choice wasn't in vain.

Concerned glances flickered between Krista and Aisha. Brooke took a few deep breaths to cool the heat in her veins. It was totally normal that they were talking way too much about Ethan. An unbearably attractive firefighter who worked out shirtless in his yard and was making Brooke's life difficult. What else was there worth talking about?

"I would rather leave the past in the past." Brooke was pleased at how calm she sounded.

"Well, at least invite him to the party. Show some neighborly spirit." Krista had her lawyer face on.

"Good fences make good neighbors."

Krista tsked. "You never know how being friendlier with him could help. You try to control so much of your life, but sometimes you just gotta let stuff happen."

The look Brooke shot her was as full of exasperation as she could make it. Krista was a great lawyer, maintaining confidentiality while getting clients to open up, good at spotting the loopholes in arguments and pushing people in just the right way to get them to shift their views on things. In this particular instance, however, Brooke was using everything she'd ever learned from Krista and wasn't going to budge.

"Look, he's coming home right now." Aisha gestured out the window. "I can run over now and ask him to come." When she moved from her spot, Brooke's stomach dropped, and she cried out.

"Don't." Her heart hammered. What was going on? Her friends weren't normally this insistent. Or maybe she was just on edge. It had been a big day, and not just because of the inspection. She was officially the executive director of the shelter. Being on the board had kept things at a distance since her role there was overseeing and advising, not leading. Now, every choice she made would directly impact the shelter's future in one way or another.

"I have enough on my mind right now. I can't add neighbor stress to everything."

"Even if he's a good contact to have, since he works for the city?" Krista just had to get in one final argument.

Unfortunately, it was one Brooke had already made to herself. "I have plenty of friends in city hall, and they'll all be here Saturday. I don't need another."

They were technically Gran's friends, and all several decades older than Brooke. So far, they'd all miraculously observed without the typical Adamsville comments and gossip as she waded through the endless administrative and legal process of getting the shelter up and running. Hopefully that wouldn't change now that she'd had a second tense interaction with Ethan.

That might not be true if she added a third.

"I know what you need." Aisha grinned and stepped back from the window, waving a hand at her completed masterpiece. "A distraction."

"I don't have time for a distraction right now." Brooke threw up her hands. The living room wasn't even halfway done, and there was still the rest of the house and the outside to decorate. "There's too much to do."

Schedules and to-do lists swirled in Brooke's brain. Between the party and the shelter, her week had to be timed to perfection if she was going to get it all done. It was already a huge relief that Krista and Aisha were helping her get ready for the party, but they both had jobs during the day. The shelter was Brooke's responsibility.

Half the supplies still hadn't arrived. There were the rest of the kennels to put together. The volunteers needed a schedule, and the one person she'd hired as an employee to help her was on vacation until this weekend. Once the remaining inspections were done, she had to get all the paperwork from city hall at some point, because of course, they didn't give you the paper on the actual day of the inspection.

Brooke literally did not have time for distractions.

On any other day, the wide, mischievous smile that Aisha gave her and the sneaky look she exchanged with Krista would have lifted Brooke's spirit and given her hope. "When's the last time you went on a date?"

A what now?

Brooke let out a huff of air and pulled out another purple skull garland from the bag at her feet. "Right, because taking care of a guy on top of everything else I have to do would be so relaxing."

"I'm not saying you need to get married." Aisha pulled the garland out of her hands and tossed it in the air, where it landed perfectly on the chandelier above their heads. "Just a date. Some fun."

"You're the fun one, not me."

Aisha's smile faltered for just a moment at that. Guilt tugged at Brooke's chest. The offhand comment was a triggering one for her friend, who so desperately wanted to be taken seriously but couldn't temper the enthusiasm she had for literally everything. Where Krista was able to switch on and off the stony intensity that allowed her to advance quickly at the same firm she'd interned with during law school, Aisha was always exactly who she was with everyone in every situation. After an endless series of odd jobs and part-time gigs, she'd finally landed somewhere she really liked. Yet the same exuberant attitude that had gotten her the job was keeping her boss from giving her more of the responsibility she craved.

The apology was on the tip of Brooke's tongue, but even with her friends, the words felt like hot ash in her mouth. "I'm sorry" wasn't something Gran ever said, and Brooke had always found it easier to show her remorse than verbalize it. She knew she had to make it up to Aisha somehow.

"Fine." Brooke sighed and stuffed the rest of the garlands back into the bag. "We can make rosebud tea."

Aisha immediately brightened and clapped her hands while Krista squealed. "A love potion!"

The sigh that Brooke let out was a tired one. "Rosebud tea."

"Love potion, love potion, love potion . . . " Her friends chanted and danced their way into the kitchen. Following with a bit more decorum, Brooke followed them, her heart already lifting a little at the familiar ritual of the arguments over Gran's list of drinks for every occasion and emotion.

Besides, Aisha wasn't wrong. A date would be a good distraction. From all the stress and work of opening the shelter. From the grief that still stuck to her like spiderwebs in the highest corners of the house she could never quite reach. From her unfairly hot neighbor who definitely disliked her even more after today.

The tea itself was simple enough. Dried rose petals, dried jasmine, and honey. The first time Gran had made it for the three of them as giggly twelve-year-olds, she'd made it seem so . . . well, magical, even though Brooke hated to use that word. Still, there was no denying that there was something entrancing about the way she measured the flowers so carefully and brought out a special silver spoon to mix in the honey.

Brooke took the same spoon from the drawer, a burning pinch in her chest. It hurt to see the familiar utensil, but it just didn't feel right to use a regular spoon to make this.

"Am I making one cup or three?" Her hands hovered over the tins of dried flowers lined up inconspicuously on the counter next to more typical herbs, like basil and rosemary.

"Make a pitcher." Aisha rubbed her hands together. "We'll drink it all week while we get everything ready for the party this weekend."

"Maybe it'll finally give you enough courage to talk to Cody at the aquarium." Krista grabbed three mugs from the cabinet above the sink, then nudged Aisha, whose cheeks turned bright pink at the mention of her workplace crush.

"Or maybe it'll loosen Brooke up enough to invite Ethan to the party."

"That's about as unlikely as this actually being a love potion." Smoothing her hair back from her face so it wouldn't get into the tea, Brooke measured out a heaping dose of all the ingredients into the silver tea kettle Gran had only ever used for her "magic" teas.

It took a little under ten minutes for the tea to boil and brew, then the three friends sat at the island sipping the purple-tinged concoction from warm mugs. They spent the rest of the night swiping through a dating app on Krista's phone, rating the options out there, as giggly as they had been twenty years ago when they'd had the tea for the first time.

While Brooke didn't think it would make her more "open to receiving the love and attention of your soulmate" as Gran's spidery handwriting described in her recipe notebook—and it certainly wouldn't make anyone fall madly in love with her if they somehow managed to drink it—it did remind her of one important thing.

The love of her friends. That's all she really needed right now.

The last thing she needed was to have Ethan Mercer at her party.

FIVE

ETHAN

There was a party going on next door, and Ethan wasn't invited.

In the week since he'd been to Brooke's animal shelter, he'd slowly watched her house transform from a neat and tidy Victorian into the haunted house of his childhood nightmares. He wasn't sure how she had the time, even with her two friends there more than usual.

Not that he noticed their comings and goings. Just when they peeked out of the side window to watch him workout. Which they'd done quite a few times this week, to Ethan's petty pleasure.

Their not-so-furtive spying was the bright spot in his day.

How depressing is that?

He shot another glance out the window, and his mood soured even more. Thanks to the bright lights shining on Brooke's lawn, even with his normally limited night vision, he could see the endless stream of people arriving at her house.

So what if it looked like the entire town was there, but she'd neglected to invite her next-door neighbor? Going out at night was something he'd stopped doing anyway after he'd gotten his diagnosis.

Sure, he could get a ride, either from a friend or from an app. But it was more than getting somewhere that was tricky.

It was navigating dark parking lots on foot when he couldn't always see the cars. It was making his way around dimly lit bars without bumping into people and things. It was feeling like he was only catching about half of everything going on.

Rather than explain it to anyone, he'd just used the excuse of Lucky and studying for his fire inspector certification. It had only taken a few weeks for everyone at the station to get the message that he didn't go out at night, and they'd stopped asking.

Even if Brooke had invited him, he couldn't go without worrying all night. There was no point in wishing she had. He'd stopped wishing for things he'd never have a long time ago.

The ringing doorbell echoed in Ethan's ears like a fire alarm.

Heart pounding, he didn't let even a speck of hope bubble up in his chest that it might be his neighbor, trusting instead that whoever was there was the person he needed to see.

"Chief Stevens." Ethan tried to keep his voice even. The fire chief was in his late fifties and had been captain by the time he was Ethan's age. The man was everything Ethan had wanted to be before the retinitis pigmentosa had set him on his current path.

The chief was also frowning slightly, a child-sized witch's hat on his head.

Ethan's white-knuckled hand held the door open, letting in a blast of humid air. Late October in South Carolina wasn't usually this warm. "Is everything okay, sir?"

"Everything is fine, Mercer." Chief Stevens rocked back on his heels and put his hands in his pockets. "Just wondering if you were going to the Adams' family Halloween party."

"Um, no, sir. I wasn't invited."

"Hmm." The older man cleared his throat. "You can come with me. I thought you might want an opportunity to meet more people in town."

Ethan shifted on his feet. "Oh?"

The chief cleared his throat again and gave him a pointed look. "I think maybe you'd like to say hello to Miss Adams?"

The dread that fell on Ethan's shoulders was only slightly less heavy than it was for a three-alarm fire. His grip tightened on the door.

Of course Jerry had mentioned what a total jackass Ethan had been to Brooke. Though Ethan had been polite and efficient for the other inspections they'd done that week, it clearly hadn't changed how Jerry saw him. Ethan was new in town, hadn't recognized an important family when he should have, and none of that would change if he didn't start getting out there more.

Now here was the chief, asking him to come with him next door to what looked like the party of the year.

The hope he'd been so careful to keep under wraps started to seep into his veins. The universe was giving him what he needed, yet again, even if the thought of facing Brooke made his stomach roil and palms sweat.

"I don't have a costume."

"Neither do I." The fire chief shrugged and pointed at his too-small witch's hat. "I borrowed this from my granddaughter for the night. People don't usually go all out for this thing."

"Are you sure?" Ethan glanced over the chief's shoulder at Brooke's house. "It looks pretty serious over there. Very Addams family. Two Ds."

The older man chuckled. "You know, I never made that connection before. Maybe that's why they do it. Michele Adams hosted these things for fifty years." He paused, the frown back on his face. "We thought they were all over when she died, since Brooke didn't have it last year. Mrs. Adams was a stickler for doing things properly."

"Like her granddaughter?"

Chief Stevens raised an eyebrow, and Ethan's heart shot into his throat. "Exactly."

"I think I have something that could work." Mind racing as fast as his pulse, Ethan stepped back from the door to let the chief inside. "Can you give me five minutes?"

"Of course." Chief Stevens pursed his lips and twisted them to the side. "Need any help?"

The words hit him in the gut, but Ethan kept his face blank. "I'm fine, thanks."

Without looking back at the older man, he headed to his bedroom.

He's just being nice.

The chief asking if he needed help was a new and uncomfortable development. For the time being, Ethan wasn't seeing anything that differently, at least not during the day. His condition made it harder to see at night long before there was any impact on daytime vision. The decision to stop being a firefighter had been his. The department had tested him and said his eyesight was still good enough to keep working.

But Ethan didn't know how long that would last. The changes to his schedule that he would need sooner rather than later because of his poor night vision would have caused issues. It wasn't fair to the rest of the crew if you could only work half a shift.

Chief Stevens was the only one who knew about Ethan's diagnosis and had been the one to put him forward for the assistant fire inspector job. Not even Jerry knew the reason why, and the choice had caused a lot of chatter around the station. Why would a young, seemingly perfectly healthy, single guy suddenly abandon a ten-year career in firefighting?

Since he'd only been on the crew for a few months and he'd stopped going out at night, the number of Ethan's friends had dwindled to zero in a matter of weeks. Walking around town with Lucky got him attention, but chatting a few minutes at the dog park hadn't fostered any lasting connections with people, and he didn't have a dog anymore. Without friends to tell him who was who and to help him navigate Adamsville society, the inspector job would forever be out of reach.

Now that Chief was here, providing something Ethan desperately needed, he wasn't about to waste the opportunity to meet more people.

Giving Brooke and her friends an up-close look at what they loved to gawk at from her window was just a happy side effect.

As Ethan rifled through his drawers, searching for the bike shorts he knew were in there somewhere, a deep ache suddenly spread through his chest, and he drew up short to rub the spot over his heart. His sister Rachel was the one who always made him wear this costume, and she was two states away now. Tugging on the tight spandex, he promised himself he'd ask someone to take a quick picture tonight to send to her.

Topping off his look with a baggy sweatshirt, it could almost be a regular outfit rather than a costume. Chief said as much when Ethan finally emerged from his bedroom. When Ethan told him who he was, he got a bemused brow crinkle and a shrug. But he didn't jeer or comment.

Another sign this was the right choice.

The short walk from his house to Brooke's wasn't as bad as most times when he went out after dark. Once the sun set, it was hard for Ethan to get around, but Brooke's yard was almost as bright as a sunny afternoon. There were spotlights illuminating the ghosts and bats in the trees, and jack-o'-lanterns lining the path to the front door. He peered down into one and Chief chuckled.

"I already checked. They're LEDs, not candles. No fire risk."

Ethan stood up and the older man put a hand on his shoulder. "Nice to see you paying attention. It's what we need in an inspector."

That spark of hope in Ethan's belly burned brighter. Even if Jerry didn't think Ethan was right for the job, the chief was clearly invested in his success.

"You know, I've really been learning a lot from Jerry. It's been great these past few months." Not a total lie. Though, since he was only part-time, Ethan wasn't doing inspections every day. It hadn't been a problem filling the hours when he'd had Lucky, but there was only so much studying and working out he could do. "Since Lucky's gone, I'd be happy to learn whatever else you think could be useful at the station."

"Now there's a thought." They arrived at the door, which was halfway open, inviting them inside without the need to knock. Ethan's hope ignited into a flame.

"But don't worry about that tonight." The chief squeezed his shoulder. "Just have fun. Get to know people. Be social. It'll be important no matter what you do for us."

The flame of hope was instantly doused in a familiar wave of disappointment. The chief was telling him the same as Jerry, that Ethan should be more visible, more involved in the community.

Why was this so complicated? All the signs had pointed to this being the direction to go, so it shouldn't be this hard. It felt like he was running a race, and they kept changing the rules without telling him. Small talk and glad-handing weren't aspects they'd ever mentioned before, but now, all of a sudden, they were essential.

At least as a firefighter, he'd known that things were unpredictable. He could trust his gut and follow the instinct he'd trained to notice all the little signs of danger. Though he thought it would be just as straightforward, this inspector job was turning out to be nothing like that.

Wishing things could be different is pointless.

Trust whatever the universe has planned.

It only took a moment once Ethan stepped inside for his troubled and anxious thoughts to melt away into awe. Inside was even more decorated than outside. The theme was clear—purple skulls covered every available surface. Skeletal spiders lurked in corners and dangled from the ceilings. When he glanced at them again, not all of them looked fake.

Despite the theme and the spooky mood, the atmosphere was bright. He'd been worried about fog machines and dim lighting, but Brooke seemed to have prioritized practicality just as much as the decorations.

A quick scan revealed clear pathways to access all the exits and there was plenty of space to move around. Small groups of people were centered around tables and seating areas placed strategically around the room to let people maneuver at ease between them. The music was at a reasonable level, not blaring, but loud enough you could tell what it was and use it as a conversation starter.

Calm swept over Ethan. This would be okay. This was why he always said yes to things. They always turned out okay. With the chief next to him, he could meet people and talk to them and start to build his trust and reputation in town.

"I think I see Marshall from the paper." Chief Stevens put a hand on Ethan's shoulder, then stepped away. "Have fun tonight."

Aaand calm feelings gone.

Ethan moved farther into the room, keenly aware he was dressed in very tight spandex shorts and the longer he stood there without talking to anyone, the more awkward he got.

Of course that was the moment that Brooke came out from the back of the house. The instant she spotted him, a scowl appeared on her face. Painted in white and black and red, the effect was downright chilling.

Even with the zombie makeup, she was the most beautiful woman there. His eyes were drawn to her as he moved around the perimeter of the room, smiling at people as she passed them, then dropping her expression the second she locked eyes again with Ethan. By the time she made her way to stand in front of him, arms crossed and terrifying makeup inches from him, he'd already considered turning around and leaving.

The curiosity of what she would say to him kept him rooted to the spot.

"Are you here to shut down my party?"

He felt the edges of a smile tug at his lips to hear the familiar fire in Brooke's tone. "No, I came with Chief Stevens. He said no work tonight, just socializing."

"So why are you standing alone?"

Did her eyes flick down to his shorts, or was he imagining things?

"I don't know anybody here except for him."

She blinked a few times, her lashes dark against the vivid blue of her irises, and her teeth scraped across her lower lip, smudging the white makeup there.

Then she narrowed her eyes and put her hands on her hips. "Really? You haven't talked to any of these people before?"

He shook his head. "Would you care to introduce me to any of them?" It was a long shot, but he had to take it.

"No." Then she turned on her heels and left him alone in the doorway, unsure if he wanted to laugh or cry.

So much for that idea.

Ethan did a slow walk around the room, stopping at each table to see what there was to eat and drink. They all had slightly different, very detailed themes. One was food in the shape of skulls, another was spiders. One drink table was all purple punch and soda, the other spirits. All this creativity was mind-bogglingly impressive, and Ethan couldn't help but wonder what other hidden talents Brooke might have.

Beyond disliking him, of course.

"You must be Brooke's neighbor." Ethan turned to find a woman smiling at him, her poof of blond curls familiar. His pulse ticked up a notch. This was one of Brooke's friends. Tonight her hair was tucked under a headband with cat ears and lines of makeup painted dark whiskers on her cheeks. The rest of her costume was basically an adult onesie, with a tufted tail that made him think of . . .

"And you must be a lion."

Her smile widened, the effect dazzling and a little overwhelming. Like staring into the sun. "I'm Krista, but tonight I'm Nala."

Her eyes raked up and down his body, taking in his giant Harvard sweatshirt and black bike shorts. "And you are?"

The up-close attention was just as satisfying as he thought it would be.

"Ethan."

She chuckled. "I already knew that. I meant your costume, Ethan."

His stomach twisted. Of course she knew his name. Of course Brooke would have told her friends about him. Both the incident with Lucky last year and this week's fire inspection.

What else had she said? And to who else in this room?

His mission for the night was in serious jeopardy. He'd done nothing but tick off Brooke since they'd first met and the party was for her friends. Everyone here might already think he was a jerk. Chief Stevens could be hearing all about how terrible Ethan was from his friend Marshall, who ran the Adamsville paper.

Adamsville. He looked around the large living room again, wondering if the Adams family had bought the unique and stately house, or built it. Either way, Jerry and Chief Steven's concerns about how he acted around Brooke suddenly made a lot more sense. Antagonizing her had been more of an error than he realized.

As impossible as it might be, his most important mission for the night just became getting on her good side. And one of her friends had just introduced herself.

Whatever road the universe sent him, he rolled down.

He smiled at Krista, flashing the dimples that would get him someone's number faster than you could say "firefighter" back when he still went out to bars. "I'm Princess Diana."

There was a pause, and Krista blinked a few times. Ethan's heart pounded in his ears while he willed his smile not to drop. This was all his sister Rachel's fault. Her obsession with the royals had trickled into every aspect of their lives growing up. It was his lazy, go-to costume whenever Rachel made him go out trick or treating with her. The guys at his old fire station had always loved it, if only for the chance to make inappropriate jokes.

Krista suddenly laughed, the sound drawing the attention of at least half of the men in the room, and a few women as well. "That's amazing. Fantastic job. Ten out of ten."

Ethan's shoulders relaxed, some of the worry melting away. Then he spotted Brooke in a corner, her gaze fixed on him. Though it was a little hard to tell with the dark smudges of makeup around her eyes, she looked even more furious than she had earlier.

Talking to her friends wasn't the way to soften up Brooke, apparently. Time to try something else. He looked around to see what else was right in front of him.

"Um, is there any water? The pitcher on this table is empty."

It was one of those fancy glass ones that looked like a vase. The water had been tinged purple with several silicone skull ice cubes floating around.

"Sure. There should be another in the fridge if you want to bring it out."

"Of course. Can I get you anything else while I'm in there?"

"Why aren't you sweet, princess." There were crinkles at the corners of her eyes and Ethan got the impression this was closer to Krista's real smile, not the one that drew all the stares. "I'm all set, thanks."

He nodded once and made his way toward the kitchen. There was a way to help, which meant there was a way to win over Brooke tonight. All he had to do was keep an eye out for more signs from the universe to know which way to go.

SIX

BROOKE

"Holy forking shirtballs." Krista found Brooke chatting with the owner of the Main Street Deli and grabbed her arm, pulling her into a corner. "Did you see those shorts?"

Brooke knew this had been coming from the second she'd spotted Ethan in the doorway.

In black spandex that hugged his thighs like a second skin.

It was infuriating. Everything had been going great. People were laughing, talking, eating, and drinking. Everyone was saying how nice it was to have the party again. Brooke could practically feel Gran smiling down on her. The Adams' legacy was safe.

Then Ethan had walked in, throwing her off. She hadn't planned for it, and didn't know what to do about him. Letting him stay increased the chance of him blabbing to somebody important about how he'd seen her act—one time!—around a dog, and how rude she'd been at the shelter to a town official. Throwing him out could be an even worse hit on her reputation.

She'd settled for glaring at him, hoping to scare him off. Clearly that hadn't worked, so now she was refocused one thousand percent on her other guests who weren't wearing costumes that showed off every muscle from ankle to quads.

"No, I've been busy being a good hostess."

Krista snorted, not fooled for a second. "You know who he is, right?"

With a weary sigh to let Krista know just how uninterested Brooke was, she glanced around the room until she spied his oversized Harvard sweatshirt. "A lazy college student?"

"Princess Diana."

Brooke looked again at his retreating form as he headed toward the back of the house. The tiny strips of fabric encasing the legs she'd watched do endless squats were, in fact, bike shorts the late royal had liked to wear with baggy sweatshirts. Ethan even had the chunky white sneakers and crew socks to complete the look.

"That's kind of adorable," she admitted.

"I know, right?" Krista put a hand over her heart. "I think we should adopt him."

Brooke whipped her head back around. "He's not a puppy."

"That's right, we still need to find out what happened to his puppy."

"I'm sure it's fine. Maybe he just got busy with work. Fire inspector on top of firefighter must be a lot."

"Go ask him." Krista gave her a nudge.

"Why me? You're the one who wants to adopt him."

"Who are we adopting?" Aisha appeared at their side, a smoking cocktail in one hand and a bowl of spider pretzels in the other. Her wavy, red wig looked amazing with her skin, and the sparkly seventies' disco costume brought out the flecks of gold in her eyes. Not one to be outdone, Krista was the queen of the savanna in her lion costume and mane of curls.

Meanwhile, Brooke was a dripping, drooling zombie. It had seemed like a good idea at the time to go for spooky over sexy, like Gran had always done, but now she wasn't so sure.

It had nothing to do with Ethan and how good he looked in his tiny shorts, of course.

"Are you eating all of those?" Brooke grabbed a few of the pretzels from Aisha's bowl and shoved them into her mouth. There was a satisfying salty sweet crunch, and her heightened emotions were somewhat soothed by the combination of carbs and chocolate.

"We're adopting Ethan," Krista told Aisha.

Brooke shook her head. "No, we're not."

"Then go find out what happened to his puppy, or I'll invite him to every movie night from now until the end of time."

Aisha nodded, wig jiggling unsteadily on her head. "I second the motion."

Overruled by a lion and a disco diva. "This vote was rigged. I didn't even get to present my counter defense."

"There is no defense." Aisha shrugged and handed her drink to Brooke, who sipped it gratefully. The purple gin wasn't her favorite, but it looked amazing, and it would calm her nerves, which was all that mattered right now. "He's your neighbor, and there is a potential dog-related abuse issue here."

"He wasn't abusing the dog. It just ran into my yard." She still wasn't apologizing for how she acted. Anyone in her situation would have done the same.

"Maybe something else happened. He might be mourning it and could use a new one." Krista was now picking out all the M&M's from the bowl of Chex Mix on the table they'd somehow found themselves in front of. "Your first adoption at the new shelter before it even opens. That would get you some good press. The editor of the Adamsville Daily is here tonight."

"Everyone is here tonight." Gran always invited the same group, adding to it over the years until she didn't even need to send out invitations, people just showed up. From the deputy mayor to the fire chief to the high school principal, Gran had known anyone and everyone important in town.

It hadn't felt like the time to change the guest list. The goodwill Gran had built up over the years had helped to counteract the drama Brooke's mom had caused. Three decades after the infamous departure, Brooke wasn't going to be the one to mess with a winning formula.

Other than her friends and Ethan, there was nobody under the age of fifty here. It's why she'd kept the music soft and the lights bright, the same way Gran always had. No point in making it hard for people to hear and see when they were drinking, her grandmother had always said.

"You've already made the rounds twice." Krista popped another M&M in her mouth. "Go talk to Ethan. It'll seem weird if you don't."

"We're out of pretzel spiders." Snatching the not-quite-empty bowl from Aisha's hand, Brooke headed in the direction of the kitchen where Ethan had gone, every muscle in her neck as tight as the wires holding the decorations in place.

This was not how she'd pictured the night going. If he was going to stay, she'd have to change tactics. Maybe she could keep him entertained and distracted, then he wouldn't have a chance to talk to anybody else.

It didn't take long to find him, literally bumping into him as he came out of the kitchen.

"I'm so sorry." His voice was deeper than it had been at the shelter. Softer. His eyes were still the same intense gray, but he looked down almost as soon as he met her gaze, his cheeks tinged pink.

She sucked in a breath, her mouth suddenly too dry to respond. Those shorts clung to every muscle in his upper thighs and the baggy sweatshirt was rolled up to his elbows, putting his thick forearms on display.

Then Brooke looked down and let out an audible gasp, staring in horror at the pitcher in Ethan's hand. The love potion—no, the rosebud tea—had been sitting in the fridge all week. The three friends had forgotten about it as they frantically decorated the house and prepared the snacks for the party. The tea had been sitting undisturbed for days, the light lilac now a dark purple. Brooke's heart dropped into her stomach.

It doesn't matter. It's not really a love potion.

So then why was Ethan blushing and looking at her with an expression that was most definitely not the irritation and aversion she expected to see there?

"I've, uh, been meaning to tell you what a great costume this is." His eyes swept up and down, the tips of her fingers tingling as his eyes raked over her body. "The makeup is really impressive."

"Thank you." What was happening? She held out a hand, proud it wasn't shaking as much as her heart was inside of her chest. The politeness drilled into her by Gran was the only thing allowing her to form words right now. "Let me take that pitcher for you. Please enjoy the rest of the party."

"I can put it on the table for you, no worries." He flashed her a smile, a dimple appearing like the sun on a cloudy day. "What you've done tonight is amazing. Happy to lend a hand if I can."

The tick of her pulse, already off the charts, thrummed in her ears. Why was he offering to help? Complimenting her?

Maybe it was a trick. He could be planning on dumping out the pitcher, accidentally causing a mess somehow.

Or, even worse, had Ethan spotted some crack in the facade that was Brooke's life without her grandmother and recognized she needed help?

In the brief moment before reason returned to her anxiously spiraling brain, she didn't mind the thought of Ethan helping. It sounded wonderful. Which made it all the more confusing. And dangerous.

"No, I'm fine, thanks. Here, have some pretzels." Brooke pushed the half-empty bowl into his hands and grabbed the pitcher, the brush of their fingers sending a rush of electricity shooting up her arm. She held the tea to her chest, a little roughly, and drew a shaky breath. "Did you . . . drink any of this?"

"Um, yeah?" He frowned, a line appearing between his eyebrows. "I was thirsty. Should I not have?"

"It's fine." She clutched the pitcher even tighter, heart hammering so loudly it was probably making waves in the liquid. "It's just, um, the tea wasn't done steeping. It tastes better after a few hours."

"Oh, okay." That adorable eyebrow line didn't disappear. "It tasted pretty good already."

Then he smiled at her. Warm, small, almost shy. Her pounding heart stopped short, and the air compressed around them. The smile wasn't big enough for that dimple to appear again, but it hit her right in the middle of her chest anyway. The timidity of it, the sincerity, the intensity of the emotion behind it.

It's not possible. It's just tea.

"Thanks," she squeaked out, then turned on her heels and hurried away from him.

Safely tucked away in the kitchen, Brooke dumped the entire pitcher of purple liquid into the sink. The big, shaking breaths she was taking didn't quite seem to reach her lungs. Scrambling for her phone in the depths of her costume, she sent an SOS message to both Aisha and Krista, who appeared within seconds in the kitchen.

"Ethan just drank the tea."

"What tea?" Krista frowned and looked up, like she was mentally checking off items on the food tables. "We didn't put any sweet tea on the table. Just the purple water. Ethan was going to get some more."

Of course Krista had sent him on a mission and, of course, he'd agreed. Men would walk over cliffs for her.

"Well, he grabbed the rosebud tea instead. That we made the other night."

"He drank the love potion?" Aisha clapped her hands together and danced in a circle in the middle of the kitchen.

"Shhh!" Brooke knew nobody could have heard her down the

hall over the music and the buzz of conversations, but she didn't want to take any chances. The last thing she needed was for everyone in town to overhear. Gran's potions hadn't been public knowledge, just something special between her and Brooke and her friends. As far as everyone at the party knew, Gran had been a sensible paragon of the community. Brooke needed them to see her as the same thing. Serious, professional, trustworthy, and stable.

She needed them to know she wasn't her mother. Even after thirty-two years of near perfection, the specter of her origins hung over her, ready to attack at the slightest stumble.

"You know what this means?" Aisha went on, still at her regular, too-loud volume.

"Absolutely nothing." Brooke took several quick, deep breaths through her nose. "It's just tea. It's not a love potion."

Except Ethan was being really nice all of a sudden. And the way he looked at me . . .

"Well, it's not *not* a love potion." Krista grinned, her dark eyes bright with mischief as she leaned against the counter next to Aisha.

"It's just tea."

"But it might be—"

"I need it to just be tea."

It *had* to be just tea. Otherwise, it meant that Gran could have taken something to get better and chose not to. It meant she chose to leave Brooke.

Just like her mother.

"Um, hi."

Everything in Brooke's body froze at the new voice in the kitchen. Her back was to the door but there was no doubt who it was, thanks to the look of pure glee on Aisha's face and the wide grin on Krista's face. To Ethan, it would look like the two of them were being friendly, but Brooke could see the shark-like gleam in Krista's eyes.

"Yes?" Krista asked, her voice as smooth and thick as honey from the other side of the kitchen.

Brooke slowly turned, keeping her face as expressionless as possible while her heart started pumping blood again at four times its normal speed.

"I just . . . " Ethan rubbed the back of his neck, the muscles in his forearms visible and flexing beneath the rolled-up sleeves of his sweatshirt. His weight shifted from one foot to the other, the movement drawing Brooke's eyes to his bare legs.

"I wanted to ask again if I could help with anything. You seemed kind of stressed. Out there." He waved toward the living room, his eyes darting to the empty pitcher of tea on the counter.

He was probably wondering why she'd run off, why she'd acted so strange that he'd drank some tea. There was no way she could possibly explain to him that it wasn't just tea.

It is *just tea.*

"That's very kind of you." Krista shot Brooke one of her most devious looks, and Aisha was practically buzzing with energy. Their thoughts were beaming at Brooke, loud and clear.

They, at least, were convinced the "love potion" had worked.

No, he's just helpful. It didn't mean anything. Maybe he felt bad about how he'd acted at the shelter. Maybe he was trying to look good in front of Chief Stevens.

Neither of those possibilities explained the way he was looking at her. He hadn't even glanced at the food on the counter. What guy walked into a kitchen and didn't even scan it for a snack?

One who'd just drank a love potion.

It's just tea!

Brooke took a deep breath, shook back her hair, and lifted her chin. "I'm fine, thanks. Please enjoy the party."

He let out a soft chuckle, and that little endearing line between his eyebrows made a brief appearance as his gaze fell to the floor, then back up to meet Brooke's. No quick glance at Krista in her skintight lion costume or at Aisha bouncing on her heels next to the counter.

It was Brooke he was looking at. Brooke he'd complimented. In her dripping zombie outfit, Brooke held his undivided attention.

"I told you, I don't really know anyone except for Chief Stevens who brought me."

The thump of her heart was loud in her ears as she wondered how to respond to this shy, helpful, adorable fireman who was most definitely not falling for Brooke because of a magic love potion.

In the space where Brooke's answer should have gone, Aisha said, "I don't know anyone either except for these two. And now you."

Sweet baby huskies, his dimples were back. Brooke locked her knees to keep from swooning. Krista would never let her hear the end of it.

"Could you actually do me a favor and take a picture of me?" He held out his phone while his gaze finally swept around the kitchen, as if unsure if he was making a reasonable request. "I want to send it to my sister."

Of course the shy, helpful, adorable fireman had a sister. It all made sense now. He knew how to talk to women, knew how to be nice to them. It wasn't because he was in love with her. The rosebud tea was just tea.

It had to be just tea.

"We have sticky hands from the candy, sorry." Krista held up her palms, a small smile playing on the edges of her lips as she nudged Aisha who held up hers as well.

Brooke wanted to strangle them both. Somehow a bowl of Chex Mix had appeared between them on the counter, as if they'd been preparing a new one this entire time.

"Sure, I can take it." Brooke stepped forward and reached for his phone, suddenly remembering Krista's threat to include Ethan in the trio's activities unless she got the details her friends wanted. "If you answer a question for me."

"Sure."

Brooke took a deep breath, gripping his phone tightly. "Did something happen to your puppy?"

His face went blank for just a moment before a wide smile stretched his lips. "Who, Lucky? He's fine. Just went back to the facility upstate to finish his training as a guide dog."

"You need a guide dog?" Brooke blurted out before she realized how ridiculous and rude that was. Heat pooled in her throat.

There was only the briefest moment of his smile faltering, so quick she must have imagined it. Then those dimples flashed and Brooke's knees buckled. "I was a puppy raiser. Well, first a dog sitter, then I took him on full-time when his original raiser moved away. They stay with raisers for a year or so to get used to being out in the world."

Brooke couldn't see her friends' faces anymore, but she could sense their euphoric expressions and what they were thinking all the same.

Shy, helpful, adorable, *and* a selfless raiser of guide puppies?

Gran would have been so ashamed of her. Brooke was the lowest of the low to have yelled at him and his dog. This man should be smashing things in her kitchen, telling all of her guests she had lice, or spitting in all the punch bowls. Instead, he was asking her for a favor and smiling at her like she was the most beautiful thing he'd ever seen.

What if it's not just tea?

"That's incredible." Brooke cleared her throat and held up his phone. "Say cheese."

He stuck the goofiest pose possible, with two thumbs up and a wide, silly grin. Brooke dug her teeth into her bottom lip to stop herself from laughing.

"Thanks." The appreciative look he gave her made her stomach flutter. Which was a completely normal reaction to a really hot guy in bike shorts.

A really hot guy with no earthly reason to be smiling at her like that.

Other than a love potion.

Ethan paused, like he was waiting for one of the three women staring at him to say something. When nobody did, he rubbed his hand along the back of his neck again, putting those forearms on full display again. "I guess I should get back out there and try to get to know people."

Just as he walked out of the room, he turned back to give her one more half-smile, his lips tilting up. Brooke could hear Krista and Aisha sigh behind her.

And maybe she let out a little one of her own as well, before panic came surging back with the force of a freight train.

"Well, fork me," Aisha whispered. "Gran's potions totally work."

Though she'd never say it out loud, Brooke couldn't help but agree with her.

At least she wouldn't have to worry anymore about Ethan bad-mouthing her to everyone in town.

SEVEN

ETHAN

From the safety of the hallway that connected the kitchen to the living room, Ethan's eyes drifted between the party guests. They landed Chief Stevens talking to a group of older men who were laughing like they'd all known each other for years. One of them looked familiar—maybe the deputy mayor?

Ethan let out a breath through tight lips, the slow exhale doing little to calm the anxiety swirling in his chest. He knew he should get out there and be social, but he wasn't looking forward to another failure so early in the evening. Talking to Brooke had been a disaster. There hadn't been a clear sign it was what he should do, instead he'd been following some undeniable pull toward her, hoping he could charm her.

That's what happened when Ethan hoped. Disappointment and shattered dreams.

Glancing over his shoulder, he considered his options. It wasn't worth going back into the kitchen to try again. The way she'd looked at him, as if she had no idea what to do with him, burned like he'd put his hand to a flame.

Was he really surprised he'd failed at getting her to warm up to him? Maybe a little. The bike shorts had gotten a few downward glances, and her chilly attitude probably had more to do with how stressful hosting a party like this was than with any animosity toward Ethan. Still, their interaction hadn't done much to build his confidence in his assignment to make friends with everyone in town.

At least he'd gotten a photo for Rachel.

Tucking himself away in a corner—this house seemed to be full of these little nooks perfect for hiding—he decided confronting the masses in the living could wait until he sent the ridiculous picture to his sister.

It took less than ten seconds for her to reply.

> **Rachel**
> Whose kitchen is that? Are you at a party?

Then, a moment later, as if she'd finally taken a second look at him:

> **Rachel**
> You look great. But you'd look better with the wig.

A laugh rumbled through Ethan's chest. Holy smokes, he missed her. Knoxville was a full day's drive away. Between his schedule when he was a firefighter and hers as a resident in a busy hospital, it might as well be the moon.

The more regular nine-to-five schedule of an inspector meant he could go see her more often, but he wanted to hold off until he officially had the job.

Which he never would unless he went out there and met people, but he couldn't leave his sister on read for too long or she'd worry. He leaned back against the wall, the soft murmur of conversations drifting over the spooky notes of a Halloween soundtrack, and typed out a response.

> **Ethan**
> It's my neighbor's Halloween party.

> **Rachel**
> The one who hates dogs?

> **Ethan**
> She doesn't hate them. I think she was just having a rough day.

If there hadn't been the party last year, maybe it was because she was dealing with the death of her grandmother right around the time his dog had dug up her garden. Not the greatest way to introduce yourself to the neighbor in general, but if she'd also been grieving, then he couldn't really blame her for letting out some of her emotions, could he? After all, the only reason he'd been eager for a fight that day was because he'd only recently gotten his diagnosis.

> **Ethan**
> She's starting an animal shelter.

> **Rachel**
> Maybe you should volunteer to make sure she doesn't yell at the dogs there.

He sent back an eye-rolling emoji, but her comment sparked something. It wasn't a terrible idea, actually, asking if he could help. Animal shelters always needed volunteers.

Ethan didn't plan his life the way others did. If an opportunity came up, he always tried to say yes, trusting whenever his gut tried to tell him something.

It was his gut that had told him his problems seeing at night were something more than fatigue or a side effect of smoke.

It was his gut that had told him to take up Aunt Mary on renting her house for next to nothing when she moved to Florida. It was a new town, but his sister had just moved to Knoxville so there was nothing tying him to their hometown in North Carolina anymore. With all the work he'd done on it over the past year, his aunt had agreed to give him a portion of the profits when she eventually sold it.

Now his gut was telling him the shelter was the way to get to know more people in town. It gave him a reason to go back to the dog park. Maybe even a reason to talk to his old crew, see if they could team up the way they had with the guide-dog charity that had brought Lucky into his life. It was the perfect solution to everything. There was only one problem.

There was no way Brooke would say yes.

She'd taken the picture, sure, but clearly only to be polite in front of her friends. The wide-eyed way she'd stared at him in the kitchen left no doubt in his mind that she would reject any offer of his help immediately. She hadn't even wanted him to bring water in from the kitchen, snatching the pitcher away from him like she was afraid he'd drop it and break what he was sure was priceless heirloom crystal.

Ethan
I don't think she'll yell at the dogs. But I also don't think she wants my help.

Rachel
Did you ask her?

Ethan
No. If she wants the help, it'll happen.

His sister sent a string of face-palming emojis.

Rachel
You can't just stand around waiting for things to fall in your lap. You've got to make things happen.

Shaking his head, he tucked his phone into his pocket, pushed off from the wall, and made his way toward a food table. His sister just didn't get it. She'd already been on her path in medicine when their parents had died, while Ethan had been drifting, struggling to find his way. Every time he hoped for something, it hadn't worked out. Once he accepted whatever life brought his way, things would happen for Ethan the way they were supposed to. Firefighting, Aunt Mary's house, Lucky, the inspector job. He hadn't gone looking for any of it, but it had all turned out fine. This would too, somehow.

"Ethan." At the sound of his name, Ethan turned to find Chief Stevens at his side. The older man put a hand on his shoulder and led him toward a group of men standing nearby. "Sorry for leaving you on your own earlier. I was just telling Marshall here about that fundraiser we had last year at the fire department. Somehow it didn't make it into the paper."

See, Rachel? Things happen to me. I don't make them happen.

"The 'date with a firefighter and a dog' raffle?" Ethan chuckled, remembering the long lines to buy tickets that had snaked around the corner all week. "That was wild."

"It was great!" Chief Stevens was beaming at him and Ethan's heart lifted. "Raised a ton and didn't cost us anything except the raffle tickets. Brought a lot of attention to a local charity as well."

When the guide-dog organization had first come to them with the idea, Ethan had no idea what would happen a few months later. Helping to organize the raffle had been fun, but after learning more about what they did, he'd wanted to do more.

Being a puppy raiser for the charity sounded amazing, but his firefighter schedule meant he could only offer to be a puppy sitter. The old assistant fire inspector signed up to raise Lucky, and Ethan watched him whenever he went away on long weekends. When his wife's job took him out of state, he not only left the role available, he left Lucky with Ethan. He'd already been considering leaving full-time firefighting because of his diagnosis, which meant he had the time for the puppy.

Everything worked out the way it was supposed to. Tragedy and disappointment always led to better things, as long as Ethan didn't hope too hard for things to be different.

Now here he was, talking to three of the most important people in Adamsville, and he welcomed the unexpected turn the evening had taken. The group of men went back and forth, and though Ethan didn't say much, the lightness in his chest buoyed him through the conversation. It was easier to relax around people when he wasn't also inspecting their building. Within an hour, he'd talked to almost everyone in the room.

It wasn't how Ethan liked to meet people, and he'd stayed pretty quiet, but at least it was a start. The chief seemed pleased with him, nodding and smiling and patting him on the shoulder. With a little luck, he'd mention something to Jerry about tonight, and Ethan's uncertain future would be back on track.

Not wanting to press that luck, Ethan said goodnight to Chief Stevens and made his way to the door. Someone waved at him, and he turned to see Krista. Next to her was Brooke, her gaze as cold as ever, and the confidence high he'd been riding from his successful socializing came crashing down in an instant.

He should thank Brooke for hosting. It was the polite thing to do. He'd watched her flitting around the room while he chatted with the chief's friends, smiling that creepy zombie smile that was still somehow also eerily enchanting.

Yes, he knew it was a problem to find that so attractive.

Not as big a problem as the frosty look she was sending his way.

Tonight probably wasn't going to be enough to convince the chief and Jerry he was "integrated into the community" the way he apparently needed to be for the job. And who knew what other important people Brooke had in her social circle.

Putting on his biggest, brightest smile, he waved at Brooke and Krista while heading to the door. He mouthed "thanks" and escaped into a much cooler October night than he expected. Blinking a few times, he wished he'd thought of some excuse to bring a flashlight.

No point wishing for things you don't have.

He let himself get his bearings and adjust to the dimmer light before slowly making his way down the pumpkin-lined walkway. This also gave Brooke time to come after him. If he was supposed to volunteer at the shelter, she'd follow him outside. Even if it was to yell at him, he'd take it as the sign he needed to offer his help. If she didn't come, then it wasn't meant to be.

It took him twice as long to get to his front door as it had to follow the chief to the party, and he shivered the entire time, the weather windier than it had been earlier. But no one followed him.

Ethan had his answer.

EIGHT
BROOKE

The shelter was opening in less than twenty-four hours. This was not the time to panic.

This also wasn't the time to remake her banana and matcha smoothie for the third time, but it still wasn't quite right.

Brooke leaned against the kitchen counter and took a long drink of the thick green concoction, knowing perfectly well that while L-theanine and B6 could help to calm the nervous system, no amount of smoothies in the world, magic or not, were going to help Brooke right now. Drink in one hand, she scrolled through her phone with the other, going through the endless list of things to do before the animals started arriving at the shelter tomorrow.

Right at the top was picking up all the inspection paperwork at city hall. For some reason, Adamsville—probably thanks one of her ancestors who'd been mayor—made it a requirement to come get them in person.

Though the smoothie wasn't hurting things. At least now she wasn't quite as hungry as she'd been earlier.

She'd always suspected that was ninety percent of why the smoothies seemed to help so much. Gran knew how hangry Brooke could get, especially as a kid. Anytime she was feeling sad or hope-less, the solution was always to feed her.

Sipping away, she made her way through the house, sparkling clean thanks to Aisha and Krista who had spent the night after the party and all day Sunday with her. They'd both already left for work this morning. Since the shelter technically wasn't open yet, Brooke didn't have to be there at a certain time. She was tempted to not go at all and just wish on a lucky star that everything would be ready for tomorrow.

But that wasn't who she was. She had her plan, and following it was the only way to be sure things would go the way she needed them to.

Her feet, apparently unaware of her plan for the day, led her to the side window that looked out on Ethan's backyard. There was a crush of disappointment in her chest to discover he wasn't there.

No, this is a good thing. She shook her head and continued to drink her smoothie. It shouldn't matter if she was able to creepily spy on Ethan or not. She had to avoid him at all costs. That sappy, lovesick smile he'd given her before he left her party had been as telling as if he'd told her to her face how he felt. Or rather, how he thought he felt thanks to the rosebud tea.

How long would the effects last? A week? A month?

The only solution was to stay as far away from him as possible for as long as possible.

Naturally, that was the exact moment he stepped out into his yard. Though nights had been getting cooler, the weather during the day was still warm, as if the South Carolinian summer didn't want to let go quite yet.

Or maybe it didn't want Ethan to stop working out outside, either.

Naturally, he was shirtless. The hazy outline of a tattoo—that her friends had definitely not spent hours discussing what it might be—was on full display on his back. From this angle, it looked like some kind of axe.

Her fingers gripped the glass in her hand, and she sucked greedily at the straw as she watched him do some squats and push-ups to warm up. Then came the upper body weights, then she knew next would be the lower body.

Was it embarrassing she knew his routine better than her friends' work schedules?

Probably.

Definitely.

Was it her fault she had a mind for patterns and routines? It just stored away the information, categorizing it and saving it for when it might be useful.

Not part of his regular routine, however, was the long stare he gave in her direction.

No, not in her direction.

Directly at her.

A curse word flew out of her mouth as her heart jumped into it, and she spun around, practically diving for the couch, out of sight of the window.

This was bad.

Not quite as bad as screaming at him and his dog, but definitely a top ten embarrassing moment. Possibly a top five.

There were only two reasons he was looking at her house.

One, that stupid love potion had worked and he was completely obsessed with her.

Two, he knew Brooke and her friends watched him workout.

She didn't know which one was worse.

What if it's both?

She closed her eyes and leaned against the back of the couch, eyes closed. Three deep breaths, then it would be time to head to the shelter.

Downing the rest of her smoothie in one large gulp, she stood and went back into the kitchen, averting her eyes from every window she passed. She focused her attention on cleaning up the kitchen, taking her time with it, the familiar routine soothing. A reminder that not everything was out of her control.

Just as she was about to leave, she noticed a few spots of red smoothie on her white sweater, and she cursed again. She stomped up the stairs, furious with herself for being so careless. It had probably happened when she'd surged away from the window like the creeper she was.

Finally, dressed in a clean sweater and with another splash on her wrists of the dwindling stock of Gran's homemade lavender oil to soothe her nerves, Brooke headed out the door.

Ethan was on his porch at the exact same moment.

Their eyes met, because of course they did. His gaze was drawn to her, like the rosebud tea was supposed to make happen. Next, he'd start walking toward her, unable to stop his desire from wanting to be as close to her as possible at all times.

The thing she'd giggled over and hoped for as a middle-schooler now sounded like an absolute nightmare.

Well, maybe not a nightmare. There were worse things in the world than an attractive, shy, puppy-raising firefighter wanting to talk to her.

She gave a small wave, barely an acknowledgment, the absolute minimum of politeness. Brooke could practically feel Gran's disappointed eyes on her. With a sigh, she took a step toward him, and he made his way over to the bright white fence that separated their two houses, arriving at the same time.

"Good morning," she said, her tone hopefully crisp enough to signal she wasn't up for talking much today.

"Morning." Underneath his jacket, he was dressed in a dark-beige uniform that did ridiculous things to his eyes. The deep gray of his irises wasn't a color she'd seen in anyone else. The light tan of his uniform made them look like the cloudy, stormy sky above a wide expanse of desert.

Woah there, calm down. It's just a guy in uniform.

"On your way to work?"

He gave a few gentle bobs of his head. "You? Is the shelter open already?"

"Tomorrow's when all the animals arrive. There's a ton of stuff to unpack and organize and clean before then." She took a breath and blew it out through her mouth, purposely making the most unattractive sound possible. "Oh, and go pick up all the inspection reports."

Another few bobs. Was he just rendered speechless by her beauty, the way the love potion was supposed to do? It was more likely that he wasn't a morning person, like so many other people on the planet.

"I could get those inspection reports for you, if you want."

The air left her lungs in a sharp snap of an exhale. "Um, no, that's fine. I don't want to bother you."

"Not a bother at all. Happy to help."

Now she couldn't breathe at all, her chest squeezing tight. Was this really him, or was it the tea? There was a tiny possibility that he was just a nice guy, and they'd gotten off on the wrong foot. But given how she'd treated him the three separate occasions they'd met before he drank the tea, it was hard to imagine he could get over it without a bit of help.

"Okay, um, thanks." She tucked her hair behind her ear, commanding her lungs to function properly. This was a normal, neighborly thing for him to offer. Adamsville was a small town, people acted like this all the time. "I'll be there all day."

"No lunch break?"

Oh no, was he trying to ask her out? Her stomach dropped to the grass beneath her feet. As much as she didn't want to believe it, as ridiculous as it had seemed the morning after the party, this was just too much to be anything other than magical. There was no way he'd be acting like this otherwise.

"I really need to get going." She looked at her watch. "Too much to do, too little time."

She ran off before he could say anything else, not even bothering to say goodbye. She'd see him later on today at some point anyway.

Cursing for the third time that morning, this time for her big mouth, she got into her car. This was what she got for trying to be like Gran. Polite, talkative, and making potions for every little problem that popped up in her life. She ended up with a guy in love with her and volunteering to do things for her.

Not that she needed his help anyway. Solidifying the stellar reputation and legacy of Michele Adams was something only Brooke could do. As she drove away, she told herself she wouldn't look back at Ethan. But her eyes had a mind of their own and were drawn to her rearview mirror like it would reveal the secrets of the universe.

Ethan was standing next to his car, and he ran his hands through his hair before getting in. The short brown waves were cut close to his head on the sides, and longer on the top. It was the perfect hair for running your fingers through. Krista and Aisha had spent more time than Brooke would ever admit talking about what it would feel like. Every part of him demanded that kind of attention and discussion. He was exceptional without even trying that hard.

Except for those muscles. They saw the work that went into them. But the rest you had to be born with. The hair. The height. Those eyes.

Finally no longer able to see him, she settled into her car seat and opened the window, the morning air a welcome burst of coolness across her face. The drive to the shelter was short, but full of emotional pitfalls, and today they all hit especially hard. The tightness in her chest flared hot when she passed by her old apartment. Moving out of Gran's house had been hard, but Brooke only lived on her own for a few years before she moved back in to take care of her grandmother.

The apartment block gave way to an empty field, and the morning sun hit Brooke right in the eyes. Blinking fast, she pushed away the memories of taking care of Gran the way a mother would a sick child. The way Gran had all of Brooke's life.

She didn't remember her mom, since she was barely two when she left. The only picture she'd ever seen was one Gran had from the day Brooke was born. Gran was holding Brooke and grinning from ear to ear, while her mom was sitting in the background, a small, tired smile on her face.

She'd been seventeen.

The guy that had gotten her mom pregnant had been long gone by the time Brooke was born. A few years later, her mom had left too, supposedly to go find him. At least that's what Gran had always said. She liked to paint a picture for Brooke when she was little that her parents were off living some dangerous life Brooke couldn't be a part of, so they'd left her with Gran because they loved her so much.

The reality was, they hadn't even wanted her.

Gran did though. That photo was proof that, from the very first day of Brooke's life, she was thrilled to have her. Gran had saved her from whatever terrible life Brooke might have had if she hadn't stepped in when Brooke's mother left.

Just like Brooke would be able to do for the animals at the shelter.

Pulling up to a red light, she fought back the surge of tears that suddenly overwhelmed her. Even if she was hurting from being left behind yet again, she couldn't disappoint Gran. Not when she owed her so much.

The light turned green, and she wiped at her cheeks before turning onto the street that led to the shelter.

After so many months of waiting for it to open, it almost hadn't, thanks to Brooke's poor judgment in hiring Jason. Now she had to do everything she could to make sure it succeeded. It was up to Brooke to make sure people remembered the Adams family for all the good it had done for the town. Brooke's home-staging career had been a quiet one, keeping her behind the scenes. It was nothing like the public work her family was known for. Adamsville was named for Brooke's great-great-uncle, but despite Gran's standing, the rumors still lingered even thirty years after Brooke's mom had disappeared and left her baby behind.

Parking the car in the spot directly in front of the shelter, Brooke inhaled slowly and let a tiny tendril of hope and pride wrap around her heart. The Michele Adams Animal Rescue would be what cemented the family's good name in the town once and for all.

And Brooke would be the one to make it happen.

NINE

ETHAN

The pizza place was one of his favorites. Before his diagnosis, Ethan and his new crew had come in a few times after a night out. He'd sit at the corner booth, laugh at the others while they joked around with the cooks or leaned over the counter to grab some extra parmesan. Once he'd even fallen asleep at one of the tables and only woke up when someone had poured a pitcher of soda on him. The friendships that had started to take root in his first months in town had all withered away when he'd stopped going out. He hadn't set foot inside the restaurant since he quit being a firefighter.

Ethan spun in a slow circle, letting his eyes linger on the spacing between the tables, then back again in the opposite direction along the ceiling as his stomach twisted tighter. Things weren't looking great. The last thing he wanted to do was shut down a local institution and have everyone at the station know it was because of him.

Is it better to let it stay open if it's dangerous? Everything in the dining area was just slightly off: only half the sprinklers worked and one of the emergency exit lights was out. There weren't enough fire extinguishers and the tables were too close to the booths to leave ample space for evacuation. Extension cords criss crossed the floor of the hallway that led to the bathrooms.

He looked at the owner, Mrs. Carver, an older woman with silver-streaked black hair and a flowered apron tied around her waist. She'd always been behind the counter on those long-ago nights with his former crew. Seeing the hopeful look in her eye when he introduced himself as the inspector had put a lump in his throat he hadn't been able to shift the entire visit. He cleared his throat. "There are a few things you'll need to address."

"Excuse me?" Her eyes narrowed.

Ethan's gaze darted to Jerry for help, but the older man said nothing, his expression unreadable.

"It's small things that shouldn't take long to fix."

Now he had two people glaring at him silently. He ran a hand along the back of his neck and swallowed hard. There were still a few more things to check. "Do you have any CO_2 canisters?"

She looked at Jerry, who nodded, then she waved a hand. "This way."

Ethan followed her into the back area, Jerry following right behind. The feeling of triumph from talking with people at Brooke's party was flickering away to nothing like a bonfire in a rainstorm. The assistant inspector job that had seemed possible while surrounded by Chief Stevens and his friends on Saturday night now felt completely unattainable.

As if one night would somehow transform Ethan from the introvert he was into a social butterfly, always able to say and do the right thing to the right person.

No such luck. It was awkward as anything making small talk with an irritated Mrs. Carver while he checked the CO_2 canisters and then the range hood.

This was what happened when he hoped for something. If things were meant to be, they'd happen. Anytime Ethan wanted to change things, they failed. He failed.

All he could do was follow along with what was put in his path and trust it would lead where he should go. There had to be a reason Ethan was finding so many problems while inspecting one of the only places full of good memories for him in town.

When he asked about how long Mrs. Carver owned the place, he got a short, sharp answer. When he asked for the inspection reports for the fire suppression system, she gave him a dirty look, and something clicked into place.

She'd been expecting him not to mention any of the problems. His heart sank into the depths of his belly. Is that what other inspectors had done? Maybe it had been a little thing they'd over-looked once, and it had kept piling up, year over year. Or maybe things had just gotten away from her recently. She did look more tired than he ever remembered seeing her, even though he'd always been there after midnight.

Whatever the reason, Ethan was there to help keep people safe. If she fixed everything up, she had nothing to worry about.

Yet it was Ethan's palms that were sweating, his stomach that was twisted in knots. Jerry's continued silence clearly meant Ethan wasn't handling this right, but what was he supposed to do? Tell her everything was okay when it wasn't? Make a joke and put her at ease?

I can't do this.

He'd been good at being a firefighter. Following orders, using his instincts, knowing he was making a difference. The things that had made him a good firefighter weren't transferring over into this new job the way he thought they would. When you were responding to a call, you didn't stop to think if this person's family was important in town or how getting to know them might make things easier. You saved everyone, no matter what.

"The kitchen looks great." He smiled at Mrs. Carver, and this, finally, seemed to get her to warm up to him. Whether it was the smile or the relief that in this room at least there were no issues, he didn't know. He was just grateful to have her stop looking at him like he was a bug on her famous pizza.

Heart pounding, Ethan went through the list of items she'd need to take care of, keeping his voice as gentle and optimistic as possible while Jerry waited silently off to the side. Mrs. Carved looks his way a few times, as if to double check everything Ethan was saying was correct, which did little to calm his nerves.

Finally, they both said goodbye to Mrs. Carver and headed back out to the truck. The air was a cool relief on Ethan's heated face, and he ran the back of his hand along his forehead.

"So." Ethan cleared his throat, suddenly as dry as the grass in summer where there'd been no rain for four weeks straight. "How did I do?"

Jerry paused with his hand on the driver's side door with Ethan standing slightly in front of the truck, ready to head to the passenger side. Ethan held his breath, then let it out, heart pounding in his ears.

The older man opened the door. "That was fine."

Deflating faster than a popped balloon, Ethan fought to keep his expression neutral as he made his way to the passenger side.

Fine. It was fine. That was good. He wasn't going to be getting medals or pictures colored by kindergartners in this job. Fine kept people safe, and that was fine.

Really.

The drive back to the station was a short and quiet one. Ethan knew Jerry wasn't shy about giving his opinion, so no news really was good news.

But it was like an itch that he knew he shouldn't scratch. The need to ask for more details, to know what he could have done better. Maybe he should have told her how much he liked her pizza, or spent more time explaining the issues to correct.

They'd just turned onto the street that led to the fire station when Jerry spoke again. "I heard you were at the Adams' family Halloween party this weekend."

"Oh, um, yeah." Ethan shifted in his seat and swallowed hard. "Brooke's my neighbor."

"Hmm."

Uncertainty swirled in Ethan's belly. It had felt like a good thing that he'd gone to the party, but Jerry did seem happy about it. Maybe he thought he'd gate crashed.

"I wasn't planning on going, Chief Stevens stopped by to invite me."

This, apparently, was the wrong thing to say. Jerry's face darkened, and the stony silence in the car turned icy.

It was only a few blocks to the station, and Ethan spent every one of them looking out the window with his hands twisting tight in his lap. It was an eternity before they pulled into the station's parking lot, and just as they did, Jerry's phone rang. It was a quick call, and the man's quiet demeanor didn't change much as he said various forms of "yes" and "uh-huh" and "got it."

Then he hung up and turned to Ethan.

"You can take the rest of the day off. I have to take care of something."

"Oh, okay." Ethan wiped his sweaty palms on his pants. "I was thinking I'd take all the inspection reports and licenses out to the shelter."

Jerry raised an eyebrow. "Are we providing that service now? I don't remember seeing that memo."

Ethan's heart dropped into his stomach. "No, it's just, Brooke has a lot to get ready and—"

"We can't be doing favors for people, Ethan." Jerry shook his head and smoothed his hand over the steering wheel. "You didn't give any leeway to Mrs. Carver, so Brooke doesn't get any either."

Heat bloomed in Ethan's chest. "Should I have not mentioned what I saw?"

"You could have been nicer about it."

The air in the truck pressed in around them. Their definitions of nice clearly weren't the same. This job was getting more confusing by the day. He was supposed to get to know people, understand their status in the community, but not bend the rules because of that.

It was Ethan's own fault; he shouldn't have said anything about helping Brooke. It's just . . . it had felt like a sign that morning. First Brooke had come out of her house at the exact same time as him. Then she'd mentioned a need, her eyes so wide and blue and panicked. Since Ethan was in a position to help out, there was no other choice but to offer.

He thought it would be a good way to show he was getting more involved in the community, that people were trusting him. Especially since Jerry had seen Ethan get so tense with Brooke.

Looked like he was wrong.

Ethan took a deep breath and let it out slowly. "I'm just helping her out. The shelter is opening tomorrow and she needs the paperwork."

"Hmm." Jerry grunted, clearly not happy about it. "Maybe she should have been focused on that instead of her party."

Ethan released a breath as the pieces fit together. Jerry was upset he hadn't been invited to the party. Maybe he'd expected one during the inspection but thought the way Ethan had acted at the shelter had nixed the possibility.

"I'll let her know when I see her that you wished you could have been there."

Please let that be the right thing to say.

Jerry's expression didn't change, but there was the slightest softening of his eyes. "Hmm."

Then he got out of the truck and left Ethan there, fumbling around with his doubts without a light to guide him out.

It was early in the afternoon when Ethan arrived at the animal shelter, and the sun was still shining brightly. Though this errand shouldn't take more than a few minutes, he did a quick calculation, his shoulders relaxing when he reminded himself there'd be daylight for another few hours.

The night blindness issue hadn't come up with Jerry yet, and Ethan wasn't sure how to approach it without sounding like he was asking for special treatment, even though his sister and his doctor liked to remind him he had the right to. Until Jerry calmed down about the Halloween party, however, there was no way he would bring it up.

Ethan didn't look any different, and didn't feel any different, not during the day at least. So far he'd been able to manage his schedule, but a few times he'd had to leave his car at the station and call a rideshare. Nobody said anything about it, but that only made Ethan more anxious, not less. Either they had all been wondering about it and didn't feel like they could talk to him like they used to. Or they didn't actually care at all.

Ethan's stomach was in knots as he got out of his truck. Taking a deep breath, he went through his inspection checklist in his head. While he was only there to give her the paperwork, it was good practice to verify everything again.

Address visible, check.

No parking spots blocking hydrants, check.

No moss or other materials on the roof that might increase the fire risk, check.

Satisfied, and somewhat calmer, he walked into the shelter. The reception area had completely transformed. Gone were the clinical, depressing white walls and wide, empty, cold spaces. The walls had been covered in colorful animal print wallpaper, and the floor was painted bright blue, with a few thick rugs that Ethan knew from experience would keep muddy dog paws from tracking dirt all over.

There were long benches under the windows with low, sturdy cushions in a dark, easy to clean material. There was still a clear pathway to the door, nothing blocking movement from the back to the front, but it all looked much homier, much more inviting. Like you'd want to come in and hang out with the animals and stay for hours.

"Hello?" Ethan set the paperwork on the counter. "Brooke?"

"In the back!"

He followed the sound of her voice through the long hallway of the kennels and into the storage room. Like the reception area, everything had gotten a coat of paint and some decorations. Even the kennels looked welcoming, with pillows and blankets in different colors.

"This place looks really good," he said as he walked into the storage room.

"Ethan!"

Brooke dropped the box she was holding and it fell with a thump. His heart dropped along with it.

"Is this a bad time?"

"Um, no, actually." She bent to pick up the box, and he knelt down. Their hands brushed and the heat of her skin against his danced up his arms. She stood up at the same time he did, her face red. "I just didn't think you'd actually come."

"I said I would, didn't I?"

She gave him an odd look, like someone simply saying they'd do something for her didn't always mean they would.

"I put the inspection reports on the counter out front." He bent again to pick up the box. "Where is this going?"

She swallowed, Ethan's eyes tracking the movement of her throat rather than looking into her eyes. Who knew what he might say or do when faced with those icy-blue irises.

"Up there." She pointed to the top of the shelving unit. "It's just extra blankets."

He spotted a step ladder in the corner and dragged it over with his foot. "I meant what I said. This place looks great."

She raised an eyebrow. "Did you expect it to have fallen into disrepair so quickly?"

His cheeks heated as he climbed the ladder. She still thought he didn't like her. So much for trying to be nice and helpful.

"No, I meant the decorations and everything." He put the box on the shelf then looked down to see her eyes widen and cheeks flush.

"Thanks." What might have been the barest hint of a smile tugged at her lips. She tucked her hair behind her ear. "I used to be a stager."

"What?"

She nodded her head in the direction of the hallway, to the rest of the shelter and all the work she'd clearly put in over the past week since he'd last been there. "It's what I used to do. Stage apartments and houses for real estate companies."

"Why'd you stop?" He made his way down off the step ladder then leaned against the shelves and crossed his arms. Her body mirrored his, arms tight against her chest as she shrugged her shoulders.

"Someone had to run this place."

"You could hire someone."

"I did." She choked out a laugh. "You saw what he did to the place."

"That explains it." The words were out of him before he could stop them.

"What's that supposed to mean?" There was that edge of fight in her tone, and Ethan rushed to make sure it didn't turn out exactly like the last time he'd been at the shelter.

"I mean you never would have made all those mistakes we saw on that first inspection." Ethan ran a hand over the back of his neck, but it did nothing to relax the tense muscles there. "Like hiring that guy who messed up the electric panel. I know I don't know you that well, but I can tell you have an eye for detail. You pay attention to all the little things. Like at the party. Everything was skull-themed and purple. Even the ice cubes."

"You noticed that?" Her lips turned up in a smile, small but real. "Thanks."

A moment of silence stretched between them. While Ethan's heart danced circles inside his chest, he concentrated on the distant woosh of passing cars on the street, and the soft tick from the clock in the reception area. There were so many things he wanted to say, but he had no idea where to start. That he was sorry to hear about her grandmother passing, that he realized now why she'd been so upset with Lucky, that he hadn't meant to make things harder for her that day.

Just as he opened his mouth, a phone rang. She reached into her pocket and walked out into the hallway, leaving him deflated and alone in the storage room.

He folded up the stepladder and put it in the corner, cheeks blazing. When he walked into the shelter today, he'd been hoping for a chance to offer more help. Spending more time with Brooke hadn't even been on his radar, but that little smile of hers had made him hope for... well, he didn't know what exactly but this hot flare of disappointment reminded him again how ridiculous it was to hope.

It didn't matter. If there was another opportunity, he'd take it, but the phone call had been a sign as clear as day that he wasn't supposed to say anything else to her today.

"What do you mean you quit?" From halfway down the hall Brooke's angry words pierced through Ethan's brooding. "You haven't even started yet."

There was silence as she listened to the person on the phone. Every muscle in her hand was clenched tight, her shoulders hunched up to her ears. Before Brooke spoke again, she took two deep breaths, like she was trying to calm down. Her words were only slightly less angry than before. "It's fine. I understand. Thanks for letting me know."

She ended the call and put her hands over her face. Her back was toward Ethan, and he waited to see if she'd say anything. A full minute passed, the only sound her ragged breaths echoing in the hallway.

"Um, is everything okay?" He already knew the answer, but he had to say something.

She turned, and her face was so drawn, so sad. It reminded him of that day he'd first seen her. Underneath the anger at Lucky, there had been so much pain, and it was back again. His chest split in two.

"Everything's great." She sighed and ran a hand through her hair, tangling her fingers briefly in the long, sleek black strands. His palms ached with the need to smooth it down for her. "I just lost the one paid staff I have for these first few weeks."

"But you're opening tomorrow."

Her smile was brief like before, but with none of the warmth. "I know."

"So it's only you now?"

She shook her head. "I agreed with the board when they didn't want to approve another paid position after what happened with the old director. Everyone else is a volunteer. Maybe one of them will want more hours." The hand in her hair moved to rub her forehead.

And here it was. Like a lighthouse in the middle of a storm, the universe was showing him what was next for him. First this morning with her rambling about needing to pick up the reports. That brought him here, in this moment, so that he could make the offer he couldn't figure out how to do at her party.

"I could help."

"What?" Her gaze shot to his, forehead puckered and eyes hard.

"I'm only part-time at the station." The words rushed out of him. "I have the time."

Brooke stared at him for a few moments, as if trying to figure out if he was serious or not. "The role was for an office manager, someone with experience at a shelter, I don't think that—"

"I don't mean that job. I can do whatever you need."

"Whatever I need?" He could almost see the plans taking shape in her mind. "It might be boring stuff like picking up food and changing newspapers."

"That's fine." Heart pounding, he tried to keep his voice even and his excitement under control. This was how he could do it. Integrate into the community in a way that wouldn't make Jerry weirdly jealous. Ethan could get to know people in a way that didn't make him anxious. Build trust with them. Starting with Brooke.

She narrowed her eyes and leaned against the wall in the hallway. "Why would you help me?"

"Why wouldn't I?" He took a step in her direction, knowing he couldn't tell her the real reason. It would sound too self-serving without the whole context of his diagnosis—and that was something he definitely wasn't going to mention. "We're neighbors, right?"

"Neighbors," Brooke repeated the word slowly, like she was tasting it, running it along her tongue.

Stop thinking about her mouth.

"As you're well aware, I can lift lots of heavy things." He lifted his arms to grab the doorframe of the storage room and flexed, just a little.

This brought a blush to her cheeks, and he gave her a smile, the kind that he used to use on women back before his diagnosis. Before he stopped hoping for a different future than the one he'd been given.

"I can do other things. I've gotten very good at paperwork." That was all it felt like he did most days. Registering permits, looking up laws, calling the contractors to check when they couldn't tell if the number was a four or a nine.

"Well, it's not like I can really say no to another volunteer." She ran her hands through her hair again and smoothed out the rug in the hallway with her foot, the pained expression on her face told him just how much she wished she could. "Thank you for offering."

"So I'll see you tomorrow?" Dropping his hands from the door-frame, Ethan kept his voice calm, but wanted to get the yes before he left. He needed that yes. Everything in his life seemed to hinge on it.

She inhaled, and counted something on her fingers. "The day after."

"I'll see you Wednesday."

She sighed, the sound heavy and resigned, like she was fighting some internal battle against herself. "See you then."

Just like that, everything was fine again.

TEN
BROOKE

The text from Krista came right as Brooke tripped over one of the countless boxes behind the desk while she was looking for the scissors she'd left somewhere the day before. In the chaos of the first animals arriving, she'd let the deliveries pile up. It had been a hectic day, but it had been wonderful seeing the end result of a year of work.

It wasn't entirely unlike staging in that way. Organizing, decorating, setting everything up.

Except when she staged houses, she got to walk away. A few pictures for her portfolio were all she took with her, and she never saw those places again.

There would be no walking away from this. The shelter was her life now.

And she couldn't even find the stupid scissors.

Her pulse pounded in her ears and a frown tugged at her lips as she started opening drawers, her hunt growing more frantic the longer it went on. Her phone buzzed again.

Brooke closed her eyes and took a deep, calming breath.

Help was good. Help was needed.

If it had been anyone other than Ethan, she'd be thrilled. The two volunteers who'd shown up that morning had taken the dogs that had gotten dropped off on opening day for walks. Both were only part-time, like all her volunteers, so they'd gone home right after.

Ah ha!

The scissors were under a stack of papers, definitely not where she'd left them. One of the volunteers must have put them there.

Maybe help wasn't needed.

It's not a big deal, she reminded herself as she ripped open the top box in a stack five high. *It's just scissors.*

Except it wasn't just scissors, was it? The box contained pet shampoo, and she didn't even remember ordering it. Only her second day open, and Brooke already felt like she was just barely treading water. More help wasn't what she needed. Nothing was going as planned. She needed someone to take over for her.

Her sleep, already worse since Gran died, had become nonexistent. It had been weeks since she'd been able to go to a workout class or finish a book. The shelter was taking over her life, and despite the warm and fuzzy feelings yesterday at seeing all the animals arrive, it wasn't fulfilling in the way she thought it would be.

A loud meow drew her attention down to the floor. A cat blinked up at her, its dark-gray fur matted against its skinny frame. It wove its way through her legs, meowing pitifully, though Brooke knew she'd fed all the animals less than an hour ago.

"How did you get out of your cage?" She laid the scissors on the desk, took a mental picture of exactly where she left them, then bent to pick up the cat.

"I don't recognize you." Brooke stroked along the cat's bony spine, and it purred, rubbing its face against her chin. Her stomach fell. "Did you just wander in here?"

There'd been a chip scanner in one of the boxes she'd unpacked yesterday, and she held onto the scruffy feline while she hunted around for it in the drawers of the desk, relieved that at least one thing was easy to find. The cat rumbled happily against her as she waved the scanner over its body.

Heaviness settled into her chest, and she did a second full scan. There was no sign of a microchip.

Great. On top of the almost immediate success of the shelter, nearly full to capacity within a day of opening, now they had strays wandering in.

Just follow the plan—

Nothing is going as planned!

Tears pricked the corners of Brooke's eyes, and she took a shaky inhale, the cat still warm in her arms.

Of course Ethan picked that exact moment to walk through the front door.

"Good morning." His smile was wide, his eyes bright. He looked thrilled to be there.

Too thrilled. Brooke's face heated. Not even the volunteers had looked that excited, and they'd both talked her ears off about their love of animals.

Could the rosebud tea really be the reason? It might have been responsible for his offers of help Monday, but today was Wednesday, four days since the party, surely the effect would have worn off by now.

It had been steeping for days by the time he drank it though . . .

Brooke glanced at the clock above the door. "Good afternoon."

He turned to follow her gaze, and his smile widened even more when he saw the clock was a cat with a swinging tail. The dimples Brooke had tried so hard to forget about since her party were on full display. "What can I do to help?"

Brooke kept a hold on the cat and blinked slowly, her exhales longer than her inhales. Whatever happened, she had to make sure Ethan didn't know just how upset she was. If he was still under the influence of the love potion, who knew what he might do that he'd regret later once it had worn off? It had been tempting to refuse his offer to volunteer, but Brooke wasn't in a position to refuse help at this point. She'd said yes because she had to, for the good of the shelter.

It had nothing to do with the edge of a tattoo peeking out from the neck of his long sleeve tee shirt, or the way his muscles flexed under the thin material.

"Maybe we can start with a tour?" The cat nudged Brooke's face and meowed. "Since I'm not sure what you'll be doing yet, it'll be good for you to know where everything is, just in case."

"Sure." His eyes lingered on the cat. "Maybe we can start with this guy here?"

"This is—" Giving all the animals names had been a bright spot in the chaos of the past two days. Staring into Ethan's stormy gray eyes, looking for any signs of rosebud-tea-influenced infatuation, the name popped right out of her mouth. "Cloudy."

He leaned on the counter and reached out a hand to scratch under the cat's chin. "Hey there, Cloudy. You seem pretty friendly for a stray. Or do you just like who you've found?"

His voice was low and rumbly, and absolutely not the reason Brooke's voice cracked on her next words. "I'll introduce you to the others."

There was an uptick in Brooke's pulse as she walked into the back, the cat still purring happily in her arms. Yes, everything had been approved during the inspection, but that didn't mean he wouldn't still be on the lookout. Who knew how long until the potion would wear off, and he was still in a position to make things difficult for her when that happened.

"This isn't to just keep an eye on things, is it? Like, to catch me in some fire code violation?"

"What?" From behind her in the hallway, he sounded hurt. "I want this shelter to stay open. That's why I'm volunteering. If I see something, I'll just tell you and you can get it fixed."

"Oh." She stopped, and in that moment of immobility, Cloudy finally decided to wriggle out of her arms. She quickly slipped him into the nearest open cage, but the second before she closed the door, he shot out of it like a streak of lightning.

"Gotcha." With the ease of a wide receiver catching a pass, Ethan's outstretched arms were waiting for the cat to slide right into them. Cloudy climbed up to give his face a curious sniff, then settled his paws on his shoulders to peer at the other animals, a king surveying his domain. Ethan laughed, the sound hitting Brooke right in the middle of her chest. "I guess he doesn't like the idea of being locked up."

"I can't let him wander around." Brooke pushed her hair back from her face. "Thank you for catching him. It was like he was aiming straight for your arms."

"Saving cats is kind of a firefighter thing." Ethan smiled, dimples winking, and ran his hand along Cloudy's back. "I guess I just have attractive arms."

Heat pooled in Brooke's cheeks and she turned away.

Ethan cleared his throat. "For cats, I mean."

The empty cage clanged, and Brooke focused her attention on latching it shut so the noise wouldn't bother the other animals. "I guess we'll finish the tour with Cloudy coming along."

"Sounds good."

Without looking back at him, Brooke continued down the hallway, stopping to show Ethan where the food was kept and the feeding schedule on a whiteboard hanging by the back door.

"This is the yard where the dogs can run around."

"Have they been out yet today?"

Brooke shook her head, then finally let herself turn to catch his eye. Dark, stormy gray looked back, almost the exact same color as Cloudy's fur, and full of an intensity she couldn't keep pretending was natural. She sucked in a breath and leaned against the wall.

"Just a quick walk this morning with some volunteers." Was her voice always that breathy? Must be the exhaustion from running around for two days straight.

"I could take them out while you finish up whatever you were doing when I walked in."

"That would be—" Her fingers traced the edges of the whiteboard next to the door, where they'd keep track of which dogs were outside. "Very helpful, thank you."

She held out her hand. "Let me take this guy. He may have wandered in from outside, but now that he's here, he's staying in."

A rough meow let them know just how unhappy Cloudy was about being disentangled from Ethan's arms and clung to him even tighter. Cats were always grumpy, but this one seemed to be aiming for a first-place medal as Ethan struggled to hand him off to Brooke.

The brush of their arms sent flames shooting along her skin, and she was grateful for how wriggly Cloudy was. It let her focus her attention on the cat instead of on how electrified every single one of her nerves was from touching Ethan through two layers of clothes.

It was only because she knew what was underneath that shirt that she was acting this way. It was a completely and totally normal reaction.

When she finally pulled her gaze up to meet his, the heated look in his eyes was completely and totally normal too.

For someone who'd recently taken a love potion.

Ethan

The cat clung to Ethan like he was his lifeline, his claws digging into his sweater. Instead of focusing on that, he focused on Brooke, the deep blue of her eyes shot through with worry.

"Oh jeez, he's ruining your sweater." She reached forward to pluck the cat's paws off him, her hands brushing against his arm, and the world around him melted away. There was just him and Brooke.

And a very grumpy cat.

"It's an old one." This was a lie, but he wasn't going to add yet another thing for Brooke to stress about. By the time she'd managed to disentangle the cat completely, there were two holes in his sleeve. "It's fine."

It really was fine, but he could see moisture collecting in the corners of Brooke's eyes, and he reached desperately for something to distract her. There was nothing though, no ideas, no way to be useful, other than what she'd already asked him to do. "I'll go take the dogs outside."

She nodded once, not looking at him, her watery eyes fixed on the cat in her arms.

It took a few minutes to get the four dogs outside. Each one jumped excitedly, sniffed his hand, then snuffled in little circles around him before finally following him to the door. All except the fourth dog, an older basset hound, who gave Ethan a sleepy "woof" before padding outside next to him.

The second they were all outside, Ethan inhaled a slow, deep breath. The weather was finally cooling off, but still in the sixties and dry. Years of paying attention to the weather and how it might impact a fire weren't much help with what he was doing now, but it was an instinct he didn't think he'd ever be able to turn off.

The yard behind the shelter wasn't big, only about as long as the building itself and around twenty feet wide. It had a big tree that would give nice shade in the summer over a bin full of toys and a bench for people to sit. He chose to stand, grabbing a few toys and tossing them around. Lucky's favorite had always been the squeaker toys, and his heart ached a little to see one in the box.

It was soothing his soul to be around dogs again, even if these were all the complete opposite of Lucky. He'd been bred specifically to be a guide dog and was so desperately wanted. There'd been a waiting list just to be a puppy raiser for the organization, and the only reason he'd ended up with Lucky was the same reason he was working with Jerry. The former inspector—Lucky's original puppy raiser—had moved out of state.

According to the notes next to their kennels, these dogs had all been abandoned by their owners. Or, in the case of the basset hound, whose owner had died, given to the brand-new shelter by the owner's children who didn't want him.

If Ethan could, he'd take all of them home. To have your circumstances change overnight and suddenly not be wanted anymore was something he understood deep in his core. The ache in his chest wouldn't be soothed by adopting every single dog that came through the shelter though.

He tossed a ball, and the three younger dogs thundered after it in the small yard. The basset hound stayed near Ethan, his face turned up to the sun with his eyes partially closed. Ethan squatted down and gave him a scratch on the head that quickly turned into a full cuddle, and Ethan felt the hole in his heart from Lucky start to scab over. He'd volunteered to get the social contact he'd been told he needed, but he hadn't expected to get this much satisfaction from spending time with dogs again. And this was only his first day.

"Can you stay until five today?"

He jumped at the sound of Brooke's voice and turned to see her head sticking out of the back door. Her cheeks flushed pink. "Sorry, I didn't mean to scare you. I just have to go pick up more kennels, and it looks like traffic is bad right now, so I thought I'd go a little later."

It would be close to sunset by then, and Ethan would have trouble driving. Not complete night blindness the way it would be if it was full dark, but he didn't want to risk it. Indecision rippled in his belly, the words getting stuck in his throat.

He swallowed thickly before answering, not wanting to lie but also not willing to tell her the truth. "I'm sorry, I can only stay until four today."

He braced himself, ready for the disappointment or for her to push back, asking for a reason.

Instead, she shrugged and turned to go inside. "Okay, no worries. I can go tomorrow."

Before she could close the door, he called her name. She stuck her head back outside.

"Why do you need more kennels?"

She let out a sigh, a heavy one that hit Ethan in his belly. "I've gotten over a hundred emails since we opened, asking if we can take more animals. I don't want to say no, but I haven't even started working on getting the ones we have adopted."

He bit back a question about having enough space, knowing she'd take it badly. He was still, after all, working for the city and for her to even share her plans with him showed a certain level of trust. All of that would be ruined if he put on his fire inspector hat, even for a moment.

"I could work on getting them adopted."

She stepped out into the yard, and one of the dogs came bounding up to her. She bent to give him a cuddle but kept her eyes on Ethan. "How?"

That was a great question. He continued his own cuddles with the hound, the slow, firm movements soothing both his mind and the dog. Thoughts came in a furious rush, and he sorted through them as quickly as he could before landing on the simplest of them.

"Let's have an adoption event this weekend."

"This weekend?" The panic in her voice made the dog she was petting startle. She cleared her throat. "How? I don't even have a website set up."

"I could ask the station to put it on their social media." He didn't know if this was actually possible, but asking would cost him nothing, and it gave him a reason to head to that side of the building again. "Usually it's just photos of the guys in uniform. We have quite a few followers."

More like a few hundred thousand, which was ten times more than the town's actual population.

There was a flush in her cheeks, and she bit her lip. "Oh?"

"Do you . . . " He raised an eyebrow. "Follow them online?"

The quick glance she gave him and deepening color in her face was all the answer he needed.

A spark of jealousy shot up his back so fast he had to stand up to let out some of the pressure. It seemed all of her peering out the window during his workouts weren't about him in particular. Thanks to social media, she also had easy access to the flexing muscles of his former crew as they went through their daily prep in uniform. Ethan had never wanted to be part of the photos, and now he wished he had. Then at least she'd have been able to see him when he was doing good and saving lives.

Hoping for something different is pointless.

He might not be a firefighter anymore, but he could at least help save these animals.

"I've seen you put together an incredible Halloween party in less than a week."

Blush still spreading across her cheeks, she scraped her teeth along her plump bottom lip. "The decorating only took a week, but the planning was a lot longer."

He waved that away.

"This is way simpler than a party. You'll totally be able to figure it out." Now the flush on her face was almost a deep purple and the look she shot him was one of gratitude. His heart soared to realize he could have this effect on her.

"I'll do whatever you need to get ready."

Brooke stood up and found a toy to throw so the dog would run off. He held his breath, waiting to see what she thought of the idea. It might be too much, too soon. This was a very capable woman, who already had friends to help her. The only reason he was even here was because she'd been put on the spot at his offer to volunteer. Hoping for more chances to help wasn't just a risk. It was practically a guarantee he'd be disappointed.

She turned to face him, her eyes bluer and brighter than the cloudless sky above them, and a smile tugged at her lips, cherry-red from worrying.

"Sure, let's do it."

ELEVEN
BROOKE

Everything is going to be fine. Just follow the plan.

The words whirled in Brooke's brain, but they didn't quite make their way down to her stomach, which was tumbling around like she was on a roller coaster. Backward. In the rain.

It had nothing to do with the adoption event taking place today. Setting up something this massive in such a short period of time was well within Brooke's wheelhouse. She'd staged apartments in just a few hours that went on to sell for tens of thousands over asking price. It wasn't the logistics and timing that had made her hesitate at Ethan's suggestion.

It was because she should have been the one to think of it.

This was just the kind of event Gran would have put on. She'd always found countless ways to give her time, money, and clout to different charities in the area. While Brooke knew it shouldn't matter whose idea an event like this was when the important thing was helping animals, that didn't stop the little voice in her head telling her she was failing Gran's legacy.

Caught in a torrent of conflicting emotions she could barely contain, Brooke glanced over at Ethan, who was helping Krista set up a table in the parking lot of the shelter. Brooke's fingers tightened around the clipboard in her hands. Of course her friends had been thrilled to hear that Ethan had volunteered so much of his time this week on the adoption event.

Brooke still couldn't quite believe he would do all of this just to be helpful. The reality of the love potion was hard to accept, but it explained so much.

Like why his eyes kept finding her in the chaos of setting up for the event. Why he kept giving her small smiles and waves that did nothing to settle her stomach.

"Everything looks great." Aisha appeared at her side, a stack of blank adoption forms in her hands. "I think you'll end the day with a lot of empty cages."

"That's the plan."

Thanks to the volunteers she'd already had lined up, all the animals had been processed and pictures put up on social media. A full website was something Brooke would have to work on at some point, but even without it, they'd still been able to get the word out about the open house—all thanks to Ethan's connections at the fire department. For all Brooke's protests at her party that she didn't need any more friends in city hall, it was turning out to be quite useful to have Ethan as a volunteer.

Yet another thing she hadn't predicted but should have. The order and rules that had guided her life until a year ago were all falling to pieces around her.

At least her friends would always be there to help.

Maybe Ethan too.

But if it was all because of the rosebud tea, eventually that would wear off, and he'd realize how incomplete she was, how many cracks were hidden behind her perfect facade. Then he'd do what any sensible person would do and leave. Nobody wanted to clean up someone else's messes forever.

"Where should I put these?" Aisha held up the forms.

"Hmm?" When Brooke finally pulled her eyes away from Ethan to face Aisha, her friend had a wide grin on her face.

"I'll figure it out." Aisha winked. "You just relax and enjoy the view."

Face heating, Brooke snatched the papers from her and grumbled her way over to the table furthest away from Ethan and Krista. The sharp, piercing notes of Krista's laugh filled her ears, but Brooke kept her eyes averted. She didn't have time to wonder about Ethan's motivation or how the shirt he was wearing managed to cling to every single muscle she knew was underneath. She had to make sure everything was flawless. She had to make Gran proud and leave nothing for the town to complain or gossip about. The facade had to stay perfect.

Just like staging, it was about getting people to picture a new life for themselves then removing the friction from the decision process. Partnerships with local vets ensured that neutering and the first round of vaccines and physicals had already been completed prior to adoption. The shelter also provided the carrier, the first week of food and, tucked in a practical but adorable paw-print-patterned folder, all the information they had available about the pet's temperament and known medical history. It had been a lot to set up in just a week, but like Ethan had reminded her, she'd done a fantastic job with the Halloween party in the same amount of time.

It was the reminder she'd needed that Gran's legacy maybe wasn't in quite as much danger as Brooke worried it was.

Carlisle, a basset hound and the oldest animal they had right now, let out an uncharacteristically loud bark, and Brooke jumped.

"I didn't see him before." Aisha's wide eyes followed the volunteer who held the leash. The dog was moving so slowly, the volunteer had to pick him up and carry him. "What's his story?"

"Same as every other animal in this place." Brooke sighed. "Owners couldn't take care of him anymore." Or in this case, the late owner's children hadn't wanted to.

Her eye twitched when Carlisle barked again, loud enough to make one of the volunteers shriek in surprise, then laugh when she saw that such a small, old dog had made such a loud noise.

Brooke could lie to herself all she wanted, but this was nothing like staging. The clean, orderly days that she used to love were long gone, and she had to accept that she'd never have them back. Her world was now a maelstrom of barks and meows, of messy litter boxes and unruly canines tugging at leashes.

Ethan, at least, was in his element. Since the moment he'd shown up at seven a.m., he'd been running around getting supplies, setting things up, and countless other small tasks. It was like he thrived in the mayhem. The never-ending list of things to do barely phased him.

As if drawn by her swirling thoughts about him, once Ethan finished setting up the table with Krista, he made his way over to Brooke. When she turned to Aisha, Brooke found that her friend had scampered off in the other direction.

Brooke pursed her lips, heartbeat thundering in her ears like the roller coaster in her stomach was heading up a steep incline. Ethan's rolled-up sleeves showed off his muscles along with the edge of his tattoo, the tip of an axe peeking out from his sleeve. She kept her eyes on that instead of his face as he approached.

"It's a fire axe."

"What?" Her eyes shot up to his face and landed on the amused smirk of his lips.

"The tattoo I've seen you checking out."

When I work out shirtless in my yard was the implied end to that sentence.

Brooke swallowed. "Do you use one a lot?"

He hesitated, then nodded. "I used to."

Before Brooke could ask what he meant, he gestured to the shelter.

"Do you need any help bringing out the smaller animals?" He cleared his throat. "Is Cloudy up for adoption?"

"Um, no." She glanced down at her clipboard, checking a note she'd put there herself yesterday. "He hasn't been to a vet yet."

It was because he kept escaping every time they tried to bring him to the appointment, not because Brooke had developed any sort of fondness for the little ball of fur the exact same color of gray as Ethan's eyes. Cloudy was annoying, actually, always underfoot whenever he was out of his cage, almost tripping her at least once an hour.

"So, what about the others? Should I bring them out now?"

Keeping her eyes on the clipboard, she looked at the schedule. They were ten minutes ahead, thanks in no small part to everything Ethan had been doing. He was like a one-man crew, able to lift more and move more in the same amount of time as five other volunteers.

It didn't help that those same volunteers would often stop what they were doing to stare at him working. Especially once he'd rolled up his sleeves.

With the same amount of energy it was taking the volunteer to carry Carlisle, Brooke pulled her gaze back up from her clipboard to look Ethan in the eyes. Which were as intense as they always were.

Back to staring at the arms it is.

"I think we can wait a little. Take a break. You've been working nonstop all morning."

"It's fine. I like moving around. It's been hard being behind a desk the past year."

The question was there, on the tip of her tongue, to ask him about his job, why he was only part-time now, why he'd been a puppy raiser, or any of the other hundreds of things she wondered about him. She was sure he'd tell her if she asked, thanks to the lingering effects of the potion.

Though she wasn't the only one who was curious. Krista and Aisha had been wondering all week what his story was. That's the only reason she was interested. To give her friends the information they so desperately craved.

Brooke glanced down at her clipboard again, seeking out the comforting scrape of her teeth against her lip as she considered what was still unchecked from her list. "Do you mind helping with one more thing then?"

"Lead the way."

They made their way inside and through the shelter to the storage room in the back, with Brooke acutely aware of Ethan right behind her. His eyes on her back prickled along her skin, and the heat of his eyes warmed her entire body.

This was a bad idea. She should have asked one of her friends to help her instead. Or one of the other volunteers. A few more had shown up than she'd expected and while that had relieved some of Brooke's anxiety about today, in the long run, it would add more to her plate. Volunteer management was one more task she'd have to manage.

They got to the storage room, which was filled with boxes. At least this was one thing she could delegate to a willing and—so far —trustworthy person. "Could you put together some adoption kits?"

She opened the top box to pull out a stack of flattened carriers with the shelter's logo on it.

"There are carriers for the cats and leashes for the dogs. I don't know how many we'll need, so you don't have to unpack all of them."

"Whatever you need." She looked up and he flashed her a smile, all dimples and bright eyes, and her breath caught in her throat. "Happy to help."

"Thank you." The words came out in a rush, like she was unused to saying them. She was, in a way. Her friends didn't need to hear it every two minutes. They knew how she felt.

At least thanking Ethan was a lot easier than apologizing would be.

"Of course." He hesitated in the doorway, his eyes shifting from side to side. "Um, I don't think there's room for both of us in here."

"Oh, right." She slid out from behind the box and passed him in the doorway, their bodies not touching but coming very close. She paused, just for a moment, when they were face-to-face, his breath hot on her neck. Their eyes met, and the already warm space grew infinitely hotter. The roller coaster her body had been on all day climbed higher and higher along with her pulse.

Her breath came out in a slow, shaky exhale, her voice barely above a whisper. "I'm not breaking any fire codes, am I?"

"You're good." He kept his eyes on her for a moment longer, then he slid past her into the room, their arms brushing. The roller coaster flipped her upside down. "The boxes aren't blocking the door, it's just too small of a space for two people with them in it."

"Right." She inhaled through her nose, a little steadier. "You're really good at your job."

He let out a puff of air, a sound that was half chuckle, half sigh. "You're probably the only one who thinks so."

"Really?"

He stayed quiet and pawed his way through the boxes, separating everything into piles.

Alrighty then. Looks like he doesn't want to talk about it.

"Well, you're definitely my best volunteer."

He nodded, his eyes fixed on a pile of leashes he was detangling, but there was a pink tinge to his cheeks that set her stomach churning again.

Oh fork, she was embarrassing him. And herself.

"I'll be outside if you need me."

Brooke hesitated at the door. She wanted to say something about how nervous she was, about how unqualified she felt opening this shelter, and how she knew how it felt to not be sure of yourself. Everything that she kept bottled up inside felt like it could be safe with him.

But it might not be. The potion would wear off eventually.

So instead of saying anything, she turned around and left, the searing memory of his arm bushing hers lingering on her skin.

TWELVE
ETHAN

As he pulled into the shelter's parking lot, relief settled onto Ethan's shoulders like a heavy blanket on a cold night. After spending all day listening to Jerry point out mistake after mistake in paperwork Ethan had definitely double checked, it was all he could do not to run inside and bury his face in a dog's fur. Nothing about his inspector job was turning out how he thought it would. He wasn't even sure he should be at the shelter right now.

Except this was the one place that felt like he might actually know what he was doing. The adoption event had been great, and the compliment Brooke had given him echoed in his ears for hours. She'd even said thank you not once, but twice. The words seemed like they'd been pulled out of her, her lips unused to saying them. It still felt like a victory, like proof that Ethan could change someone's mind about him if he just kept trying his best. Like maybe he could change Jerry's mind too.

Eventually.

When his boss had mentioned that morning how nice it had been to see the fire department promote the shelter's event and pointed it out as the kind of community collaboration he liked to see, Ethan told him he'd been at the event. Instead of hearing "nice work" like he'd expected, Jerry's face had clouded over and reminded him he shouldn't be doing favors for people.

Clearly he was still brooding about missing Brooke's party, so Ethan hadn't told him about volunteering at the shelter on a more regular basis. What if it made Jerry even more upset?

Still sitting in his car in front of the shelter, Ethan rubbed his hands over his face, throat tight. He should probably just go home.

No, he'd promised Brooke. She'd accepted his help, and he didn't think she accepted it from many people other than Krista and Aisha. He had his volunteer slot now. She'd even put his name in pen on the schedule, her handwriting just as neat and orderly as everything else she touched. Backing out now would make things harder for her, and everything inside him wanted to make her life better.

Better for the animals, I mean.

He reached into the back of his car and grabbed a spare tee shirt to change into. In his rush to leave the station, he'd kept his uniform on and, as he'd learned last week, it was a magnet for animal hair.

Right as his shirt was halfway off his body, Brooke walked outside with a few dogs on leashes. She caught his eye through the window and waved, a flush spreading across her cheeks. Ethan's pulse did a funny little somersault that wasn't entirely unlike what happened to him right before he ran into a burning building.

He quickly finished changing and got out of the car.

"Hi." She looked down at the dogs, like she wasn't sure what to do with them.

"I think that's my job." He reached out his hand for the leashes, and their fingers brushed, sparking that familiar heat that always seemed to be simmering between them. "Are you supposed to be here today?"

Shaking her head, a whiff of lavender, herbal and woodsy and warm, breezed toward Ethan. Brooke gestured toward the shelter.

"Amanda had to leave early, and I have a lot of paperwork to finish. Walking the dogs was just procrastination."

"Oh, you can do it if you want—" His cheeks heated, and he tried to hand back the leashes. Barging in and taking over wasn't what he was here to do. He was here to do whatever she needed.

"It's fine." Brooke flashed that little smile again, and his chest squeezed tight. "I should get back to it."

Biting her bottom lip and sending Ethan's pulse racing, Brooke turned on her heels and went back inside.

Indecision rippled through him. Paperwork was what he liked the least about his inspector job, but he did have some tricks for getting through it faster. Should he go in and offer to help her with it? Or just do what he was here to do?

The terrier tugging at his leash settled the question for him. A half hour later, he was back at the shelter and Brooke's car was still there.

When he walked in, she was bent over the desk, her mouth turned down in a frown and the end of a pen clenched between her teeth. The papers spread in front of her were in three neat stacks, Post-its scribbled on top of them. A clear travel tumbler with a straw was next to her, the dark-brown concoction inside only halfway finished.

"Everything okay?"

"What?" Brooke looked up and then around, her blue eyes wide and weary, like she didn't quite know where she was. "Oh, yes, everything's fine."

This was clearly a lie, but he wasn't about to point that out. "I'll get these guys fed then."

"They all have notes on their cages about what they eat."

"I know." He bit back a smile. "I noticed last week."

This kind of organization was impressive, but also had to be exhausting, if the expression on Brooke's face was any indication. She was still stunning, her dark hair shiny and straight, that plump lower lip tucked under her teeth as she concentrated on the computer screen. Stunning, but clearly drained, like when he'd do a full forty-eight-hour shift with nonstop calls and no nap.

Ethan went into the back to put the dogs back in their kennels. Before he went to the closet to get their food, he stopped by the desk.

"Could I take a look?" He leaned next to her at the desk, far enough away that he wasn't in her personal space, but close enough he could just almost smell the lavender. Was it her shampoo? A lotion? He inhaled. "I do a lot of paperwork at the station."

"You mentioned that the other day." She frowned. "I thought you were an inspector."

"I don't have the inspector job yet. This has been like—" His fingers danced along the desk, careful not to disturb any of the papers there. "An extended training period."

"So you're doing that on top of your firefighter job?"

His stomach twisted, and he picked up a loose paperclip, slipping it back onto the stack of papers it had fallen off. "I'm not a firefighter anymore."

Saying it out loud was still painful, tight, and hot like a burn that wasn't quite healed.

"Why not?"

He met her eyes, but the words didn't want to come. The cat clock on the wall ticked away the seconds until she looked away, a flush creeping across her cheeks.

"Never mind. It's none of my business." She turned her attention back to the computer, her fingers typing away as she answered an email, leaving Ethan to stand there awkwardly with his heart in his mouth.

It was a simple question. One he should get used to answering. The burning in his chest and throat would always be there whenever he talked about his condition. Might as well get used to it. He'd already avoided the topic once, when she asked him to stay late. The memory of her compliments from the adoption event still glowed bright, warming him, encouraging him to share the truth.

When Brooke finally looked up from the computer, her eyes flicked to the ground, to the clock on the wall, to anything but him. Ethan took a step forward and put his hands on the desk so she'd look at him.

Her eyes were such a piercing blue he needed to see them, to feel the depths of that cool, icy stare and sink into it. He took a deep breath.

"I have retinitis pigmentosa."

"Okay." She blinked, her lashes heavy on her cheeks before that startling blue gaze was finally fixed on his. "What is that?"

Saying the words out loud to someone he barely knew was scary as hell, but at least she sounded curious. If she'd reacted any other way, he'd have run out the door. Instead, he kept talking.

"It's a degenerative eye condition. I'm losing my vision, slowly. I don't know how long until it's gone completely. Probably decades, but then this inspector opportunity came up right after my diagnosis and well . . . " He dropped his gaze and smoothed a hand along the desk, wiping away dust that wasn't there. Brooke would never let there be dust on any horizontal surface. "It seemed like a good idea to start something else now, before it's too late."

There was silence from Brooke, and a ticking from the clock above their heads. Ethan tried to take deep, calming breaths but only managed a few short, shallow inhales through his nose.

"You never wanted to be an inspector?"

He shook his head, still not looking at her.

"How much can you see now?"

At this, he finally glanced up and found her head tilted slightly and her teeth scraping along her bottom lip. It grew redder with each pass, and the beat of his pulse in his tongue ticked up a notch.

"I still have good vision." The words were thick and he cleared his throat. "I didn't actually have to quit being a firefighter."

"So why did you?"

"Driving at night is hard. I've almost stopped entirely. That's why I can only volunteer during the day."

Her eyes lit up, like that solved a puzzle she'd been working on.

"My field of vision is still pretty wide, but that can change quickly, even if the journey to full vision loss will probably take much longer."

That was more than he'd ever said to anyone about it, including Chief Stevens. After getting his initial diagnosis, he'd spent about an hour looking it up online, stumbled across a few forums full of personal accounts and distressing details, then had never typed the words again. His doctors told him whatever he needed to know. Researching on his own wouldn't change whatever was going to happen to him. It hadn't changed anything after his parents' accident.

So it was beyond surprising how good it felt to talk about it. Like the sizzle of water dousing a flame, or that first cool blast of fresh air when you finally take your helmet off after a call.

"You don't know for sure when vision loss will happen?"

He shook his head and leaned further along the desk, closer to her. Close enough to see the tiny cut in her lip where she'd worried it too hard with her teeth. "It may not ever fully happen. Sometimes people still have a little vision their whole life. But the definition of legally blind is very different from what people assume blindness is."

This was what had stuck with him the most from the minimal amount of research he'd done. The label of "blind" that he'd undoubtedly have one day would not mean the same thing to everyone. It didn't even mean the same thing to the people who had it. If no one could really define it, then why should he worry about when it would happen?

It had been the opposite when his parents had died. The hours he'd spent trying to determine if the weather was to blame, or if they'd missed a recall notice, or if that particular stretch of road had repair issues, hadn't changed anything. The police, the lawyers, the insurance, they'd all told him it was "just one of those terrible accidents that sometimes happen."

Then there'd been the weeks of sleepless anxiety, worried the same thing would happen to him, or to Rachel. He could remember the exact moment his attitude had shifted, and he'd realized that hoping things could be different was pointless. A random conversation with a friend, and his entire perspective had changed.

Now he was here, with Brooke, exactly where the universe wanted him to be.

"It's not like one day I'll just wake up and things are gone. This is gradual, over many years, but it can feel like a big jump, depending on what it is."

She nodded slowly, absorbing all of this, and her eyes focused on a spot just beyond his shoulder. When no more questions came and silence stretched between them again, a crinkle of doubt etched itself into his heart. Maybe it had been too much. Maybe this had been a mistake. Maybe she wouldn't want him volunteering anymore.

He stepped back from the counter and looked up at the clock, the cat's eyes and tails swinging back and forth with every loud tick.

"That sounds really hard."

His head whipped around, Brooke's words hitting a spot in his chest directly next to his heart that he didn't know was tender.

"It's fine." A small chuckle forced its way out of his mouth. "There's nothing I can do about it. No sense in worrying."

These were words he'd repeated to himself countless times, but somehow saying them out loud made his skin prickle. It wasn't a lie, but for the first time, it didn't feel like the entire truth either.

"Well, you're a lot calmer about it than I would be." She tucked her hair behind her ears and grimaced. "I don't like not knowing things."

Ethan chuckled again, a real one this time, easy and unforced. "Really? I'd never have guessed."

She rolled her eyes and shoved his arm. His skin burned at the unexpected contact. The desire for more surged out of nowhere, like a wildfire in the middle of a drought. It felt just as dangerous too.

"You're really not worried about it?" Her tone was teasing, but her eyes were serious.

"I let fate decide for me and things seem to work out." He put his hands on the counter again, bringing him that much closer to her. "After all, wasn't I here on the right day to hear you needed help?"

Her lips twisted to the side, and he fought the urge to reach out and trace their jagged edges with his finger.

"The week I got my diagnosis was the same week someone moved out of state and left an open inspector spot. And that same person had been raising Lucky, so I got him too. Things always happen the way they're supposed to."

Brooke was shaking her head. "I don't think that's true. Luck favors the well prepared. If I wasn't controlling things, nothing would happen."

"I think they'd happen no matter what." He gestured around the reception area, the colorful walls bright in the afternoon sun. "This shelter would have opened even if you weren't in charge. That Jason guy was here before."

At this, Brooke turned away, her face scarlet.

The lightness in his chest evaporated, his heart dropping into his stomach. "I said something wrong." It wasn't a question.

"It almost didn't open because of me." Her words were tight, like she was holding back tears. He'd only ever seen her cry once, when she'd yelled at Lucky. There was an itchy feeling all along his skin at the thought of seeing it again. "I found Jason. I pushed the board to approve him because I wanted the shelter to open as soon as possible. He turned out to be a crook. It was my fault."

Ethan had figured as much, given the state of the place when they'd first inspected it, but he wasn't going to tell her that.

"Maybe it was meant to happen, so that you could be here instead." He smiled. "You're doing a great job."

It was like her entire body shut down at this. Her eyes looked away and she turned her shoulders inward. It was almost painful to watch, to realize that he'd said absolutely the wrong thing, yet again.

Did she really not see how incredible the space was? How clean and organized it was, how happy the animals were, how successful the adoption event had been?

None of the words swirling around in his brain seemed like the right way to say all of that. If the words were supposed to come, they would.

This time, they hadn't.

"I'll go get the dogs fed."

"Thanks," she said without looking up from her paperwork.

He walked into the back, feeling more like a failure than he had this morning at his inspector job.

Maybe because this was something he'd actually wanted. Being at the shelter and around the animals was the only place he felt like himself these days. He wanted to be here, but even more than that, he wanted to help Brooke. To make her life easier, to make her feel better during a difficult time. It was how she'd made him feel when she'd thanked him, when she'd listened to him and stayed curious.

That was the danger of wanting something. He'd never actually get it unless he was supposed to. There was no point in hoping for it. Whatever was going to happen would happen, no matter what he did.

THIRTEEN

BROOKE

Alone up front with her endless piles of paperwork and bills, Brooke dropped her head into her hands, not sure why it felt like a hole had opened up in her chest. She'd gotten what she wanted. At work in the back, Ethan had stopped saying the kinds of nice things Brooke didn't deserve. Alone was what she wanted. Alone was safer.

So why did the space feel empty and too big without him next to her? He was like that perfect lamp giving just the right light to a room, or a pillow the exact shade of green to match the weird wall color the seller had chosen for whatever reason. Her stager's eye knew how to spot something that fit perfectly. While she knew it was because of experience and preparation, someone like Ethan would call it her gut instinct.

Her gut liked having Ethan around.

Her gut trusted Ethan when she didn't even trust herself. Why else would she have blabbed so much about Jason? She'd just barely stopped herself from admitting everything else that was going wrong.

The numbers on the page swam in front of her eyes, and she put down her pen, then dropped her head in her hands.

This was hopeless. Barely two weeks in and she'd spent twice as much as she'd budgeted, thanks to the unexpected veterinary costs of some of the animals they'd taken in. The idea had been gnawing at her since the first day, but now she was almost sure. People were using the rescue just to dump the animals with health problems they decided they didn't want to handle anymore.

It was hard, she knew it was, and she could sympathize. When Krista's dog had gotten hit by a car in middle school and Aisha's cat had gotten sick in college, the amount of money their families had paid to try to get them well again was absolutely staggering. Seeing someone having to part with a pet they loved because of the cost made her wish Gran had suggested some other kind of animal nonprofit rather than a rescue. Maybe something that gave out grants or partnered with local vets to find people who needed help the most.

But no, Gran had specifically stipulated a rescue, with a physical location that wasn't her house as a place to board animals. After a lifetime of allergies keeping her from having pets or adopting the countless strays she came across, Gran wanted there to be a place where animals could be safe and cared for. Lifting her head slightly to look around the reception area, Brooke knew her grandmother would have been proud to see what a great space it was. Unfortunately, the money that Gran had left for it wouldn't be enough to keep things going for much longer.

It would have been enough if Brooke had managed things better. She'd hired the wrong people, trusted the wrong people. Including herself. First with Jason, then with the office manager quitting the day before it opened. Running a shelter was nothing like staging apartments, and the same financial rules that had worked for her for years were no use now.

If only she could see the world like Ethan and blame the universe for everything. Then she wouldn't be carrying around the weight of her mistakes. Then she wouldn't be the one who had to figure out how to fix them all. Alone.

"Brooke?" Ethan's voice was a welcome distraction from her maudlin musings about her multitude of failures.

"Yeah?" She took a bracing sip of her chocolate coffee smoothie —Gran's favorite recipe for energy—and headed to the back. When she got there, Ethan was standing in front of the cages with a frown on his face.

"Did this one get adopted?"

"No." She stepped forward to double-check, and their shoulders brushed. He didn't get out of the way, but she didn't expect him to. The love potion was still in effect, it seemed. He never would have told her quite so much otherwise about his medical situation.

Retinitis pigmentosa. She'd never heard of it before, but it sounded like such a challenging situation to be in. Yet here he was, helping her, instead of focusing on himself and what he needed to do to prepare for a very uncertain future.

Sure, some of it could be chalked up to his go-with-the-flow personality, but the rosebud tea was clearly influencing him. Otherwise, why would he have shifted so much attention to Brooke and her shelter? It was the opposite of what Brooke would be doing in the same situation.

Those last months with Gran had been completely absorbed by her care and researching how to turn back the clock. Brooke had been an anxious mess even before Gran had finally passed, then she'd gotten even worse, as Ethan and his dog had witnessed.

Well, it wasn't quite the same. His diagnosis wasn't fatal, though it was life changing, or would be, eventually. Not that he was the type of person who'd let something like that change him. Unlike Brooke, who felt like she barely recognized herself and this new life, Ethan seemed so at ease with whatever was going on. He wasn't spending every spare moment working or up all night worrying. He was using his free time to walk and feed abandoned dogs. He was giving her compliments.

That's why she couldn't tell him about the financial issues the shelter was already having. He thought she was doing so well, and she liked at least one person thinking she was capable.

Even if it was only because of some magical tea he'd accidentally drunk a few weeks ago. Without it, the cracks would be obvious to him, and he'd be long gone.

Pulling herself away from where her body was touching Ethan's, Brooke felt rather than saw his disappointment at the distance between them.

It's only because of the tea.

"This is Cloudy's cage." She turned and scanned the small space that held the kennels. There was no gray tail hidden in any of the other cages. "I guess he figured out how to unlatch it."

"I've never seen a cat do that."

"I've never seen a cat like him." Brooke sighed and ran her hands through her hair for what felt like the hundredth time today. It was getting frizzy at the ends, the careful flat ironing she'd done that morning long gone. "He just appeared one day, no microchip, no sign of an owner, and doesn't seem to follow any of the normal cat rules."

She started a slow walk down the line of cages, clicking her tongue to see if that would draw his attention. It never had in the past, but it at least kept her mouth busy.

"What exactly are normal cat rules?" She could hear the humor laced in Ethan's voice, and when she looked back at him, there was the smallest, cutest smirk on his face that made her own lips tingle.

She quickly turned her head back around and let her eyes trace along the top edge of the cages. "Unfriendly, independent, hisses at any attempt at closeness."

"Hmm."

Heat raced through her body. If it weren't for the rosebud tea, he'd probably be thinking that sounded a lot like her.

"Cloudy is like feline Velcro. He'll be attached to your leg nonstop if you don't put him in his cage for a break." She paused for a moment, squinting at a patch of gray in a corner that, when she tilted her head, turned out to be just a shadow.

"Sounds like he's found his human," Ethan said from behind her. "Even if she doesn't realize it yet."

"Is that fate deciding things for me?" she teased, and just barely stopped herself from shivering at the low rumble of his responding chuckle.

"Or just realizing animals have their own personalities and opinions." They kept up their slow walk down the hallway. "When did you last put him in his cage for a Brooke break?"

They'd arrived at the storage room, which was normally closed, but was open since Ethan had been getting food for the animals.

"Right before you got here." Brooke pushed open the door to reveal Cloudy sitting on the top shelf, happily munching away at a bag of kitty kibble he'd managed to knock over.

From behind her, the warm, smooth laugh of Ethan enveloped her like a hug.

"Guess he didn't want to wait his turn."

Brooke shook her head, biting her lip to stop from smiling. It was kind of funny, but her heart sank as she watched more dollars go down the drain—or in this case, into a cat's belly. It wasn't wasted, of course. The animals had to eat. But she'd calculated the amount based on weight and age for all the cats, and this wasn't part of that plan.

"Bad kitty." Brooke dragged a ladder from the corner of the storage room and set it underneath the shelf. Cloudy was too preoccupied to hear her reproach or her approach. Still, she kept her steps as quiet as she could until her face was level with the truant feline.

"Gotcha." Before the cat could scamper away, Brooke had snatched him up and held him close to her chest, tucking his feet into one hand.

The movement was quick, but unpracticed, and Brooke felt her foot slip on the step beneath her. She teetered on the edge, unable to throw out her hands for balance, and the other leg lifted to compensate. The room swam as she spun on her one unsteady heel balanced on the edge of the step.

"Woah!"

One second, she was convinced she was headed for a direct impact with the floor. In the next, before she could even blink, she was in Ethan's arms, staring up at him, breathing hard with Cloudy still clutched to her chest.

"Careful." A small, adorable smirk lit up his face. His eyes were glued to hers, just begging for her to get lost in their stormy gray depths.

It took a few shattered inhales before she could speak. "Thanks."

Their gazes stayed locked, neither of them moving. Brooke's neck was cradled in the crook of Ethan's elbow, her cheek flush with his broad shoulder. The muscles supporting her flexed, but there was no other change in his stance. The smirk slowly slid off his face and his expression shifted into one full of longing and want.

"I'd never let you fall."

His words were soft and full of heat. The air in the small storage room was heavy, and breathing suddenly became ten times harder. Warmth spread through Brooke's chest, but that could have been from Cloudy. The cat's contented purr was almost indistinguishable from the hoofbeat drumming of Brooke's pulse in her ears. Everything in her tightened, and her hand squeezed into fists, apparently forgetting they were holding a cat.

The ringing screech of Cloudy's meow finally broke whatever spell had fallen over Ethan.

With a move that was infinitely more practiced than Brooke was at holding a squirming cat, Ethan lifted her up and set her on the floor. Then, he took Cloudy from her, his hands brushing against hers with a sizzle as the cat meowed in protest. Or maybe in relief to be free of Brooke's unyielding grasp.

"I guess he does like you best." Cloudy struggled in his arms, trying to get back to Brooke—or more likely, his interrupted meal. Ethan kept a tight hold on him, and walked out of the storage room, calling over his shoulder, "I'll get him back in his cage."

Brooke was alone again, heart hammering and head swimming. Being in Ethan's arms, even briefly, had the opposite effect that it was having on Cloudy. It was all she could do not to run to him and demand he wrap his muscles around her. It had been the safest she'd felt all year. Maybe even the safest she'd ever felt.

Something inside of her shifted, just a little. Like a cloth on a pane of a dirty window letting in a single ray of light, the idea of something more became visible for the first time. Maybe she didn't have to carry all the weight by herself. Maybe Ethan might be strong enough to help her.

Then he was there, at the door to the storage room, an open, enraptured smile on his face, and darkness covered up the light.

No. As long as the potion was still in effect, she couldn't do that to him. If someone was going to be in her life in a serious way, she had to know whatever they were feeling was real.

Otherwise, she was just that same silly little girl, hoping her mother would come for her one day . . . until she grew up to be a silly woman, thinking a magic potion could fix all of her problems.

FOURTEEN
ETHAN

The message from Rachel was followed by a string of sad-faced emojis mixed with smiling dogs and cats. Ethan grinned and snapped another photo of Charlie, the floppy-eared beagle puppy that had just arrived today, and sent it to his sister. Then he added it to the shared folder online, where all the volunteers put their photos of the animals. It had been Ethan's idea, something they'd done at the station with not-so-gentle nudging from the guy who ran the fire department's social media accounts.

Ethan had been nervous to suggest it to Brooke. After the incident with Cloudy, she managed to make herself scarce any time Ethan was working. There always seemed to be errands for her to run or animals to take to vet appointments. Or she simply wasn't there at all. It was nice to know she felt like she could trust Ethan on his own at the shelter, but it also felt like she was avoiding him. Maybe because of the way he'd looked at her while he'd held her, so warm and soft against him, for way too long to be considered just polite and helpful. Maybe she was embarrassed about what she'd shared about Jason and feeling like it was her fault.

Or maybe she didn't want to see him because of what he'd told her.

Sure, she'd reacted with curiosity at first about his diagnosis, but as the reality of it sunk in, she must have realized how much it would impact his life. Hell, he could barely wrap his head around it, but someone like Brooke would put the pieces together much faster than he had.

Still, when she was rushing out one day and said that he should send any photos he took to the shelter's email, he'd mentioned the shared-folder idea, and her face had lit up. That small victory had gotten him through the past week of nearly silent inspections with Jerry.

When Ethan had told him about his new volunteering routine, all he'd gotten in response was a mumbled "Adams again?" and a frown. Ethan had hurried to explain that it let him interact with lots of families and businesses in town, and whenever he mentioned working with Jerry, they all had good things to say. This resulted in a pair of raised eyebrows from his boss, and a tiny nod. Which could be a good sign. Or not. Only time would tell.

The actual volunteering was great, something that he could sink into and not have to think too hard about. It was a little like firefighting. There was a lot of sitting around on some shifts once the actual work was done. You had to figure out ways to stay busy and entertained. Though Ethan didn't have the guys he used to work with, he had the animals, and some of them were just as entertaining as full-grown men doing pull-up contests to pass the time.

As if to prove he was more interesting than firefighters, Charlie stood on his hind legs and barked.

"Good boy." Ethan grinned and snapped another picture for Rachel, then went to get the dog a treat.

When he got back to the reception area, Brooke rushed in,

apologizing. She stopped mid-sentence to stare wide-eyed at him. Her hair was up, the ponytail so tight it was tugging at her face, making her look even more surprised.

"Oh, Ethan. I didn't realize you were here today."

Ignoring the tug in his chest at the clear disappointment in her face, he smiled. "Amanda called me and we switched."

She frowned at this, as if considering if she should have been involved in this decision. "I guess that's okay."

He raised an eyebrow, heart hammering. "I mean, if you'd rather I go—"

"No, no, you're here now." She set down her bag and a travel mug with a straw on her desk. "As long as you're not too tired."

"I'm fine. I used to do forty-eight-hour shifts running in and out of buildings that were on fire. Three hours hanging out with animals isn't exactly exhausting."

"Of course." Her cheeks turned pink. "I just mean you've been volunteering a lot. I feel like I'm taking advantage."

Please take advantage of me.

He cleared his throat. "I'll let you know if it's too much. Don't worry."

She nodded, not quite meeting his eye, and took a sip from her drink. A bright pink substance shot up the straw. It looked like the same one she'd had a few other times.

"That looks good. What is it?"

"Oh, um, nothing."

He rolled his eyes. "Relax, I'm not going to ask for a taste." As if he needed another example of how much Brooke wanted to avoid him.

"It's just a smoothie." She bit her lip, her perfect white teeth scraping across the plump pink and drawing his eyes like some secret was hidden there. "When I was little, my grandmother called them magic potions."

"Oh yeah?" He pulled his eyes up to hers to see if she was joking. But Brooke wasn't the kind of person to joke. He knew that much about her. Everything about her was so serious, so organized, so logical. This idea of her believing in magic was a charming crack in the glossy image she was always projecting. Maybe helping her meant getting her to trust him enough to show more of those cracks. Then she wouldn't be so tired all the time. "So, what's magical about this one?"

"Nothing." She shook her head and turned away. "Forget I said anything."

"No, come on, I'm not teasing. Really. What's in this one?"

She inhaled and her gaze raked his face, like she expected him to start laughing uncontrollably. He pursed his lips and schooled his features into the most attentive, non-judgmental expression he could manage.

"This is just berries and kale." She put a hand on the mug and gripped it tight, her knuckles popping out. "But Gran always added lemon balm. She said it was good for a bad mood."

Brooke rolled her eyes, like that was the most ridiculous thing she'd ever heard. But the softness in her voice when she mentioned her grandmother was unmistakable. She might not believe it, but her grandmother had, and that was important to her.

"And you're in a bad mood today?"

"You could say that." Brooke brushed a hair aside that had escaped her tight ponytail.

"I can tell."

She raised an eyebrow and put a hand on her hip. "Oh yeah, Sherlock?"

"Your hair is up." He gestured at her dark mane, resisting the urge to tuck aside another lock that had escaped the smooth style. "My sister's always grumpy when she puts her hair in a ponytail that tight."

"Maybe it's up because my hair looked awful this morning, which doesn't help my mood." She tugged at the end of it. "The bad mood isn't caused by the ponytail. It's a symptom of it."

"If you say so."

She shot a glare at him and his heart stuttered.

"Drink more of your smoothie," he teased.

She huffed and rolled her eyes again, but her lips curled up and she bent her head to take a sip. Then she glanced up, eyes narrowed. "This is just because I'm thirsty. And need vitamin C."

"Whatever you say." The grin on his face was impossible to get rid of. It was going to be there all afternoon.

"How have things been?"

They switched into work mode, Ethan running her through the calls and emails they'd gotten and giving a quick report on the new animals and how they were adapting.

"I also made a few updates to the adoption interest form."

"What?" The panic in her voice was instant, and guilt shot through him. He should have known better than to spring this on her.

"It's just something I've been playing around with." He moved over to the computer on the reception desk and opened up the files. "See look, if you change this around . . . "

The pinched expression on her face loosened the longer he spoke. By the time he'd finished explaining his new idea, she was practically beaming.

"Ethan, this is amazing." The warmth in her voice washed over him, the compliment like an oasis in the middle of a desert. She even put an arm on his shoulder and squeezed, sending pings of electricity through his body. "Thank you so much."

Heat hit his cheeks, the unexpected praise not quite sitting right. "You don't have to do it this way. It's just an idea."

"We'll absolutely start using it. It'll save so much time." She was standing right next to him, her eyes focused on the screen while her shoulder was just inches from his. The nearness of her was overwhelming, that mystery lavender scent invading his senses. It was the closest they'd been since he'd caught her falling from the ladder, the warm weight of her body against his feeling so right when everything else in his life felt like he was doing it wrong.

He inhaled slowly and shifted on his feet, the computer mouse slick under his palm. Her words seemed honest, but no one had ever said anything like that to him before. It wasn't that he didn't trust her, he just worried it was based on pity. "It's really not a big deal. If you're just trying to make me feel better, because of what I told you, then—"

"What on earth are you talking about?" He didn't turn to look at her, but he could feel her gaze on the side of his head, hot and fierce. "Ethan, this has nothing to do with your eyesight. You said yourself it's not impacting anything right now other than how well you see at night. There's no link between that and your ability to come up with good ideas to help the shelter. This is the third one you've had in less than a month."

The heat in his body shot up to inferno levels. When she put it like that, it was hard to remember why he was feeling so insecure about it.

"I guess it's just different from the inspections." Ethan rubbed his hand along the back of his neck. "Jerry has a really specific idea of what I need to be doing."

It would be nice if he shared those specifics with Ethan. For weeks he'd been following Jerry's directive to "integrate" himself with the community, but Ethan wasn't now sure if it was supposed to be for his benefit—or Jerry's. Whatever Jerry's issue was with Ethan helping Brooke, he wasn't about to stop volunteering when it was still helping him get to know people in Adamsville.

And helping Brooke.

"Well, that's there. Here, I want and need all your ideas." Brooke was biting her bottom lip again. "I hope you realize how hard it is for me to say something like that."

He couldn't stop a grin from spreading across his face. "You mean admitting you need help?"

"So much help it's not even funny." In a flash, her expression shifted and her eyes turned watery. Ethan's grin faded as she dropped her head into her hands. "Things are falling apart, and I don't know how to fix everything. I don't think I can."

Her words were soft, an embarrassed whisper that wrapped around his heart and squeezed. How many people had she talked to about this? Did her friends even know?

"I think you're doing a great job." He reached out and put a hand on her shoulder. He'd said the same thing the other week, and she'd turned away. This time, she leaned into his touch, and the energy that zinged between them was so hot, he was grateful he knew how to put out a fire if it happened. "This place looks amazing."

"And is making negative money." She stepped away from his hand and spread her hands across the papers on the desk. "I could manage my staging business, but it wasn't as complex. I used one or two vendors for the furniture and the clients all came through referrals, so I didn't need much marketing."

"I bet you were a really good stager. Like, where did you even find name tags in the shape of paw prints for the cages? And the carpet in the back tracks zero mud. It's amazing."

Her lips turned up a little before falling again.

"I just knew what to pay attention to. But here"—she shook her head—"there's too much going on. I can't keep track of all the orders and the vet bills and the adoptions. It's just not adding up. Most of the money Gran left went into the building. The rest needs to come from donations and fees. We'll have to close before we even get started."

Oof. Money wasn't Ethan's strong suit. Living on his own meant things weren't expensive, and he'd never really needed to budget. Rachel still had to remind him to do his taxes every year.

However, he did know about fundraising.

"What if you did some kind of carnival or raffle?" His tone was hesitant, prepared for her to shoot it down, even after she'd just told him she wanted his ideas. A simmering fear of rejection was lying just under the surface. Where had it come from? He didn't used to get this worried about things.

Now that he'd gotten a taste of it, he wanted her praise, he realized. And wanting things was dangerous.

"What would we raffle?" Her gaze danced around the room, so helpless and lost. It wasn't an expression he'd ever seen on her face before. His brain searched for something, anything, to make that look go away. "We can't give away the animals. And we can't buy anything."

The idea came as fast as the flare of a fire doused with lighter fluid, and he let the grin spread across his face again.

"What about firefighters?"

FIFTEEN

BROOKE

Krista's eyes were shining bright as flames as she raked her gaze over the dozen men gathered on stage. "You know how I feel about firefighters, but strictly from a financial perspective, this is the best idea you've ever had."

At least her multitasking skills meant she was able to ogle and set up chairs at the same time.

"It was Ethan's idea." Brooke might not apologize, but she gave credit where it was due, and this was brilliant.

They'd already unfolded close to two hundred chairs, but Brooke wanted an extra few rows to be sure they could fit everyone who'd officially RSVPed via social media. The online tickets alone had already brought in enough to cover the most recent vet bill she'd gotten for two kittens someone had found behind a dumpster. She wasn't sure people knew or even cared what cause they were supporting. They just wanted a date with a firefighter.

"Why isn't Ethan being auctioned off with the others?" Aisha was sitting at the end of the row, focused on untangling the rolls of tickets they'd sell at the door as people walked in. Half of the dates would be won in raffles, and the other would be auctions, happening live tonight.

The past week had been a whirlwind of preparations to get ready for the event at the Adamsville community center. It had been ages since Brooke had been in here, not since Gran had watched her perform in plays as a child, and the memories hit her in waves. At first it would be intense, then it ebbed, only to come back even stronger.

Watching Ethan talk and laugh with his former colleagues was helping it to stay ebbed.

"Because he loves Brooke, obviously." Krista nudged Brooke with a snicker.

"That's not why."

"Your cheeks are on fire right now," said Aisha, standing up and looking toward the stage. "Should I go see if there's someone to put them out—"

"No." She lunged across a row of chairs to grab Aisha's bright-yellow sleeve, clinging to the silky fabric.

Tonight her friend was wearing an amazing jumpsuit whose intense color made her skin look impossibly dewy. Krista was in what they called her luscious lawyer mode in a dark skirt that hugged every curve and a crisp white shirt that somehow remained unwrinkled despite the flurry of activity setting up the room.

Brooke knew she looked good, too, the light-blue dress a perfect match for her eyes. She'd even made herself a "beauty enhancing" smoothie before leaving the house. It was still hard to believe it could really be magical, but after weeks of witnessing the effects of the rosebud tea on Ethan, she figured it couldn't hurt. If nothing else, she got some vitamin C and hydration, which had the uncanny ability of turning the exhausted and drawn complexion Ethan saw at the shelter into something more shimmery and vibrant.

Not that she'd done any of this for Ethan.

Brooke let go of Aisha's sleeve. "Don't interrupt him. He looks busy."

Happy was what he looked like, actually. She'd never seen him like this before. Like he wasn't worried about anything, like he was totally at home.

That made sense, of course. He'd worked with these men on days-long shifts, fought fires beside them, handled emergencies Brooke couldn't even imagine.

The crinkle of his eyes when he smiled and the laugh so loud it carried across the room were pulling at something deep in her chest. The aching center of her that had felt unmoored since Gran's death recognized something steady in Ethan. This was one thing that had nothing to do with the rosebud tea. It was just who he was.

At first, she'd only told him about the financial struggles to get him to stop lavishing praise she didn't deserve. Now she was glad she'd done it. Not just for the shelter, but so that she could see such a happy, comfortable look on his face.

Krista looked at her watch. "It's almost time for the doors to open. Let's go."

The next hour was a blur of faces, money, and noise. Brooke smiled so much, her cheek muscles spasmed. Her back hurt from standing, and the noise was so overwhelming, she actually hid in the bathroom at one point for almost ten minutes before Aisha came looking for her.

It wasn't that she didn't want to have the event. It was incredible. They were raising so much money. But this had never been her thing, just like hosting the Halloween party had never been her thing. Of course she'd done it perfectly—she'd never let Gran down or give the town any reason to speak badly of the Adams family. Brooke wasn't her mother. It was just that being the face of these events was a lot more pressure than she'd expected.

The chaos of the past few months was miles away from the calm of an empty apartment and the contemplative puzzle of finding the exact right furniture that would ensure the sale went above asking price. She missed it like an ache, like a piece of her was missing. Tonight it was worse than it ever had been, thanks to the unexpected reminders of Gran that kept popping up. Everything in her body was wound as tight as the watch she checked every five minutes to see how much longer the night would last.

At least once the auction started, nobody paid any attention to her. All the eyes in the room were focused on the strong, muscled bodies parading up and down the stage, flexing and striking poses like they did this every day.

Brooke's eyes kept sliding off the stage, however, and toward the back corner of the room, where Ethan was standing.

"They're taking a break." Krista appeared at her elbow with a tall glass of something sparkling and pink. "Drink this and go talk to Ethan."

"He's busy."

"He's doing absolutely nothing. He's been in that same corner all night, leaning against the wall and staring at you."

"He has not been staring at me." She would have seen it at some point, since she'd been staring at him all night.

Which was why she noticed he wasn't completely at ease anymore. Before the break when the lights had gone back up, it had been dark in the large space. He'd mentioned it was harder for him to see at night. It was why he always took afternoon shifts and never evenings, why he stopped being a firefighter, when he clearly missed it.

The research she'd done on retinitis pigmentosa had been minimal, using only a few brief moments every night before crashing into bed, exhausted from the shelter. Even if she'd had the time to look it up properly, it wasn't really her place to learn about it. He was just her neighbor. A volunteer.

The guy in love with her because of a magic potion.

"Just go over there and talk to him." Krista waved around the room. "Thank him for this idea, at least."

Brooke kept her eyes on the stage, knowing she'd already thanked him already, many times, at least once a day as they were preparing for the event. Not that Brooke had had much to do. This was something the fire department had done before, and Ethan had taken the lead in organizing everything with Krista and Aisha, while Brooke focused on keeping her head above water at the shelter.

The days that he was volunteering at the shelter were her favorite. Things were lighter when he was there, more fun. It was the same feeling as when she drank Gran's special blend of flowers and herbs that made up her "bad day tea." Her head knew that what really helped was that Gran would listen without judgment whenever she gave it to Brooke.

Her heart, however, was more willing to believe in magic.

This belief was what had broken her completely a little over a year ago. All she'd wanted was for Gran to get better, and the woman who'd raised her on magic potions hadn't even wanted to try. From the moment she'd gotten her diagnosis, Gran hadn't had a single smoothie, but Brooke kept hoping she'd change her mind right until the very end.

Now, Brooke had let herself give in to that hope again, and it meant all these feelings stirring inside of her for Ethan were for someone who'd been tricked into spending time with her.

When the potion wore off, when he saw her for who she really was, her heart would be broken all over again.

"You look great." A voice in her ear made her jump, and she fell back into a wall.

She turned her head. No, not a wall. Ethan's solid, muscled chest. Thanks to her friends—who had conveniently disappeared—she knew exactly what that chest looked like, covered in sweat, doing push-ups and pull-ups in his yard.

"Thank you." She stepped away from the intoxicating pull of his body and turned so she could face him, look him in the eye. "You're looking quite dapper as well."

Red tinged his cheeks and he looked away. "I had to borrow this suit from one of the guys."

"I thought you've done these events before?" Brooke's heart

flip-flopped in her chest and sank into her stomach. Had she been wrong to let him take the lead in organizing the evening? What qualifications did he have, besides rippling muscles and the ability to not dissolve into a pool of despair whenever the numbers in a spreadsheet weren't adding up?

"I have, but behind the scenes." He nodded at the stage and Brooke's heart rate slowed. "Promoting it online, setting up the sound system, things like that. I've never been one of the dates. I'd just come and hang out, help out with the tickets or whatever."

"Well, you did a great job with this." Reassured she'd been right to trust him, Brooke tucked her hair behind her ear. "I couldn't have done it better myself."

His eyebrows raised high, and the corner of his lips tilted up. "Wow. Coming from you, that's high praise."

She shoved his arm, and he stumbled a little, grabbing her arm to steady himself. The pressure of his fingers was like a mini explosion of fireworks along her skin. "You've really never been one of the dates up for auction?"

His gaze was on her arm, where their bodies touched, not on her face. "It always felt so awkward. I like meeting people if I'm out with friends and they can be like a buffer, but I get nervous and shy when I have to interact one-on-one with people."

"Oh?" She let out a disbelieving chuckle. "That hasn't been a problem with me."

It was the closest she'd ever come to talking about that day with him. About how rude she'd been, how much she still hated herself for acting so irrationally, so unlike what Gran would have wanted.

"You seem to be the exception." His eyes now finally met hers, his lips tugging up at the corners. "I'm not sure why."

She sucked in a breath. It was the tea. The love potion. Even though weeks had passed, the effects were still there. From the compliments he gave her, to the way he was looking at her right now with his hand on her arm. None of this was really how he felt, and she should tell him.

He'd think she was absolutely insane, but maybe that's what it would take to break whatever spell he was under.

Her heart tumbled around in her chest. Did she really want the spell broken?

From the stage, the MC took the mic, and they both turned their attention to him. Ethan dropped her arm, but stayed next to her, so close she could feel the heat of his body.

"Alright, thank you so much for your generous bids for these amazing guys." The crowd cheered at the MC's words. "We're at almost five thousand for the evening, and we'd love to hit that goal. Unfortunately, we're all out of firefighters, so please consider making a donation while you enjoy the dancing and drinks."

Brooke plastered a smile on her face as people turned to look at her while they clapped.

"Are you okay?" Ethan's voice was quiet. "I'm sorry we didn't quite make as much as you wanted."

"It doesn't matter if we hit it. Honestly, any amount is a huge help."

It's what Gran would have said. She'd be grateful and gracious about all the donations, and Brooke did her best to nod and smile and everyone who caught her eye.

Next to her, Ethan let out a low, assessing hum. "I don't know if I believe you."

"I know it seemed like a reasonable goal when we set it, but the town isn't really that big." She brushed the hair away from her face and kept her eyes on the crowd, the smile still stretching her lips. "It's not like people can spend thousands just for an hour with a firefighter, no matter how fit and sexy they are. The max bid all night was only two hundred dollars."

Beside her, she could feel him thinking, considering, seeing through all of her lies. She bit the inside of her cheek to stop from crying.

"Maybe I could do it."

"Really?" She turned her head and was surprised at just how

close he was standing to her. The dimpled smile on his face filled her entire field of vision. "But you just said you don't like talking to people you don't know."

He shrugged. "It's for a good cause."

She blinked, trying to get back to her safe, logical place. "So was the fire department, but you never did it for them."

"Do you want the money for the shelter or not?" He raised an eyebrow.

Of course she did. "But anyone can bid on you. What if you get someone who picks their teeth at dinner?"

"It's just coffee and a visit to the shelter to see the animals, not an entire meal."

"What if they smell? Or want you to join their MLM? What if their MLM is for smelly deodorant?"

"Then I'll be sure to give them your email instead of mine." He winked at her.

She crossed her arms over her chest. "You're not thinking this through. Is this really how you live your life, just seeing something come along then doing it, no planning, no consideration for what might happen later?"

"It's worked out for me so far."

"I'm serious, Ethan."

"So am I." He grinned, his dimples twinkling at her. "I mean, not about the email thing. But I'm going to do it."

Brooke bit her lip, pulling at the skin there with her teeth, ruining the lipstick she'd spent an inordinate amount of time putting on earlier. Not because of Ethan, of course. Because Gran would have expected her to look her best when representing the shelter. And she definitely wasn't jealous at the thought of someone bidding on Ethan. Only concerned that he'd be put into an uncomfortable situation just to help her, which was unnecessary given how much he'd already done.

"This wasn't the plan though." Brooke desperately grasped

onto the most logical of all arguments, knowing even as the words left her mouth the answer that Ethan would have.

With a flash of his teeth that made her knees tremble a little, he said exactly what she knew he would. "When an opportunity presents itself, I have to say yes. Who knows what the universe has in store for me?"

And with that, he made his way up to the stage to talk to the MC.

The lights from the stage were brighter than Ethan expected, and it put the entire audience in shadow. He knew it must have been like that for the others, but this was different. It was true blindness for him beyond the lights lining the bottom edge of the stage. He blinked, but nothing changed. It never did, and that's what had triggered the doctor's visit last year.

He took an unsteady step and put his hands on his hips, while the MC spouted some nonsense about his love for hang gliding and long walks on the beach. Everyone he'd introduced had been the same ridiculous, over-the-top, completely fabricated bio, just to get a laugh out of the crowd.

"And you know Ethan loves animals, since this former firefighter's been volunteering at the shelter!"

The crowd went wild at that nugget of truth.

The bidding started small, like it had for everyone. Twenty dollars, then fifty, then a seventy-five, then a hundred. This was the easy part. The actual date would be the real challenge. But it would be worth it, for Brooke.

For the animal shelter.

No, for Brooke. He inhaled slowly and beamed out at the

crowd he couldn't see. Sharing his diagnosis with her had opened something up inside of him. It did no good to deny that he felt something for her, that he had since probably the first fiery moment he'd seen her.

His head swam and he stumbled, using every last one of his expertly trained muscles to stay upright. There wasn't much he could do about this realization on stage in front of hundreds of people.

When they got to five hundred dollars, the highest of the night so far, Ethan realized it was only two women bidding against each other, pushing the amount higher and higher. He shifted his pose and tried to catch their voices.

"Five hundred and twenty!" one cried.

"Five hundred and fifty!" the other shouted right back.

The MC was entirely useless in this exchange and was looking at Ethan with an odd smile on his face, like he didn't know what was happening but was enjoying it immensely.

Ethan would give anything to see better in the dark right now. There was not even the hint of a dress or hair to help him. He turned his head slightly so his ear was in the direction of the voices.

"Six hundred!"

"Six fifty!"

There were murmurs in the crowd. Ethan still had no idea who was bidding on him. He held his breath, which puffed out his chest, and the bids went even higher.

Finally, a third voice shouted "one thousand," and Ethan's stomach dropped to the floor. The MC was quick to proclaim a winner loudly over the shocked gasps that echoed around the room.

"Congratulations to our very generous winner." The room erupted into applause and Ethan made his way to the side of the stage where the stairs were. He kept one hand on the wall as he walked down, a smile plastered on his face that he didn't feel in the slightest.

What the blazes had just happened? Who had bid so much on him?

There was the spark of hope, that maybe, just maybe it had been Brooke. There were moments, in the way she'd look at him, or in the heat of the air around them, that he was sure something was going on between them. Then she'd protested so much about him doing it, so maybe she was jealous. Maybe this had been her opportunity to tell him that she felt whatever he was feeling too.

At the bottom of the stairs, he paused, back against the wall. Reality sank in, along with the familiar feeling of helplessness when faced with not being able to see much in front of him.

No, it couldn't be Brooke who'd bid on him. If she had that money available, she'd just put it directly into the shelter, no need to do it in a public way. He swallowed, hoping whoever had won the auction was making their way over to him now. He'd gotten on and off the stage on his own, so it didn't feel like he could ask for help now. The lights were still low in the room while the MC introduced a local band who'd be playing for the next hour or so as people mingled and hopefully bought a lot of drinks at the cash bar. Earlier he'd been talking and joking around with some of the firefighters, and it had felt better than he'd imagined it would after so many months of his new solitary life. Almost like he was still one of them.

The dimness of the room reminded him that wasn't true anymore.

A heaviness settled in his stomach as the minutes ticked by. It was a churning, swirling, heavy dread that was somehow also in his throat, threatening to come flying out. He shifted on his feet, his shoulder creeping up as he flattened his hands against the wall. He tried to focus on the smooth, warm wood paneling beneath his fingers and not the rising acid hitting the back of his tongue.

"Hey," said a voice at his side and he turned. His eyes had adjusted just enough to the low light that he could just make out Brooke's familiar features. Her dark hair was down tonight, shiny even in the darkness, her smile a flash of white, her eyes a burning beacon of blue. The churning in his stomach settled and his heart lifted.

"Hey." He shifted his weight but kept his hand on the wall. "Did you—I mean, are you the winner?"

"No." Her tone was an odd one he'd never heard before, but not entirely unlike when she'd yelled at him during his inspection of the shelter. A challenge was simmering below the surface, an unhappiness she didn't seem quite able to put words to without being impolite. "I thought you might need some help. I read it can be hard going from bright light to a darker space, and you were just kind of hanging out here by the wall."

Even though he could barely see, it was like the sun had come out. She'd *read* about his condition? This shouldn't surprise him, considering what he knew about Brooke and the organized way she ran her life. Still, his chest warmed and unspeakable gratitude filled him. He had to blink furiously to relieve the pressure behind his eyes.

"Thanks." He cleared his throat, not entirely sure how she could help. No one had ever offered before. Though, to be fair, he'd never told anyone the details so they'd know to help. He'd been dealing with things on his own until now, but maybe he didn't have to. "Could I take your arm?"

She held out her hand, and he put his into hers, then she guided it up to the crook of her bent elbow.

He was grateful to her. That was the only reason he was warm all over right now. The only reason his palm was tingling from the contact with hers, the only reason his hand on her elbow felt like something forbidden, like a sugary snack late at night or eating the entire bag of M&M's instead of just a handful to quell his craving. He wasn't craving her. He couldn't be.

Or maybe he'd wanted her for so long, it was just part of who he was now.

She started walking slowly away from the stage and into the dimly lit room. "Where are we headed?"

"Toward whoever the winner is, I guess."

"That would be Krista."

"Really?"

Brooke let out a short laugh. "You sound surprised."

He was, but more surprising was the thread of disappointment weaving through him. Maybe he'd misinterpreted Krista's attention at the Halloween party, since he'd been so fixated on Brooke. Maybe Brooke had only ever watched him from her window because of her friend.

Maybe he wasn't meant to be with Brooke at all, and this was his sign.

"You're really good at this," he said, changing topics completely.

The muscles in her arm flexed a little under his hand. "What? Leading you around?"

"Yeah."

There was a pause, and he could picture her teeth digging into her lip as she considered what to say. The room was a mass of dim shapes, slowly getting clearer the longer he focused, but it was exhausting.

"I used to help Gran around. She lost a big part of her vision near the end."

The floor shifted beneath his feet, and he gripped tighter to her arm to avoid stumbling.

"What happened?" He felt her muscles tighten beneath his hand. "If you don't mind me asking. You never really talk about it."

They were still making their way through the crowd, toward the edges of the room. It was noisy, everyone in high spirits thanks to the auction and the bar. This wasn't exactly the ideal place to talk about it, but then again, it was almost easier with so many people around. It felt less intimate.

"It was cancer that actually . . . " She took a shaky inhale. "The vision loss wasn't linked to that. It was just regular age-related degeneration."

"I'm sorry for your loss. I've been meaning to say that for a while."

There was a pause, a long one, and he wasn't sure she'd say anything. Then, softly, "It was over a year ago."

"But you still miss her."

It wasn't a question and Brooke didn't respond. Ethan could have said more about his own loss, but it had happened so long ago it wasn't so much missing his parents as it was a memory of missing them. If he told her about them, then he'd have to explain how their death had led to everything else in his life, how each element had fallen into place once he'd given up trying to control every little thing. She already thought he was irresponsible, accepting things as they came. No need to remind her of just how different they were when she was already guiding him around, fully aware that he wasn't like the others who'd been up for auction tonight.

While he stayed silent, Brooke kept leading him slowly around the room, quietly letting him know where there were chairs and tables so he wouldn't bump into them.

It was so easy, so natural, like they'd been doing this for years. It wasn't something anyone else had ever done for Ethan, and he wasn't sure he'd ever want anyone else to do it. Brooke didn't make him feel annoying or like a burden. It was the way she did so many of the things she did well: with focus and attention and a deeper understanding and care than she ever let anyone suspect while making it look effortless.

"There he is!" Krista's excited squeal met his ears long before Ethan was able to see her clearly. His eyes were slowly adjusting, especially now that they were in the bar area, which had its own, much brighter lighting.

Safely delivered to his destination, Brooke dropped her arm and his hand fell to his side. His fingers curled into a fist. He didn't want her to stop touching him. Even if the only reason was to lead him when he couldn't see that well.

"Now, when will we have our coffee date?" Krista asked.

Ethan slid his eyes to Brooke, who'd moved further away from him, her eyebrows pinched tightly together. This wasn't Krista's usual flirty, exuberant personality he was slowly but surely getting used to. Well, she was still sparkling, but her tone was different, more friendly than flirty.

"Um, whenever it works for you." He ran a hand along the back of his neck. "My schedule is pretty flexible."

"How about tomorrow? Ten o'clock at the Batter Me Up Bakery?"

"Sure, sounds good."

Before Ethan could think to ask about the weird tension between the two friends, there was a voice behind him and a hand on his shoulder.

"Ethan, so great to see you tonight." The lights had brightened and his eyes had adjusted, but even without that, he would have recognized Chief Stevens's voice.

"Hi, Chief."

"Is this the lucky girl?"

"Yes, this is the woman who won the auction." Ethan gestured. "Krista . . . "

"Waters." Krista smiled, a brilliant one that was clearly intended to charm the chief. It worked as planned, and he took her outstretched hand with a dazed look on his face, as if he was unsure if he should shake it or kiss it.

"Have we met before?" Chief's eyes crinkled at the edges as he tilted his head.

Did a shadow pass over Krista's face? Ethan still wasn't seeing everyone properly. "I was at Brooke's Halloween party, but I was busy in the kitchen. I didn't get a chance to say hello to everyone."

Chief nodded, still holding her hand. "That must be it."

"I'm also a junior partner at Mendoza, St. Claire, and Forcett."

"A lawyer?" He whistled. "Well, lucky Ethan."

Her tinkling laugh echoed in the room, and a few heads turned. "You mean lucky me, paying a grand to finally get a guy to sit and drink coffee with me without bailing halfway through."

It was a joke, or at least meant to be a joke, but Ethan heard something else behind those words. He glanced again at Brooke, whose eyebrows had smoothed out and her expression had turned into a curious one. Her gaze darted between Ethan, the chief, and Krista.

"Nonsense, they must be lining up for you." The chief patted her hand reassuringly.

"None as charming as you." The words were perfect, Krista was perfect, and Ethan was left wondering again if he'd just misinterpreted everything up until then. The same people-reading and status-tracking skills that he lacked for his inspector job would also have come in handy right about now.

At least Jerry had come tonight. Aisha had stopped by the fire station a few days ago with some treats to thank people for participating, and she had made sure to invite Ethan's boss to the auction. That had seemed to mollify whatever lingering resentment Jerry still had about Brooke's party. Ethan wasn't going to spend time worrying if it would make a difference or not for his inspector job. Like so much of his life, it was out of his control.

The chief chuckled, wished them a good night, then moved away, giving Ethan a short nod that he knew meant he wanted him to follow.

"I'll see you tomorrow, Krista." Ethan gave her his typical charming smile, the one he hadn't used much in the past year, and she preened. Behind her, Brooke's frown deepened, and Ethan ignored the jump in his chest to head toward the chief.

It felt wrong to ignore something his body was telling him to do —talk to Brooke, ask her what was wrong, ask her if she'd maybe thought about bidding on him—but he couldn't deny the facts. The universe had presented him with a date with Krista, so that was what he was supposed to do. Wishing for things to be different with Brooke was pointless. If it was meant to be, then it would happen without Ethan needing to do anything.

Despite knowing it would eventually lead to disappointment, when his eyes met hers right before he turned away, a spark of hope for more stubbornly lit up his chest. It stayed there the rest of the night.

It took all the restraint in her body for Brooke from laying into Krista at the auction. Oh, her best friend knew she was mad. Aisha could feel it, too, and kept glancing between the two of them, her eyes wide and anxious, as three women broke down the tables and tidied up the room. But no matter how hard Brooke's pulse pounded in her ears and how tight her fists got at her sides, she kept her mouth shut.

It was what Gran would have done. Waited until they were somewhere private, not air their dirty laundry in front of everyone. The firefighters were all still there as well, helping them put everything away. She wasn't going to start yelling in front of all of them, not when they'd just put themselves up for auction to help Brooke. She thanked all of them at least ten times, and got selfless smiles in response from the adorable, muscled team.

At least Ethan was long gone, having left with Chief Stevens. Brooke had worried all night about how he'd get home, then reminded herself he was an adult who'd been dealing with this for over a year. He knew what he needed and would ask, just like he'd done tonight when he'd asked for her arm.

Then she'd led him right to Krista, the traitor. If she'd wanted to give Brooke money for the shelter, she could have just written a check. She didn't need to make such a public spectacle of herself. And of Ethan.

The second they got into the car, Aisha in the backseat and Krista behind the wheel, Brooke exploded.

"I can't believe you did that." Brooke's voice echoed in the small car, a sonic boom of irritation so loud someone across the parking lot turned their head toward them. "What were you thinking?"

Without even so much as a glance in her direction, Krista pulled out of the parking spot and onto the road, as cool and sweet as ice cream. "That you needed an excuse to see Ethan outside of the shelter. And I just gave you one."

"You—wait, what?" After preparing for a fight for the past half hour, Brooke's shoulders slumped, and she flopped back in her seat. Her heart was still racing, and she swallowed a few times before speaking again, somewhat calmer. "What do you mean?"

"Obviously you will go to Batter Me Up tomorrow at ten. Not me."

Brooke turned to look at Aisha in the backseat, who shrugged, the butterfly clips holding up her hair sparkling from the streetlights they passed. "I was just there for the food and to ogle firefighters."

Krista sighed and pulled to a stop at a red light. "Brooke, you were turning three shades of purple while those two teachers were bidding on Ethan."

Pouting, Brooke folded her arms across her chest. "That's not true."

It was very true. The two women had been at the Halloween party, where Ethan must have made an impression. She hated thinking about him with someone else, but she had no claim to him, other than her love potion. To take advantage of that would be contemptible. Her friends, however, seemed to have completely forgotten about that.

"I'm just worried about the effects of the rosebud tea on him."

"That was weeks ago!" Aisha said, leaning forward to pop her head between the two of them in the front seat. "There's no way the effects last that long. A week tops is what Gran always said. Then you're on your own."

Brooke made a noise of protest. "It steeped for a week, so it was super strong. It would have to be, since I was so horrible to him."

"But you haven't been lately, have you?" Krista said.

"Well, no." Their interactions at the shelter had gotten friendlier whenever Brooke wasn't completely stressed out. And there'd been those close calls in the storage closet, where their bodies had been touching and he'd looked at her like . . . she shivered, despite the heat blasting in her face.

"There are lots of reasons he'd like you." Aisha held up a finger. "First, you look absolutely banging in that dress, second—"

"More importantly," Krista's voice rang out in the small car. "You clearly like him. The potion has most definitely worn off by now, so it's time to do this thing for real."

Brooke stayed quiet, hands smoothing out the wrinkles in her "banging" dress, considering the not entirely untrue points her friends were making.

"I just thought that you could use a bit of a push." The light turned green, and Krista's eyes turned back to the road. "Maybe I was wrong."

The words hung in the air between the three friends, filling the car with their ridiculousness. Krista was never wrong. They all knew it.

Admitting it, however, was only slightly less painful than apologizing. If Brooke had to choose between the two, it wasn't really a contest.

"You're not wrong." The words were harder to get out of Brooke than it was to get Cloudy into his cage at the end of the day.

"I knew it!" Aisha leaned forward again and threw her arms

over the back of Brooke's seat to hug her shoulders. "You're super into him. That look on your face is so familiar."

"You mean because you have it whenever you talk about Cody?" Brooke teased her, squeezing her arms.

"Exactly." Aisha leaned back, a smile on her face. "One day, I'll actually manage to talk *to* him."

The ongoing saga of Aisha's crush at the aquarium was something the three friends had spent many late nights analyzing, and Brooke was tempted to change the subject to talk about him instead. Maybe offer to whip up another batch of rosebud tea for Aisha to take to work.

Krista had other ideas, of course.

"Brooke will be able to talk to Ethan all she wants tomorrow, thanks to me." Krista settled back in her seat with a satisfied smile and turned in to Brooke's neighborhood.

Brooke's hands fiddled with the hem of her dress. Talk to him about what? The shelter? Her nonexistent dating history and zero hobbies?

"As long as you're sure you don't want to be the one to go on the date?"

The look Krista shot her could only be described as a horrified smirk.

"No thank you."

Heat pooled in Brooke's chest, insulted on behalf of Ethan. "Is there something wrong with him?"

"Of course not." Krista rolled her eyes. "I just don't have time right now for any romantic complications. I'm too busy with work."

This tracked with everything Krista had been saying for years —except when she had a few drinks and started talking about "J," the mystery man from last summer. Then tonight, there'd been that offhand joke to Chief Stevens about needing to pay someone to sit through a date with her. Brooke wasn't entirely convinced there wasn't something else going on with Krista, but it would do no good questioning the tight-lipped lawyer tonight when she was so focused on Brooke.

"What if he's disappointed to see me? He'll be expecting you."

"Are you kidding? He was holding on so tightly to your arm, I don't think he would have let go if you hadn't stepped away."

Brooke bit her lip, then quickly released it. Her friends would know the sign of her nerves and the last thing she wanted was for them to think something was off. It wasn't her place to say anything about Ethan's vision, and there was no way to explain why he'd had to hold on to her.

Without even thinking, she rubbed her arm where his hand had been.

The smile on Krista's face was almost reptilian in its satisfaction. "See? I'm right. You felt it too."

They were in front of Brooke's house, so instead of responding to that, she told her friends goodnight and reached over to give them each a hug.

There was no way of knowing how Ethan would react. Brooke hated going into anything without all the information available, without being ninety-nine percent sure she could handle it. Just look at the shelter, where things had been as much of a disaster as she'd expected.

Except it's not so bad now, is it? Now that she had Ethan. Now that she'd been saying yes to things that she hadn't fully expected or planned.

First his idea about the adoption event, then all his improvements to the systems, and finally the auction tonight. Sharing the load with her friends was easy. They'd always been there for her. Love potion or not, Ethan had shown time and time again. Maybe he could be there for her too.

She sighed and made her way up the stairs to get ready for bed. One way or another, in twelve hours, she'd know what would happen with him and she'd just have to trust she'd be able to handle it.

.   .   .

I can't believe I'm doing this.

From the safety of her car, Brooke watched Ethan stroll up to the bakery, pause at the door, take a breath, and go inside.

He looked so nervous. Anybody would be before a date with Krista. And if her friends were right and the effects of the love potion had worn off, then there was nothing stopping him from preferring bright and sunny Krista over dark and moody Brooke.

Might as well get this over with.

Brooke took a deep breath, got out of the car, and walked into the bakery.

When Ethan spotted her, his entire face lit up. Brooke's heart soared in response. Then, just as quickly, his expression shuttered, and her heart tumbled down her chest into her stomach.

"Are you chaperoning my date with Krista?" One eyebrow raised, a smirk tracing the edges of his mouth.

"No, I'm here instead of her."

Both eyebrows popped up. "Really?"

Does he sound excited? Brooke's heart sped up, hope lacing itself into her veins before logic could take over and remind her of all the reasons she couldn't trust it.

"Really. I hope that's okay."

"It's definitely okay." The smile he gave her in return lit her up from the inside out.

Every inch of her hoped that her friends were right, and the love potion had worn off. That this might be something real.

"I've never been here before." Ethan looked around, taking in the space and the unusually large crowd for a Saturday morning. "What do you usually get?"

Brooke tucked her hair behind her ears. "They have really good smoothies."

"Yeah?" His lips curled up. "You'd be the expert on those."

Heat rushed to her face. Of course he'd remembered. "They have fresh ingredients, which is the most important thing."

"To make them magical?"

She knew he was teasing, but her chest squeezed tight. If he had any idea that's how all of this had started, he wouldn't find it so funny.

"Only if you're my grandmother. But a lot of plants do have mildly medicinal properties." Brooke tucked her hair behind her ears. "She grew everything herself, so that made it seem a little more magical."

He stilled next to her and inhaled sharply. "You mean like the plants Lucky dug up?"

She didn't answer but met his eyes, warm and soft and full of regret.

"If I'd had any idea how much those plants meant to you, I would have never yelled at—"

Brooke held up a hand. The last thing she wanted now was to bring up the past and all the reasons he shouldn't be here with her. "It's fine, really. I've already planted another."

All it took was a single step forward from Ethan, and suddenly her raised hand was resting on his chest, and his face was inches away from hers.

"Brooke, I'm sorry."

She swallowed down the lump in her throat, using all of her energy to keep their gazes locked.

"Ethan, I—"

"Are you two going to order or not?" A gangly, red-faced teenager was glowering at them behind them in line. "You look like you're either about to make out or cry."

Ethan let out a breathy chuckle and stepped away from Brooke. With a wave of his hand, he gestured that she should go in front of him.

Now that she wasn't facing him, she let herself pull her lower lip under her teeth and slowly scrape across it.

She wasn't entirely sure what had been about to come out of her mouth. Had she been about to apologize? For what? Being rude over a year ago? For the love potion he'd accidentally drunk? There was no reason to bring either up and ruin the closest thing to a date she'd had in years.

"Order?" The nasally voice of the barista cut through her anxious thoughts.

"Chai latte."

"A chocolate peanut butter smoothie." Ethan's voice was right behind her, along with the heat of his body.

Brooke resisted the temptation to lean back, to let herself get lost in Ethan. The strength of his arms, the solidity of his chest—everything about him felt stable in a way she hadn't since before Gran had gotten sick. Taking care of her on top of her job had left no time for dating, and now she was so out of practice it made her put endless meaning in every little touch and look.

He bent close to her ear and the whisper of his breath prickled along the back of her neck. "Is there anything magical in that one?"

A smile spread across her face as they made their way to the pick-up counter to wait for their orders. He stayed right behind her, even putting a hand on her lower back at one point to guide her. Or maybe just to touch her?

"Not unless you consider the combination of salty and sweet magical." She paused. "Which I do."

"Yeah?" There was a low rumble of amusement in his voice.

"There's also the combination of milkshakes and chicken nuggets."

"Um, what?" The humor in his voice was replaced with horror, and she turned to find his eyes wide in exaggerated disgust. She giggled.

Their orders were ready, and he grabbed both of their cups. A simple thing, but so considerate, she wasn't able to breathe as he led her to a seat. He put the cups down first, then pulled out her chair. She blinked a few times before sitting down.

"You mean you've never tried nuggets in a milkshake?" she asked when her heart had stopped its furious beating to something closer to a normal pattern.

"French fries, sure, but a chicken nugget?" He grimaced, then took a sip of his smoothie.

Brooke shook her head and lifted her tea to blow on it. "Fries get too soggy. There's no heft to them to hold the shake. You need something sturdier and saltier."

He shook his head too, but there was an upward tilt to his mouth that had her heart racing again. "I guess I'll have to try it."

"I converted Krista and Aisha back in middle school, so I'm very confident in this combination."

"You've known them that long?"

Brooke nodded, then launched into the story she'd told some version of at least a dozen times. How Krista had moved to town in second grade, and they'd formed a bond over *Lilo and Stitch* and ballet. Then Aisha and her dad moved in down the street the following year, and they'd become an inseparable trio, only splitting up briefly during college.

"Even as a kid, you could tell Krista was going to be a lawyer." Brooke took a sip of her chai. Ethan had already finished his smoothie, drinking it up along with her words like he couldn't get enough. "She managed to get a rule changed in middle school that said girls couldn't try out for the baseball team, and there was no softball team."

"She played softball?"

"Absolutely not." Brooke laughed. "She just thought it wasn't fair."

Ethan laughed, too, a low chuckle that spread through her bones, warming her more than her tea could have, which had gone cold during her extended monologue.

"She's definitely a powerful personality."

There was a hitch in Brooke's chest, a pang of familiar jealousy and doubt. "She couldn't come today. She had something for work and didn't want her bid to go to waste and—"

"I'm not upset." Ethan reached out and put a hand on top of hers. "I'm . . . glad it's you."

Her stomach swirled, and she swallowed hard. It took a few shaky inhales before she could even gather her thoughts enough to come up with a response to that.

"I'm glad too."

There was so much hanging in the air around them, so much unsaid. The weeks of working together and the simmering tension over their first few meetings mingled with the undeniable attraction that Brooke was now almost certain was no longer due to the rosebud tea. It might have started thanks to a magic potion, but this felt like something real.

Ethan cleared his throat. "Maybe we could get nuggets and milkshakes sometime?"

His hand was still on hers, and he made a little circle with his thumb, sending tingles along her arm that made their way through her entire body. Her breathing grew so ragged again, she could only manage one breathy word in response.

"Yeah?"

"How about tonight? If you don't have to be at the shelter?"

It took less than half a second for Brooke to mentally confirm she was free. The new system Ethan had come up with for potential new owners to book appointments had saved an incredible amount of time. Only two people now were needed on the weekends, which meant Brooke could actually have something resembling a social life.

Like going on a date with her hot neighbor tonight.

"I'm free."

"Great." The smile on his face was different from any she'd seen before. Lighter, brighter, full of hope. He stood up. "I have a few things I need to do today, but I'll come by around six?"

All she could do was nod and bite her lip to keep from grinning like there'd been Gran's "good mood potion" in her cup instead of chai. Twenty-four hours ago, she'd been anxious about the auction, convinced the shelter was a failure and that Ethan still hated her.

Now she was finishing one date with him and had another planned for tonight, while the shelter had enough money for at least the next three months.

All because of Krista, who'd been right, like always.

A groan slipped out of Brooke's mouth as she watched Ethan walk out of the bakery, and she let her head fall into her hands.

She could practically hear Krista gloating from her apartment across town.

The walk from Ethan's house to Brooke's wasn't quite as well lit as it had been for her Halloween party, but it was familiar. Ish. The path from his front door to the sidewalk and then to her front door was one he'd only taken twice, but at least it was short. Even though he felt ridiculous for needing to use a flashlight, he knew Brooke wouldn't say anything about it or think worse of him for it.

Maybe nobody else would either, but he couldn't be sure. He stopped halfway up the path to Brooke's door and let the light skim across the yard, now empty of decorations, remembering Chief Stevens's awkward offer to help the night of the party. And his offer last night to drive him home from the auction, even though Ethan had already ordered a rideshare. Letting Brooke in hadn't been easy, but it felt safe. Probably because he'd already seen her at a low point. It was easier to trust someone with your own struggles when you knew the other person wasn't perfect.

Not that he thought Chief Stevens or Jerry or any of his former crew were perfect. But they weren't going around advertising their daily battles.

When he got to Brooke's door, he held his breath and knocked, doubt suddenly burrowing into his belly and biting his insides. He hadn't thought about where they'd go. Would she be okay driving? That didn't feel very much like a date. She might not say anything about the flashlight, but he wasn't like her grandmother. Would she change her mind when she realized how uneasy places like restaurants and bars made him? Someone Ethan's age should be able to go out at night. Even his former crew had joked at the auction about his new hermit-like life, asking if he turned into a pumpkin at midnight.

Of course, they teased everyone. The fire station was a nonstop battleground of taunts and digs that Ethan hadn't realized how much he'd missed until he'd been with them all again last night. The life he should have been leading had never felt so close or so far away. Though it wasn't exactly the kind of environment that made it easy to open up about more serious things. The jokes helped them all deal with the grim reality of the job. Was it really the job he missed or the camaraderie? Probably a little of both.

When Brooke opened the door, she had a small, shy smile on her face, and Ethan's doubt melted away. He wasn't with his former crew tonight fighting fires, but he was with Brooke, where he was supposed to be. Whatever happened would happen. It wasn't up to him.

"Hey." She opened the door wide and bit her lip, the familiar gesture setting his heart thumping against his ribs. "So I did something. I hope you're not mad."

"Uh-oh." He couldn't help but grin.

"It's not a big deal." She tucked her hair behind her ears. It was smoother and shinier than they had been that morning, like she'd taken a shower since then, and done her hair. Done it for him, for this date. Her cheeks turned pink, and his ribs practically shook from the effect that had on his pulse. The scent of lavender wafted over him. "I just ordered food to come here. I hope that's okay."

"Why would I be mad about that?"

"Well, it's very controlling."

"You say this like I don't already know this about you."

She chuckled a little at that, and her shoulders relaxed, the tension easing from the lines of her face. She waved a hand, and he followed her into the house. The foyer looked strangely huge and empty without the giant papier-mâché skull that had greeted him last month. "I just figured you wouldn't want to go out somewhere in the dark, even if I'm driving. Restaurants can be so dim, and I didn't want you to be uncomfortable."

The emotion that hit Ethan in the chest wasn't something he was familiar with, so he had a hard time identifying it. It was warm, starting behind his ribcage, then pooling in his stomach before spreading through all of his limbs until it felt like he was glowing.

This was more than just being helpful when he asked.

"That's fine." The words came out halfway choked, and he cleared his throat. "Thank you for thinking of that."

She looked at him with a funny expression, her head tilted and lips turned slightly down. Her fingers rested on the edge of a side table covered in neat stacks of mail. "Of course, Ethan. It's not a bother or anything. It just takes a little planning and consideration."

Consideration. Was that what he'd been missing these past few months? The past year?

There wasn't a guarantee everyone would show him that when faced with his situation.

"I guess I don't really give people the option." He ran a hand over the back of his neck and sighed. "When I stopped driving at night, they just stopped inviting me out."

"Really?" Brooke sounded surprised. "You seemed to get along with them okay last night. No one ever offered to drive?"

Ethan's chest pinched. They had offered, but he'd been the one to say no, rather than explain what was going on.

Those bright-blue eyes were observing him closely. "Who have you told about your diagnosis?"

"Chief Stevens. My sister." He paused and looked away, his

eyes landing on the mirror above the table. The back of her hair was so straight, and so smooth. "And you."

"That's it?" At the sound of surprise in her voice, he flicked his gaze back to hers and found her wide-eyed with eyebrows up to the ceiling. "Ethan, people can't help you if they don't know."

His shoulders shot up to his ears. "I don't need help."

"Not help, then." She shook her head and leaned back against the table. "Gran was the same way, waiting until she was almost doubled over in pain before giving any hint something was wrong. People can't adapt if they don't know what you need."

"I don't need anything." The words were harsher than he intended, and she sucked in a breath. His hand flexed at his side, wanting to reach out to reassure her. "I'm sorry. I just don't want to talk about it."

"Sure." Her shoulders slumped and her gaze landed somewhere over his shoulder.

Great. The mood was off now. He'd ruined it. It was a sign that this probably wasn't going to work, and he should probably just leave.

His hands flexed at his sides. "Look, we don't have to do this tonight—"

Before he could finish, the doorbell rang, and Brooke shot up straight, the table shaking from her sudden movement. "That's the food. Please, go into the living room, make yourself comfortable."

Comfortable didn't seem possible, but he did as told and walked further into the house. The living room had seemed massive at the party, filled to the brim with people, but now it just looked cozy. The furniture was centered around a massive coffee table, with the TV off in a corner like it was rarely used. This was a room for friends to hang out and eat and talk. He could easily picture her here with Krista and Aisha, laughing and teasing. Less easy to picture was the same happening in his house next door. Since Lucky left, it felt so empty and lonely.

With a sigh, he plopped onto the couch and put his head in his hands. He was just as empty and lonely as his house, and now he was ruining everything with the one person he felt comfortable around. If things were going to work out between them, it shouldn't be this hard.

"So I got three different kinds of shakes and five different nuggets."

At this, he looked up, and she was standing at the wide entrance to the room with two giant bags of food in her hands and balancing a tray of drinks on top. He quickly stood up to take them from her, the absurdity of what she'd just said sinking in.

"I would say I'm surprised, but I'm actually not." A smile started to tug at his lips, and before he knew what was happening, he was laughing, then Brooke was laughing, and the tension from just a few moments before had disappeared like it had never been there.

"I just like being thorough," she said through giggles as he followed her into the kitchen to lay out everything on the counter. "I don't want you to try it once and think it's not for you because it happened to be a bad milkshake."

"I don't think that's possible. How can you make a bad milkshake? That's like bad pizza or a bad donut."

"Oh, you'd be surprised." Brooke lined up everything on the counter. There were six shakes in total, that she paired up two by two—one for each of them, he realized with a thud in his chest. Then she reached up into the cabinet, and her shirt lifted to show a flash of skin at her waist. Ethan pulled his eyes away just in time and had his gaze fixed on her face when she turned back with a stack of small plates.

"There's a specific ratio of ice cream to milk that gets you the ideal consistency." She put one plate in front of each milkshake duo and then put a single nugget from each little box in the same order on each. "If you need a spoon, it's too thick. If it's too liquid, it's not a good fit for nuggets."

He nodded slowly, as if this was completely logical and not the most ridiculous thing he'd ever heard. After adjusting the position of the plates so they were exactly in between the two milkshakes, she took out a glass and filled it with water, then put it right behind the entire setup. It was all very scientific and organized and . . . Brooke.

This careful attention to details was what made her so considerate, he realized. While he could tease her about it, he secretly loved it. It was reassuring to know someone had things under control, when so much of his life felt out of his control. Leaving things up to Brooke sounded a lot better than leaving it up to the universe.

"Okay." She stood back from the counter and rubbed her hands together like this was the most fun she'd had in weeks. Like there was nothing she'd rather be doing on her Saturday night than converting him to the culinary wonder that was chicken nuggets dipped in milkshakes. "So you'll take the first one at the top of the plate, at twelve o'clock, and dip it into the shake. Then you'll drink some water and move on to the second, and then third."

"Got it." He tried to keep the smile off his face but knew he would fail miserably. It stayed there throughout the entire ridiculous experiment.

After each bite, her eyes would rake across his face, observing each little reaction. Her gaze on his lips heated his pulse, distracting him. As her teeth worried at her own lip, his breathing grew uneven. At one point, she caught his hand before it reached for the plate in front of him, the zing of electricity hot where their skin touched.

"That's not the right nugget." With gentle fingers, she led his hand to the correct one, and he swallowed hard. Brooke's eyes tracked the movement. "More water?"

"Sure."

It was like some kind of torture, having her watch him without being able to touch her. His fingers itched to smooth the furrow in her brow, to tug that lip out from the prison of her teeth and trace the edges of it with his own.

And yet, in the middle of all his agitation, he was completely relaxed. The best thing he could do was exactly what she was telling him to do, and it meant he had nothing to worry about. Knowing that his next move was already decided for him was incredibly soothing, yet also exciting since he didn't know what would happen. By the time the last bite of nugget was dipped in the third and final shake, his heart was beating so fast, he could barely taste it.

Brooke frowned. "How was that one? You don't look happy about it."

"Because I'm thinking about kissing you, not the nugget."

"Oh." Her eyes went wide before darting around the room. They finally landed on his lips, but the gaze was different from what it had been the past twenty minutes. She licked her lips, and before he could think too hard about it, he closed the distance between them and brought his hands up to her cheeks.

"Is that okay?" Their mouths were inches apart, her shaky inhale warm across his skin. "I'll taste like nuggets and milkshakes."

Her mouth turned up. "My favorite."

With a surge of her body, her arms were around his neck and they were kissing. Not the tentative, slow, first kisses he'd given and received in the past. This was eager and wild, something that had been building for weeks, maybe even for the past year, and was finally being released. Like a balloon that had gotten too big, the explosive pop engulfed every sense. A shockwave rippled through Ethan's body, and he vibrated at a pitch ten times higher than usual.

The longer their lips crushed together, the longer their tongues explored and breaths mingled, the more certain Ethan was that they would never stop. This was just where he lived now, entangled with Brooke. It was absolute heaven, no reason to fight it. This was exactly where the universe wanted him to be.

His hands made his way down from her cheeks to her shoulders and then her back, pulling her closer, like if he tried hard enough, they could just become one body and the kiss would never have to end.

What finally brought it to an end was the ringing of Brooke's phone. Even that only made them pause long enough to take a breath before diving right back in. By the third ring, however, he could feel her pull away, her hands slowly releasing their tight grip on his shirt where they'd been hanging on like he was a buoy in a stormy sea.

The harsh ring of her phone sliced into their breathless, gasping silence.

Without a word, she turned, taking two big steps away from him, and reached into her back pocket for her phone.

"Hello?" Her shoulders lifted and fell as she tried to catch her breath. Ethan leaned against the counter, just as breathless as she was, but at least he didn't have to talk to anyone right now and pretend that he was okay.

He was most definitely not okay. Whatever this was between them, it was more than a simple crush on his cute neighbor. This was something that would engulf him, drag him down, and consume him completely.

It was exactly what he wanted. Brooke was everything he wanted.

And, miraculously, she wanted him too.

"Slow down. What happened?" Her voice held a tinge of panic that he knew from countless fire calls, the pleading of people as they saw their entire lives go up in flames.

In an instant, like he'd been trained to do, Ethan switched into emergency mode. His mind cleared, the lingering heat of their kiss pushed aside so he could be ready for whatever information was about to come his way.

"I'll be there in five minutes." She ended the call and turned to him for a brief moment, her face etched with lines of worry. Then she ran to the door of the kitchen and called behind her, "There's a fire at the shelter."

"What? How?" His mind raced through the possibilities as he hurried to catch up. Given how small the building was, there were only a few options.

"I don't know." Her voice trembled. "Amanda only stopped by because she forgot her jacket there. She said she saw flames outside through a window. She called 911 right away, then grabbed the animals, then called me, now—"

"Brooke, stop." She was already at the door, pulling on her jacket inside out, shoving her feet into two different shoes.

"I can't. I have to get there. What if something happens to them? They could all be—" Her breath hitched, and a sob echoed in the foyer.

He put his hands on her shoulders and waited until her eyes were on his. Like he'd done so many times before, Ethan pushed aside whatever personal feelings he had for a person or place and focused on what needed to happen next. There was no point in worrying, and no time. All of his energy and attention was on Brooke and what she needed right now.

"You said she got the animals and called 911, so there's nothing else you can do until we get there."

"You're coming?" The surprise in Brooke's voice was mirrored in her open-mouthed expression.

"Why wouldn't I?" He dropped his hands and stepped back. "You're driving, right?"

There was just the smallest beat of hesitation, and a few rapid blinks. "Yes, of course."

Doubt found its way into his stomach again, but he ignored it. There was no point, no time for it. There was an emergency, a fire. It was what he knew best, and he would be able to help. It didn't matter how he got there, as long as he did. He'd figure out the rest later. It would all work out somehow. It always did.

NINETEEN

BROOKE

The ride to the shelter was quiet, the kiss still tingling on Brooke's lips, and the warmth of Ethan's hands on her body clinging to her like those last sleepy moments of a dream.

A dream that had quickly become a nightmare. The closer they got to the shelter and the longer they stayed silent, a chilly fear filled the car, a poisonous gas sucking out all the breathable air. When she inhaled her third shaky breath in a row, Ethan put a hand on her arm. Just for a moment, barely even a touch, but it still made her shoulders drop and breathing even out.

"Thank you for coming." Her words echoed in the dark car. They sounded rote, hollow, like she didn't really mean them but was saying them because she knew she should.

"Of course. You need the help. I can help."

Where her words had been cold, distant, his were warm and earnest. Brooke's chest tightened. There was no reason for Ethan to be there, but he'd volunteered, just like he always did. He was helpful and open to everything and said yes to whatever came his way, even when it wasn't his job anymore. It had been easier to accept it when it was from the effects of the potion. Now she knew it was just who he was.

Which somehow made her feel worse.

It was easier to focus on the danger the building was in rather than the danger her heart was facing if things with Ethan didn't work out. Now that the love potion had worn off, this was all for real. That kiss had been real, and everything tonight was real, including his desire to help her. How long until he realized just how deep the cracks in her ran? All she'd done since she'd met Ethan was fail. Half the town probably already knew there'd been a fire at the shelter. Before long, the whispers would start, and everything would fall apart. Brooke would lose everything, including how Ethan was looking at her right now.

"This might wipe out everything we raised yesterday." The words tumbled out of her before she could stop them, reminding Ethan just how much of a catastrophe her life was.

"You have insurance. It'll be fine."

"How can you be so calm?"

His hand, still on her arm, squeezed. "This isn't my first fire."

Right. This used to be his job. Her shoulders relaxed even more. Ethan would know what to do.

Even though Brooke should be the one to know instead.

There hadn't been sirens on the way, but when they pulled up in front of the shelter, there was a fire truck taking up the entire parking lot, lights flashing. When she stopped the car across the street, the headlights illuminated the open door, and they could see people moving around inside. When she unbuckled her seatbelt, Ethan grabbed her arm.

"Do you want me to go first?"

"What?"

"Just in case there's bad news." His eyes were steady on hers, his voice calm. "I'll know whoever's in there. I could get the information from them."

There was a live wire in her chest, sparking hot. Would it look better or worse for Brooke to send someone else in her stead? "I— I'll be fine. It's my responsibility."

He nodded, but a wrinkle appeared between his brows. "If they haven't used the hoses, it must not have been that bad."

Relief flooded her veins, extinguishing the sticky mess of panic that had been coursing through her. "Really?"

"Actually, I can't tell from here if they did or not." He shifted in his seat, his lips turned down. "I'd need to get closer to be sure. You ready to go?"

Not even a little bit.

"Okay." They got out of the car and headed toward the truck, where a woman in uniform was tucking something into a storage compartment.

Ethan's arm fell lightly across Brooke's shoulders, and she realized he probably wasn't seeing all that well right now. She slowed her pace, falling into the reassuring role of guide, letting him know where the curbs were, and when they were almost at the truck.

Having something to do that she was good at was reassuring, and a tendril of calm snaked its way around her chest. Even in the midst of the anxiety and fear of the night, she could still be valuable. Ethan had said what he thought she needed to hear to soothe her nerves, even though he hadn't really known what was going on. It was something her friends would have done. Or Gran. She wouldn't leave him alone in the dark.

Then there was the press of his body against hers, comforting in ways she wasn't able to fully process at the moment. At least her heart had stopped beating so quickly, and her breathing was coming a little easier.

The firefighter turned and noticed them. "Ethan." Her eyes widened. "What are you doing here?"

Ethan's hand tightened on Brooke's shoulder, and he stayed quiet.

"He volunteers at the shelter." Brooke stuck out her hand, then withdrew it, her face heating. Were you supposed to shake hands with firefighters? "I'm Brooke Adams. I run the shelter."

"I'm Sarah. Everything inside is totally fine."

Totally fine. Brooke's lungs took what felt like her first breath in hours. Beside her, she felt Ethan relax. From the news or because he now recognized the firefighter, she couldn't tell.

"What happened?" Ethan asked, his voice taking on a tone of command and assurance that sent unexpected tingles along Brooke's spine.

"It looks like someone tossed a cigarette into the dumpster at the edge of the lot. The flames got high, but nowhere near the building."

All the adrenaline flooded out of Brooke, her limbs going rubbery. She leaned into Ethan as he got more details from Sarah, letting the sound of their voices wash over her without picking up the details. They were using all kinds of special terms, and the discussion of why the flames were that high got very technical very quickly. When another firefighter came out to talk to Sarah, Brooke reached up and put her hand on Ethan's where it still rested on her shoulder.

"Thank you for coming. You didn't have to."

He leaned in closer, his words a warm whisper in her ear. "I'm just glad I was there when you got the call."

Like he was meant to be. Even if Brooke didn't believe in fate, she could see why Ethan did.

"I care about this place," his soft voice continued. "Not just because it's yours, but because it's important for this town to have it."

Important. That's what this place was, and Brooke was responsible for all of it.

The night air pressed in all around her. She put a hand over her chest and rubbed.

Everything was fine tonight, but for how long? This kind of roller coaster of emotions wasn't what she was used to, it wasn't what she wanted. It was all getting to be too much.

"I don't think I can do this." The words were barely a whisper, so quiet in the night she wasn't even sure Ethan heard her. The

Adams' name and Gran's legacy were too much for her. Was this why her mom had run away? Is that what Brooke wanted to do?

He squeezed her tighter against him. Of course he'd heard her. "You are doing it. You're here."

Warmth flooded her, and she couldn't find the right words to answer him.

"I'm standing right here with you," he said as he rubbed her arm.

It was like he'd doused her with cold water.

He won't always be.

Ethan believed in fate, not magic potions. If the guy who kissed her like she was the answer to all the world's problems ever found out just how fake his feelings for her had been when all this started, he'd see it as a sign they weren't supposed to be together. He'd be gone in a second.

The gate in the middle of the fence surrounding the backyard opened just a crack.

"Brooke?" Amanda stuck her head out and the look of relief that washed over her made Brooke feel even guiltier for all these feelings of running away swirling inside of her. If she didn't do this, nobody else would, and it was too important to Gran and to the town to let it fail.

As they made their way over to the gate, Ethan's hand fell from her shoulder to her hand.

"Are all the animals okay?" Brooke asked.

Amanda nodded, then stepped aside so they could squeeze into the backyard without letting any dogs out. The gate closed behind them with a click.

"I didn't want to bring the animals back inside right away. They're all so agitated."

As if to prove her point, the barking started immediately. Brooke knew she'd have to go inside eventually too, but for now, she let herself fall into the chaos of four loud dogs running around her.

"You did an amazing job. Thank goodness you were here."

Amanda smiled weakly at the praise. Beside them, Ethan bent to give a few cuddles to Chip, the big mastiff who'd arrived that week and taken a liking to him, the way that all the dogs seemed to. There was just something reassuring about him that even animals could sense, apparently. She could use some cuddles right now. But that would have to wait even longer, until whatever she had to do inside was over.

"It was so freaky, I could have sworn the entire yard was on fire, the flames were so bright . . . "

Brooke tried to focus on everything Amanda was telling her, when all she wanted to do was curl up next to Ethan and let someone else take care of everything.

"What about the insurance?" Amanda asked suddenly.

"What about it?"

Amanda tilted her head. "You'll call them, right? Just in case there's an issue later because of the smoke or something?"

"Right." That was her job, after all. She rubbed her forehead, then heard Cloudy meow pitifully from his carrier sitting on the bench. Making her way over to him, relief flooded into her heart, followed closely by guilt. Another week and she still hadn't gotten Cloudy's profile up on their website. Something always seemed to come up, and it didn't look like she'd have time this week either. She stuck her hand into the carrier and gave him a scratch on the head, her mind already whirling with the list of everything they'd have to do. Clean up, find somewhere to put the animals while they did that, deal with insurance and whatever meetings or proof they'd need to be sent—

Another meow, this one louder and angry, pulled her out of her racing thoughts.

"What?" she asked the cat, bending down to look into the carrier. Cloudy's bright-yellow eyes glared at her. With a sigh, she unlatched the door and scooped him up. Once a skinny, ruffled bag of bones, he was now a plump, fluffy ball of fur. From the warmth of her arms, he purred happily. "This is just for a minute, since I know you must be scared."

"I was scared when I couldn't find him." Amanda's voice was laced with an apology. "I looked everywhere, and he turned up in the storage room—"

"Eating kibble?" Ethan appeared at her side and gave Cloudy a scratch behind his ears. "He was probably just looking for his favorite human to rub against."

"Ethan can you . . . " She hated to ask him for more, and didn't even know what she needed right now. Though if he wanted to keep standing close to her, the nearness of his body heating her from the inside out, she wouldn't complain.

"Let me go see what's happening inside. I'll let you know what they need from you." His voice was that serious one again, and for a moment, she had a brief flash of what he'd been like as a firefighter. Calm and collected in an emergency. Reassuring and rational.

It shouldn't have made her this attracted to him, not now in the middle of everything else, but it was like sinking into a warm bath. He would take care of everything. She didn't have to worry.

From the depths of her arms, Cloudy rubbed his face against her, his purring getting even louder. Brooke sat on the bench next to his carrier and watched his bright-yellow cat eyes close in pure bliss.

It wasn't in her nature to let someone else take over. But this didn't feel like giving in or admitting a failure on her part. It felt like letting Ethan shine, the way that Krista did whenever she had legal questions, or when she called Aisha to just vent and her friend told her some funny story about penguins so that she'd laugh.

It felt like sharing the load, not admitting defeat. It made her feel stronger, not weaker.

It was reassuring in the same way Gran had been. Steady support, never wavering.

Until Gran had left her.

Which was exactly what Ethan would do eventually.

The effects of the love potion had been enough to get him interested, but there was no guarantee he'd stick around after tonight. Between the chaos that her life was becoming and the lies about the rosebud tea, it was only a matter of time before everything fell apart. Letting him take the lead now would just make it that much harder when Brooke was doing it on her own again. The warm bath she'd sunk into would cool and then she'd be left shivering and wet and alone.

When Ethan returned outside, he was accompanied by Sarah and a man who looked to be about their age, his helmet red instead of black like the others. Ethan would know what that meant, but Brooke didn't. She took a deep breath, put Cloudy back into his cage, then turned to greet them.

"Thanks for coming by so late." She gave them a smile just to be polite, but her chest felt like it was caving in.

"That's our job." Sarah gave her a smile. "We'll just double-check everything out here looks okay."

Brooke's eyes found Amanda's. "You don't need to stay. This could go on for hours. I've got it covered."

She frowned. "Are you sure? Don't you need help getting the animals back inside?"

"I'll handle it." Then she drew all of her courage to look Ethan's way. "You should go home with Amanda."

He took a step toward her and his face clouded over. "I can stay."

Tears prickling the back of her eyes, she shook her head. "I don't need your help."

"Don't need it or don't want it?" His question was quiet, meant only for her. Sarah and the other firefighter were inspecting the outside of the building, and Amanda was gathering her jacket and purse from where she'd left them in a corner of the yard.

"Amanda can take you home. I'll be fine."

"That doesn't answer my question." The thrum of authority in his voice was so tempting. It would be so easy to just let him do everything for her. In his mind, fate was the reason he was here, so it must be his destiny to take charge tonight. Brooke knew the truth, and soon he would too.

"I want you to go."

His lips twisted to the side, and he inhaled slowly through his nose, like he was getting ready to say more. Then, in a heartbeat, he deflated, like he'd decided she wasn't worth it. His face was blank, a calm mask that looked just like the one the firefighters wore, then he turned away to follow Amanda out of the yard without looking back at Brooke.

The shaky inhale did little to settle the itchy, achy feeling that slowly seeped into every part of her body. The milkshakes and nuggets felt like they'd been days ago, not less than an hour.

"Ma'am?" Sarah was calling her. Brooke turned and blinked away the tightness that had kept up behind her eyes.

It was better this way. It was better for Ethan to leave now, before things got too serious. Before he realized that their foundation wasn't fated, and that the cracks in Brooke's life were getting deeper by the day.

Before he realized that she wasn't worth sticking around for.

TWENTY

ETHAN

Monday morning, bleary-eyed and heavy-hearted, Ethan headed to work as soon as the sun was peeking over the horizon, feeling more defeated and hopeless than he ever had.

No matter how many times he went through it in his mind, he couldn't figure out what had happened Saturday night. One minute Brooke had been leaning against him, grateful and relaxed. Ethan had felt like the king of the world, finally able to help Brooke in a way that felt familiar to him.

Then, in an instant, it was all gone. What had happened to Brooke while he'd been inside talking to Sarah and Jake? Had Amanda said something? Or maybe it was seeing Jake, Chief Stevens's son and the fire captain on the crew that night, looking impossibly official in his uniform and his red captain's helmet—something Ethan would never have—that made Brooke realize Ethan wasn't who she needed anymore.

Whatever the reason, Ethan hadn't bothered sticking around to find out. When the signs were that clear, there was no point in pushing back. He'd wanted her too much, and like always, he'd ended up disappointed.

When he pulled into the parking lot of the fire station, it was still so early, Jerry's truck wasn't there yet. A little spark of anticipation pulsed in his chest. There was time for a quick stop to see Sarah and the others who'd been there on Saturday. It had been surprisingly enjoyable to see them again so soon after Friday's auction, even if the circumstances weren't nearly as fun. He could thank them again for getting to the shelter so quickly. He hadn't had a chance before Brooke had practically pushed him into Amanda's car, inexplicably eager to be rid of him.

Or maybe there was an explanation that Ethan just didn't want to look at too closely just yet.

Even the day he'd gotten his diagnosis hadn't been this miserable. At least then, he'd had Rachel to talk to. This weekend she'd been working, and he hadn't even told her about the date. It would take more explaining than was possible in a text to catch her up enough on his current state of doom and gloom for her to give any useful sisterly advice.

As his feet turned him left instead of right in the station, a sense of achingly familiar calm settled over him, but there was a wistful undercurrent that soured it. This was where he wanted to be, but not where he was supposed to be. Saturday night had felt like that too. He'd been with Brooke when she'd gotten the call, so clearly he was meant to go with her. But then it hadn't ended up being the right thing.

A few people nodded at him when he passed them, new faces unfamiliar to Ethan, who hadn't been working on this side of the station for almost a year. The closer he got to the break room, the more nervous he got. Maybe this had been a bad idea.

The second he walked into the room, five smiling faces turned his way, and five voices cried out in unison.

"Ethan!"

It was all the same people who'd been there Saturday night, just like he'd expected. It was the very end of their forty-eight-hour shift, then they'd have four days off. The schedule was one thing he missed about this work. The people were another.

He hadn't expected them to miss him just as much.

There were slaps on his back and high fives and so much talking after spending the entire day on Sunday on his own, Ethan was more than a little overwhelmed. They'd all been at the auction Friday night except Jake, but that didn't stop the joking and teasing from picking up right where it had left off. Just like he'd always done, Ethan slipped into the role of quiet observer, chiming in when he could, laughing along like he'd always been there.

Maybe I should stop by to visit more often.

"How's it going with Jerry?" Jake asked, something quivering on the edge of his lips.

"Fine."

They all raised their eyebrows at him.

"Really." Ethan cleared his throat and shoved his hands in his pockets, shifting back on his heels. "It's just not as fast-paced as I'm used to."

"Is that why you showed up at the animal shelter last night? Looking for some excitement?" They all chuckled. "Definitely not the call I was expecting on a Saturday night."

"I'm volunteering there. Brooke's my neighbor."

"Is that all she is?" Jake elbowed Ethan in the ribs and they all laughed again.

Ethan's chest tightened, the question stinging almost as much as the rejection from Brooke. She'd been so grateful when they got to the shelter, leaning on him, finding comfort in him standing next to her. Then he'd gone inside and come back out with a few of the firefighters in uniform, and it was like she'd realized he wasn't the person she needed.

After all, who was Ethan compared to these guys? Nobody. He hadn't even been able to see the truck properly until Brooke had led him to it. Hadn't been able to tell it was Sarah standing there until she'd given her name to Brooke.

"I've got to get to work." He checked his watch, knowing that Jerry wouldn't be in the office for at least another half hour, but he couldn't think of any other reason to avoid answering the question.

Jeers and whistles echoed in the room. As he waved them off and headed back out into the hallway, he thought about what Brooke had said, before the fire, before the nuggets and milkshakes. About how people couldn't be there for him if he didn't tell them what was going on.

After being treated like he was still one of them every time he'd seen them over the past few days, Ethan had to accept that he'd been the one to pull away from his crew, not the other way around. They were there, same as ever.

He was the one who'd changed.

Not that it was easy to show weakness in this kind of environment, where saving lives depended on your mind being clear and your body being in peak physical form.

Maybe that's what had happened on Saturday with Brooke. She might be considerate, taking into account his needs the way no one ever had before, but that didn't mean she wanted him around when there was a real emergency. That was for the professionals.

Which he wasn't anymore, and would never be again.

After the glimpses he'd had this weekend of everything he'd left behind, it was that much harder to open the door to the fire inspector's office and face the pile of paperwork he'd left there Friday afternoon. The weariness settled onto him, adding to the weight that had been piling up over the weeks and months he'd been doing this job.

It may be where he was supposed to be, but it definitely wasn't where he wanted to be.

A few hours later, Ethan had just finished up another nearly silent inspection. Neither Jerry nor the deli's owner said a word unless Ethan spoke to them directly. The weather had turned wet halfway through, perfect for the tense mood, with the only sound the soft plink of rain on the windows.

At least it was an easy one. No major issues, all the paperwork checked out. Ethan thanked the owner and said the paperwork would be ready in a few days. There were handshakes all around and then Ethan and Jerry said goodbye.

Out in the rain, Ethan let himself stand there, just for a second, like the rain would wash away whatever bad thing he could feel in his bones was about to happen.

"Well, that went about as well as I expected," Jerry grumbled once Ethan was in the car.

His heart sank, all his anxiety justified. "I didn't miss something, did I?"

"No. I would have said something if you had." Jerry shook his head and pulled out into traffic, the wipers on his truck at top speed.

Ethan took a deep breath, tempted to shut his eyes, like that would make this conversation easier to handle. "I'm not sure I understand the problem."

"That was the Main Street Deli. You couldn't have been a little friendlier?"

"I asked him about his day, how he got into the business, and mentioned sports." Even as the words flew out of his mouth, Ethan knew they were the wrong ones. He was getting defensive when he should be focused on showing he was open to learning. But now that they were out there, he didn't know how to stop. "He gave me one-word answers. I don't know what I'm supposed to do with that."

"You find a way. You need to build relationships with these people. I don't know how to make it any clearer."

It was as clear as mud, but Ethan bit back that particular comment. "I've been trying. I do okay at the shelter."

"It may be Adamsville, but they're not the only important family here." Jerry sniffed, unimpressed by the volunteer work he'd been the one to tell him to do. "It's not animals you need to be spending time with."

There was so much more to what he did than just hanging out with animals at the shelter, but it would sound even more defensive to list it all.

"Just tell me what to do and I'll do it."

"I've already told you. If you haven't gotten it by now, I don't know if you ever will."

Ethan inhaled slowly through his nose and kept his hands at his sides, balling them tight into fists. Jerry told him nothing before going into places about what to expect, gave no clear guidelines to the social side to consider during these inspections, and had done zero to help Ethan learn. The chief had been the one to invite Ethan to Brooke's party, then Jerry had gotten jealous. The chief had introduced Ethan to a few people at the auction, while Jerry sulked in a corner. But the chief wasn't the one who'd be making the decision about the inspector job, it was Jerry.

"I've only just started leading inspections. I can't learn it all in a month."

"Some things can't be taught."

They pulled into the station, and Ethan felt it the second it happened. The fire died inside of him, totally drenched, with no hope of sparking back to life.

As a firefighter, this was what he always wanted to see. A dead, wet, cold site meant it was safe.

The same feeling in his chest was more like a sign of the biggest failure of his life. He was so confused that he wasn't even sure if this was rock bottom or just the ledge where he could look down into the abyss. Wherever he was, he knew one thing without a doubt.

He would never be enough. He would never be a fire inspector. Jerry had all but said it outright. Why he was still training Ethan, taking him around on inspections, having him file the paperwork, wasn't totally clear. Maybe it was cheaper than getting someone else. Maybe it was due to pressure from the chief. Maybe it was his connection to Brooke, as jealous as Jerry seemed to still be about it.

Whatever the reason, now Ethan knew it in his bones. This wasn't the direction his life was headed. This had happened before, and something else always came up.

But today, the terrifying unknown sunk its claws into his chest and squeezed tight.

"Don't worry about the insurance. I'll take care of them." From a high stool at Brooke's counter, Krista took another sip of her smoothie and smacked her lips. "This is a good one. What's in it?"

"Turmeric and ginger." Brooke put her elbows on the counter and dropped her head into hands. Even though the fire had barely touched the shelter's property, only singeing a small patch of grass that wasn't even next to the building, the insurance company had opened a claim and was asking for all sorts of paperwork. "It's supposed to bring good luck and a windfall."

"Really?" Aisha looked down at the glass. It was a warm orange color thanks to the turmeric, though Brooke had only used a spoonful of the precious stash leftover from the last of Gran's plants. The new one she'd planted a few months ago hadn't produced anything yet. "How many times have you made it?"

"It doesn't matter. It's never worked for me." Unlike the rosebud tea, that had worked a little too well. Even as her stomach churned with uncertainty, she knew she'd done the right thing by pushing Ethan away.

So why am I so miserable?

"That doesn't mean it won't for me." Aisha took a large gulp of the smoothie and sighed. "Maybe I'll try talking to my boss today."

"Be careful what you wish for."

Aisha's social media and marketing job at the aquarium was only part-time, and she was hoping to turn it into something permanent—and not just because of her crush on her coworker. The problem was getting on the good side of her grumpy boss, who seemed to hate everything about her, from her bubbly golden retriever personality to the eccentric accessories she always tried to match to the animals. The result of the smoothie may be worse than Aisha expected, but Brooke wasn't about to begrudge her some wishful thinking. Especially when she'd just spent all weekend after the auction editing photos and writing an email newsletter for the shelter.

"Go for it." Krista reached over the counter and squeezed Aisha's hand. "You're amazing at what you do."

Jealousy hit the back of Brooke's throat, hot and tight. When was the last time someone had said that to her?

Ethan says it at least a few times a week.

The bright light in Aisha's eyes dimmed a little, and her lips twisted to the side. "I don't need to talk to him today. Brooke, if you need me at the shelter, I can come over this afternoon."

"I'll be fine." Brooke gave her a weak smile that she didn't feel beyond the pulling of her cheek muscles. "There'll be plenty to do this weekend."

"What about Ethan?" Krista asked, turning her gaze to Brooke.

"What about him?"

There was a beat of silence, and Krista and Aisha exchanged looks.

"Is he going to be at the shelter today?"

"I don't think so."

Another concerned look passed between her friends.

"So did things on Saturday not go . . . " Tilting her head back and forth like she was looking for the right word, Aisha tapped her fingers on her empty glass. "Well?"

Brooke had been avoiding this conversation for two days, but there were only so many times she could go over the details of the fire that wasn't really a fire before her friends wanted to know more about other things. Like who had been there with her. She took a deep breath.

Might as well rip off the Band-Aid.

"I mean, we kissed, but that doesn't mean—"

"What?" Krista shrieked and stood up, knocking over her smoothie glass. The gloopy orange mixture splattered, but amazingly, in the other direction from everyone's phones. Krista looked at the mess with a bemused expression. "Huh, it really is a lucky potion."

"You kissed Ethan?" Aisha was bouncing on her feet as she reached over for a towel and started wiping up the spilled smoothie. "I knew it."

"Did you now?" Brooke took the soaked paper towels from Aisha and put them in the trash can under the sink. Her gaze snagged on a bucket of cleaning supplies there, and the gloves that were tucked over the edge. Something about the way they were folded, the way they were right where you'd want them but not intrusive, hit her right in the chest.

The memories of Gran came flooding in, without stopping, the way they had for the first few months after Brooke had lost her. Moments like this had been few and far between over the past few months, even with the shelter open. Things had been busy instead of sad, so Brooke had just been feeling the pressure of living up to everything Gran had wanted for her.

That included finding love.

That was the only reason she was thinking about her grandmother right now. It was nothing mystical, nothing to do with the smoothies or even the cleaning gloves, which—Brooke remembered now—Krista had been the one to put away when they'd cleaned up after the Halloween party.

By the time Brooke turned around, the counter was spotless, and both of her friends were looking at her with hungry expressions.

"You really want to hear about it?" Brooke crossed her arms over her chest. "Isn't everything going on with the shelter more important?"

Krista's piercing gaze landed on Brooke—the same one she was sure left opposing counsel quaking in their boots.

"The only thing related to the shelter I want to hear about is why your kissing buddy isn't coming by there today to help you."

"He's probably working."

Without another word, Krista suddenly stood up and made her way to the living room. Groaning, Brooke followed her. There was only one thing she could be looking for.

Aisha was the one to say it, however, when she came up behind them both. "He's not working out, but his car is there."

"So, what happened on Saturday?" There was a no-nonsense tone in Krista's voice that Brooke loved when it was directed at anyone except her.

She leaned against the couch, not looking at the window. "I got a call from Amanda about a fire—"

Clicking her tongue, Krista held up a hand, eyes still on Ethan's backyard like he might appear at any moment. "Don't even try to tell us about the fire again instead."

With a sigh, Brooke knew she'd have to tell them the whole story. There'd been a few quick messages letting her friends know how the coffee date had gone, but she'd stayed vague. She hadn't mentioned him coming over for chicken nuggets and milkshakes because she knew they'd get excited about it and make it to be some big thing, when it still felt too new and fragile.

Better to pretend nothing had happened than for Brooke to

admit she'd gotten freaked out and broke things off before everything came crashing down on top of her.

"Look, you have about ten minutes until I have to leave for the office, so talk fast or I go knock on his door and ask him about it."

"Okay, okay." Brooke ran a hand through her hair and launched into the story, starting with the coffee date. Whenever she tried to skimp on details, they pushed for more, wanting to analyze every single sigh and hand gesture. Luckily, there wasn't time to do too much of that if both of them were going to get to work on time. Brooke got to speed through the most touching and intense moments of the date without having to think about them too much.

Because if she did think about them, she'd realize just how much she liked him and just how much she wished she hadn't sent him away on Saturday night.

"I totally get why you didn't want him at the shelter." Aisha sat in the armchair by the window, facing Brooke but still glancing outside every so often.

"Really?"

"Of course." With a gesture around the spotless living room. "You barely let us see you when things are a mess. Why would you want him around to see that?"

"That's not—" Brooke stopped and frowned.

Was it really that simple? It had felt much more dire on Saturday, like he was witnessing a complete catastrophe of her own making. But it had just been bad luck, someone tossing a cigarette where they shouldn't, not something Brooke had any way to control.

It wasn't like Ethan had blamed her or said anything about Brooke being incompetent. He'd done the opposite, even reminding her she was doing her best.

The only reason she'd sent him away was . . . well, now she couldn't really remember.

"Okay, maybe you have a point," Brooke said to Aisha, who beamed. It wasn't quite the same as apologizing or admitting she was wrong, but it still wasn't easy to say.

"Of course she does." Krista finally moved away from the window and slung her work bag slung over her shoulder. "We know you try to hide every little flaw, but Ethan doesn't. We know to push back whenever you try to push us away. He probably thinks you hate him."

"You should go talk to him." Bouncing in her seat, Aisha smiled and nodded at the window. "Explain that you hate it when people hover during disasters."

Brooke gave her the look that suggestion deserved.

"We'll talk more tonight." Krista hugged her tight, then waved at Aisha to follow her. It was time for them both to get to work. "Go finish your smoothie. A little extra luck never hurt anybody. Maybe he'll stop by on his own."

Luck favors the well prepared. That was Brooke's motto, what she believed in, not magical berries and plants. At least, it had been until her Halloween party. Now it was like she was a little girl again, listening to Gran's stories and drinking whatever she set in front of her, her belief in the impossible filling every cell in her body. With so much on the line, could she really let go of the control she needed to allow for magic to take the reins?

She finished her smoothie—hoping with her entire heart it was as effective as the rosebud tea—and cleaned up the kitchen, stalling for as long as she could. But then there was nothing else for her to clean, and she had to get to the shelter eventually to start on the endless tasks that awaited her there. It was now or never.

She put on her coat and walked out the door, taking the slowest steps possible as she made her way over to his house and stopping to pick every weed in her path. It was still less than two minutes before she was standing in front of his door. She took a deep breath, then another, before knocking. Three quick, hard thumps with her fist.

Then she noticed the doorbell and pushed it, her face heating in the cool November morning.

A few moments went by, then another. She checked her watch. There was no set time for her to get to the shelter, but she wasn't going to waste all morning waiting for Ethan. Her heart beat a steady rhythm from where it was lodged firmly in her throat. She swallowed it down, then blinked back what were definitely not tears.

Looks like the smoothie wasn't lucky after all.

The problem with believing in magic was accepting what it meant about her grandmother. After months of hiding just how sick she was, Gran had finally let Brooke know, and she'd moved back into the old Victorian house to take care of her. It had been okay at first, but then Brooke realized that her grandmother didn't seem to want to get better. She didn't even want to try to understand her condition, what might help, the different kinds of treatments available. She just accepted her fate, like Ethan. Their diagnoses weren't the same, but their reactions to them were too similar to ignore.

There were at least three different recipes in that little notebook in the kitchen that were supposed to help with healing. Gran had refused to try any of them. Her whole life, Gran had been her constant, and Brooke had done everything she could to make her proud. In the end, it wasn't enough. Gran had chosen to let fate take her from Brooke rather than fight to stay as long as she could.

First her mom, then Gran. Was Brooke really that easy to leave behind?

The plan to push Ethan away before he could do the same to her first had seemed so logical on Saturday night. Standing in front of his door with tears brimming, Brooke had to wonder why, in this case, following her plans hadn't made her feel better, but so much worse.

Just as she was about to turn away and admit defeat, she heard the shuffle of feet on the other side of the door. Swiping at her eyes, she plastered on a bright smile.

"Brooke?" Ethan blinked, like he wasn't sure she was really there. "Is everything okay?"

"Um, fine." She shifted from one foot to another. His hair was rumpled, and his clothes slightly askew. Well, his pajama pants were, the drawstring shifted to the side and one pant leg twisted around his leg. He wasn't wearing a shirt, the dark lines of his axe tattoo tracing up his bare arm.

She did her best not to look at his chest, but failed miserably, her next words directed at his perfect pecs. "I just wanted to see if you might have some time today . . . no, never mind. It's fine."

She turned, heat filling her face, the urge to cry coming on stronger now.

"Wait."

Brooke kept walking away, not giving in to her hopeful heart begging her to turn around. He was barefoot and shirtless. There was no way he'd follow her out here.

Then his hand grabbed her arm, and he spun her around. Yes, he actually would follow her.

"You'll freeze." She looked down at his bare feet instead of his eyes, her own still too moist. "Go back inside. I didn't mean to wake you up."

"I'm glad you did. I slept through my alarm." He wrapped his arms around her. "I have a doctor's appointment today, so I'm not doing any inspections."

From the surprisingly warm circle of his arms, she was able to bring herself to look at his face. "Oh, you should go back to sleep then. Enjoy your day off."

"Do you need me to come to the shelter?"

The ground shifted under her feet as indecision swirled in her stomach.

"I don't need you, no."

There was a flash of disappointment on Ethan's face and Brooke took a deep breath, Aisha and Krista's voices in her head. He didn't know her the way her friends did.

"But if you wanted to stop by, I could find some uses for these muscles other than giving me a hug."

"Oh yeah?" He raised his eyebrows and gave her a smirk. "Like what?"

"Can we go inside? I'm seriously worried you'll get frostbite on your feet."

"It's nowhere near freezing." He rolled his eyes and dragged her by the hand back into his house.

This was the first time she'd been in here, she realized. He'd seen her house twice now, but this was a very different space. Even when his aunt had owned it, Brooke had never been inside.

"It's so clean."

"Don't sound so surprised." He grinned and led her to the living room off the kitchen where they'd walked in. "I do a good job keeping the shelter clean, don't I?"

"You do. But I don't need you to clean today."

"Right, just my muscles."

He was grinning, and Brooke didn't understand why. She was being a pain. Too much. Too needy. Her teeth scraped her bottom lip, and she turned her face away from his grinning face.

"Hey." He touched her arm, but she kept her gaze averted. "Brooke. I don't mind. Really."

"Why not?" She whipped her head back around, eager to catch him in a lie. To see the true annoyance shining through.

"Besides the obvious?"

"It's not obvious to me." She sniffed, the tears threatening to overflow.

He ran a hand across his mouth, scratching at the stubble on his chin. "Well, I get to spend time with you. I like spending time with you."

The heat in his eyes was undeniable, and Brooke shifted on her feet, uncertain what to do with that look that no one had ever given her before. She'd seen it countless times directed at Krista, but never her.

"I also like helping you. I like feeling like I can make your life easier." He tilted his head. "Isn't that why you help me walk around in the dark?"

"That's different."

"Is it? I can't help it that I need help." He scrunched up his nose, then took a deep breath like this wasn't something he was used to saying. "I don't like that I'm in a situation where I need to ask for help when I didn't need to a few years ago, but you make it so easy. You don't make me feel bad about it or like it's a burden. You just do it."

How could she explain that it was different, that this was something that she should be able to fix and couldn't? This was always hanging over her, and no matter what she did, she couldn't unhook from that need to do it all on her own.

"I'm just not used to anyone else offering, other than Krista and Aisha." That was close enough to the truth, as close as she was willing to say out loud.

"And I'm not used to anyone offering, because I don't tell people about it." His smile was softer now, almost sad. "I guess we're a good pair."

He reached up and brushed the hair back from her face, then bent and kissed her in the middle of her forehead. It was so soft and tender, it meant more than their wild kisses from the other night.

Had it really only been two days since that had happened? Brooke sagged against him, feeling like she'd lived five lifetimes since then. The strength of his chest—still shirtless—and the warmth of his body smoothed away the last of her worries. Then he leaned down and kissed her, and in the gentle sweep of his lips against hers, she felt cherished.

He wanted to help. It didn't mean he always would, but at least she had him right now. She would worry about a plan to deal with the inevitable tomorrow. For now, she'd just appreciate what she had for as long as possible.

The knock on Ethan's door came around three in the afternoon, and somehow, he was able to drag himself out of bed and shuffle down the hall.

It wasn't the worst time for Ethan to get sick, but that's what happened, just a few days after chasing down Brooke without shoes and on very little sleep. Instead of being there for her, helping her sort through all the insurance paperwork and prepare for the next adoption event, he was at home, in bed. Useless.

It had been a long time since he'd been this sick. Coughing and sneezing, shivery one minute and hot the next. All he felt like eating was crackers and water. He tried to play it down in the messages he sent Brooke. He didn't want her to worry. This was just a bad virus, no sense in her getting sick, too, not when she had so much on her plate already.

He peeked through the peephole.

Brooke showed up anyway.

His narrow field of vision made it harder to confirm it was Brooke than he'd expected, and alarm tightened in his chest. The doctor he'd seen earlier that week had said everything was pretty much the same as it had been a year ago, but that didn't mean there wouldn't be changes over time. Taking a deep breath, he cracked open the door, and warmth filled him to see Brooke standing there looking glorious despite the dark circles under her eyes and the worried pinch to her mouth.

"I told you not to come." His voice was as stern as he could make it, but a smile tugged at his mouth, just like a few days ago, when she'd shown up unexpectedly and told him she wanted his help. Or, technically, his muscles.

That was the sign he'd needed to get out of the funk he'd been in since realizing he'd never be a fire inspector. There were still other paths open to him. Maybe it would be through someone he met at the shelter or during an inspection. He just had to stay open to whatever came his way.

For now, though, he just opened the door wider.

"I just brought you some food." The bag clutched in her hands swung at her side. "And a smoothie."

His smile widened, despite the aches in his body. "You made me a magic potion?"

She pinched her lips together and rolled her eyes. "No, I made you a smoothie with scientifically proven ingredients that help lessen the effects of illness."

Heat bloomed in his chest. "You made me a magic potion."

"I also made you soup."

"Really?"

"Well, I bought it." She stifled a yawn. "I got home kind of late last night."

Guilt seeped into his veins.

"I'm sorry. I should have been there."

"You have nothing to apologize for." She extended the plastic bag that held so much more than just food, and Ethan took it with a trembling inhale. Then she leaned forward and put a hand on the door, just for a moment, like it was as hard for her not to touch him as it was for him not to throw open the door and wrap her in his arms. "Just get better, okay? And not because I need help at the shelter."

"Why then?" He was pushing, maybe too far, but he wanted to hear her say it. Needed her to say it. She'd come so close to saying it a few days ago, when Ethan had laid it all out for her.

"Because I care about you, Ethan." She looked down at her feet, probably not even aware he was straining for all he was worth to catch every tiny movement of her face, every flex of her body. "A lot."

"I care about you too. A lot." The words were muffled, his face pressing against the door frame while he kept his eye on her. It wasn't how he'd wanted to tell her this, but when did he ever get what he wanted? This must be how he was supposed to tell her.

"I know you do." She reached out her hand and put it on top of his where it gripped the door. The longing in her face to do more was like a balm on all of his aches and pains. Then the wind shifted and he caught a whiff of lavender. If he weren't sick, he'd drag her inside and never let her go.

"What's that perfume you wear?"

"What?" Her hand dropped and she tilted her head, the afternoon sun making a halo around her face.

"You always smell like lavender."

"It's just an essential oil Gran made."

"I love it."

Her cheeks flushed, and she tucked her hair behind her ears. He itched to do it for her, to run his fingers through the silky dark strands like he had yesterday. And the day before that . . . He opened the door wider but then she took a step back.

"Take care of yourself, please."

Once she'd walked away with a wave over her shoulder and a look that heated him more than his fever, he closed the door and brought the smoothie to his mouth.

He took a sip, not really hungry, but still enjoying the feeling of knowing she'd made it for him, even though she didn't really think it would do anything.

He didn't really think so either, but knowing she made the effort warmed him from the inside out. It didn't taste too bad either.

Just as he was putting the food down on his coffee table, his phone buzzed.

Rachel
How are you feeling? Are you hydrating?

It was Rachel, reminding him why it was sometimes the worst to have a doctor for a sister.

Ethan
Of course.

He added an eye-rolling emoji and plopped onto his couch. Standing took too much energy, and he had a feeling this conversation with Rachel might go on for a while.

Ethan
Drinking a smoothie Brooke made me. There's also soup.

Rachel
Oh, cooking for you already? Must be serious.

His fingers hovered over the phone, ready to send something snarky back, but then he stopped. Leaning back on the couch, he let the cushions half bury him, a blanket draped across his lap. A nice, warm cocoon to contemplate his life.

Ethan
Maybe. This feels different from before.

The past few days working side by side at the shelter before he'd gotten sick had been . . . calm wasn't even the right word.

Settled? At home? Whatever he called it, he knew in his bones this was something more than the brief relationships he'd had in the past. Brooke coming over to ask for his help had been a sign. The soup was a sign. Bright neon arrows pointed the way to his future, and it was all Brooke.

> **Rachel**
> Does she know about your RP?

His heart squeezed. It was natural for his sister to think that was the most important part of his life to share with someone. The painful past Ethan and Rachel shared was just that—in the past. Even they barely talked about it unless they had to. But his RP would impact his whole future with someone.

> **Ethan**
> Yes.

> **Rachel**
> Wow. Okay.

It didn't mean he talked to Brooke about it. He barely mentioned it unless he had to. He was sure Rachel wouldn't approve of that, so he didn't add that particular detail.

His eyes were just starting to close, a nap creeping up on him, when his phone buzzed again.

> **Rachel**
> Are you bringing her to Thanksgiving?

It was coming up soon, and they'd already talked about it. They talked constantly. At the shelter, on the drive home, while eating dinner. They talked about everything—except his RP. It was impressive that she hadn't gotten sick since they'd been spending so much time together. The only breaks were when he was at work, where he was still going through the motions as best as he could but no longer going above and beyond. He was waiting for Jerry to either fire him or say something so terrible he couldn't ignore it and had a reason to quit. He was waiting for a sign.

What would he do instead? The answer felt so close, but from his warm couch cocoon, his feverish brain wasn't going to think about that now. There'd be time for that later, along with all sorts of other things.

> **Ethan**
> She's doing her own thing. I'm going to her Friendsgiving this weekend though.

> **Rachel**
> If you're feeling better by then.

He took a sip of the smoothie and smiled.

> **Ethan**
> I think I will be.

Friendsgiving with Krista and Aisha had slowly transformed over the years from meeting at Batter Me Up the day before Thanksgiving for a cup of coffee and hours-long gossip fest to catch up on what had happened during the semester at their respective colleges, to more elaborate meals the weekend before.

On Thanksgiving Day itself, while Aisha and Krista were driving to see their large extended families, Gran and Brooke would watch the parade together in the morning, then volunteer at a soup kitchen in the afternoon. It was a tradition she loved, something she did every year with Gran, no matter what.

Last year, she'd turned off her phone and spent the entire day in bed.

Her friends were not going to let her do that this year.

At first, they both wanted her to stop by their family's celebrations. A quick calculation of the routes meant Brooke would only have about an hour at each house if she was going to get to the soup kitchen on time. That was one tradition she didn't want to break.

So they stuck with Friendsgiving, taking place as it always had for the past ten years the weekend before Thanksgiving at Krista's apartment.

Unlike the ten previous years, however, Brooke brought a date.

"I'm so excited you came!" Krista wrapped Ethan in a hug before she even said hello to Brooke, who stood outside the door with her sweet potato pie. She shot a look at Aisha, who was standing behind Krista, waiting her turn to maul Brooke's boyfriend.

Boyfriend.

That was a weird word. She hadn't said it out loud yet, but it had popped into her head a few times this week. A few people at the shelter had said it to her too.

"What time is your boyfriend getting here?"

"It's so great your boyfriend volunteers. All mine does on the weekend is play video games."

"Holy smokes, Brooke, your boyfriend is hot."

Pie in hand, she smiled to herself as Krista's arms barely reached across his broad back.

Yes, he is, isn't he?

Aisha got her turn for a hug, and Krista finally looked at Brooke and led her inside the familiar space, taking her arm and lowering her voice.

"So, how's he feeling?"

"He's great. The cold only lasted a few days." It had been her friends' idea to make Ethan a smoothie. After years of claiming not to believe in the magic of Gran's "potions," they were thrilled she was on board now.

Just like she had been as a little girl.

"Well, that's good. I would hate for him to have missed this." Krista led her into the living room, and Brooke groaned at the sight of Monopoly spread across the coffee table.

"Absolutely not."

"It's my year to pick." Lifting her chin, Krista sniffed indignantly.

Aisha and Ethan came up behind them. "Oh nice, are we

playing after we eat?" he asked, the clueless, adorable man that he was.

Brooke shook her head. "No, we play during the meal."

"It was my idea originally," Aisha said proudly. "A rebellion against my dad's family, who always insist the kids stay at the table forever. My cousins and I never got to play together."

"I just don't like to wait to win." Krista's Cheshire Cat smile was so unlike her normal, bright one that Ethan audibly gulped.

"It'll be fine." Brooke took his hand and gave it a squeeze. "It's just a friendly game."

Krista clicked her tongue and settled herself on the couch. "Don't lie to him. I am ruthless. It's better he knows now."

"Just at this particular game or all games?" Ethan plopped down across from Krista and immediately grabbed the box from the floor. "I'm the shoe, by the way."

Delight filled Brooke's chest and her face split into a grin. This was a different side of Ethan. Competitiveness didn't seem like it would be in his nature, but she liked it. Or maybe it was that authoritative firefighter voice he was using all of a sudden.

"All games, obviously."

"Obviously." There was a devilish smirk on his face she'd never seen there before. "And you've never lost?"

Ethan picked up the shoe token and rubbed his thumb across it.

Krista narrowed her eyes. "Never." She held out her hand. "And *I'm* always the shoe."

In the history of Friendsgivings, this was the most cutthroat game of Monopoly ever. Aisha and Brooke went bankrupt early, halfway through the green beans, then ate pie while watching Krista and Ethan slowly eat away at each other.

They looked like they were having the time of their lives.

Something about the day felt complete. Or like it was making up for last year's quiet Friendsgiving mostly spent on Krista's couch napping, only waking up long enough to eat pumpkin spice cookie dough straight from the package.

Brooke didn't believe that the universe was trying to make it up to her, that Ethan had been fated to be in her life, or anything as ridiculous as that.

But she believed he belonged with them, however he'd gotten here.

As the sun set behind the window, the game was coming to a close. Ethan rubbed his eyes and looked down at the board. He blinked once, then again. Brooke's heart leaped into her throat. She wasn't sure if he was just tired or if it was something related to his vision. It was hard to stay still, waiting to see if he needed anything. He would ask if he did, wouldn't he?

She'd been reading more about his condition, since he didn't share much about it. RP was so variable, there was no way of knowing what would happen when. There were certain things almost everyone experienced, but most people were diagnosed in their teens. For Ethan to not have signs bad enough to get checked out until he was in his early thirties already put him in the minority. What other ways would this progress atypically?

All she could do was wait until he told her more or asked for help. Being prepared and researching didn't mean she knew more about it than he did, the one actually going through it. Gran had been the same, though infinitely more stubborn about it. Nothing Brooke had shown her, no articles or documentaries or studies, made any difference in what the old woman would do or try. Ethan would probably be the same.

It was painfully clear something was happening, and he didn't want to say anything in front of her friends.

After another hour, Krista finally won—and admitted Ethan was her most worthy adversary ever—and then there was more pie and a movie. By the time they headed back home, it was almost ten.

"I'm sorry you didn't win," Brooke said in the car, her body heavy and warm.

"That's more fun than I've had in a long time." Ethan laid his head back in the seat and closed his eyes, his hand snaking across the center console to rest on her thigh. "I used to play every year with my sister."

She knew he had a sister, and he would be seeing her for Thanksgiving this week, but that was about it. In all their hours of conversations, he never said much about his family. To be fair, Brooke didn't share details about hers either.

"What does your sister do?"

"She's a doctor. Pathology."

"Oh, wow."

Ethan laughed, his eyes still closed, his hand tracing lazy circles on her leg. "Yeah, the brains and the brawn."

"Ethan, you're very sm—"

"I know, I know."

"But do you, though?" Electricity thrumming from where his hand lay on her thigh, she turned into their neighborhood. Some of the houses were already lit up for Christmas. A reindeer with a flashing red nose greeted them at the top of their street. "You've had so many great ideas at the shelter. Things I'd never think of. I'm thankful for you."

His eyes opened just a sliver at that, just enough to give her some serious side-eye. She laughed. "I know it's corny, but it's true."

His lips turned up, and he slid his hand down to her knee and squeezed. "I'm thankful that Krista gave me all the leftovers, so I don't have to cook tomorrow."

They pulled into Brooke's driveway, and she laughed again, but anxiety prickled around the edges. Heart beating in her throat, she turned off the car and twisted to face him. "You really had a good time?"

"The best Friendsgiving ever."

"It's the only one you've been to!" Relief swept through her, warm and sparkling. A smile settled on her face that felt like it would never leave.

"I'll have you know we had some seriously good potlucks at the station." His gaze lowered, just for a moment, like he was remembering how much fun he used to have at that job.

Brooke's smile dropped, and she bit her lip. "Is everything going okay with the inspector job?"

There was silence in the car, though not a tense one, as he took her hand and pressed her palm against his, then laced their fingers tight, tight, tight.

"I think I may have to stop soon. It's just not for me. I'm just waiting for a sign of what's next."

There was a stunned kind of echo in Brooke's ears. A proposal hovered on the edge of her lips, one she'd been thinking about for the past few weeks, but if he was waiting for a sign, her asking might not be enough. Just like when he needed help due to his vision, he had to be the one to ask her. Giving up control like this wasn't easy, and she didn't think she could hold off much longer.

Ethan sighed and leaned his head back against the seat again, keeping their fingers laced. "I couldn't see the dice a few times tonight."

"Oh?" Her heart was pounding so hard, he must have been able to feel her pulse in her fingers.

"Yeah. Like, I had to turn my head and concentrate to track them if they rolled to the edge of my peripheral vision. That's new. I don't know what it means."

"That you're tired?"

She got that slitted side-eye again. "I think I should check in with the doctor. When I saw her last week, she said to call with updates on any sudden vision changes."

This was more than he'd shared since he'd first told her about it weeks ago.

"You've seen a doctor recently?" Her voice was as casual as she could make it, but the need to know pressed in all around her, making the air in the car hot with anticipation. The control she so desperately needed in unfamiliar situations was hard to resist. She traced the fingers of her free hand along the back of his wrist.

"Yeah, it's just an annual appointment, to see how things are progressing. No big shifts since last year." His lips twisted. "I think you're right. I'm just tired."

She nodded, though she wasn't sure if he could see her with his eyes halfway closed. "Have you ever talked to anyone else about this besides your doctor?"

Now his eyes were open, fixed on hers. "I told you it's just you and the chief who know."

"There're a lot of other people with this condition."

"It's extremely rare." His hand in hers flexed a little.

"I don't mean in this town. But online and stuff."

He sat up, taking back his hand and pressing his palms to his forehead. The sigh he let out this time was a long, tired one. "You sound like my sister."

"Just what every girl likes to hear."

That got a chuckle out of him. He leaned over, putting both of his hands on her cheeks. They were nose to nose, their warm breaths starting to fog up the window of her car.

"I'm thankful that you care so much." He kissed her gently, just a brush of their lips. Then again, harder, more eager, his hands coming around to the back of her head and their tongues twining together.

The windows really fogged up now.

He pulled back slightly to rest his forehead on hers. "Don't worry about me. Whatever's going to happen will happen."

His words were soft, almost like he was saying them to himself rather than to Brooke, and they were familiar, triggering something at the edge of her mind. Then he leaned in to kiss her again, and Brooke let herself get swept up in it, in him, in the feeling of his hands in her hair and the heat of their desire for each other.

It was only later, when she'd stumbled into her house, feeling half drunk with her lips still stinging, that she realized why she recognized his words, why they'd hit her so hard.

It was the same thing Gran had told her the day before she'd died.

Cloudy had escaped his cage again, and he wasn't in the storage room like Ethan expected. As he double checked the top shelf, just to be sure the sneaky feline wasn't hiding behind a box, a boulder-sized ball of worry settled itself in his stomach.

Was Cloudy really gone, or could Ethan just not see him? Friendsgiving was only two days ago. His vision couldn't be deteriorating that quickly. Or maybe it could; he still hadn't done any research. The doctor last week had told him everything he needed to know.

She'd also said to call if he noticed changes, but he hadn't gotten around to that yet. He had a cat to find.

"Here, kitty, kitty . . . " Making his way down the stepladder, Ethan clicked his tongue a few times.

Nothing. Not even a hint of a meow.

With a sigh that seeped into his bones and made the boulder in his stomach start to roll, Ethan walked back into the hallway. Slowly, turning his head side to side, he took his time looking around. The kennels were only halfway full thanks to the adoption event the day before, but they would likely fill up quickly after

Thanksgiving. Some of the blankets and toys were looking a little worn.

He took out his phone and added a few items to the shared note the shelter team had for tracking supplies. It was another one of Ethan's ideas that Brooke had loved and implemented right away.

She was not going to love the fact that he'd lost Cloudy.

Everyone loses Cloudy, he tried to reassure himself.

Yeah, but everyone else has normal vision and finds him again within minutes.

Phone in hand, he inhaled deeply through his nose and let it out through his mouth. If he called the doctor, and she wanted to see him right away, it was a bad sign. If she wasn't worried, then Ethan wouldn't be.

With his thumb frozen over the call button, he fought back the rising blaze of panic that threatened to engulf his chest. Nothing, not even running into a burning building for the first time, had made him feel this way. Like his entire future was wrapped up in a single phone call.

At that exact moment, the bell over the front door jangled, and Brooke's voice called out from the reception area.

"Hey!" Her head popped around the corner into the hallway and at the sight of her smile, the boulder in his belly started to shrink. "I brought you lunch."

Cool certainty beat back the panic in his body until it was barely a flicker of a flame. Here was his sign he wasn't supposed to call. Shoulders relaxing, he slipped his phone back into his pocket.

"Thanks." He joined her in the reception area and wrapped her in his arms, then kissed her forehead. She hummed with pleasure and sank into his embrace. "But I'll eat in a bit. I need to find Cloudy first."

"Ugh, he got out again? He's probably in the bathroom, behind the toilet is his new favorite hideout." Brooke shook her head against his chest. "This is why I never put him out during adoption events. Who would want a pet that keeps getting into places he shouldn't be?"

"Maybe he just doesn't like me."

"Oh, he likes you." She burrowed into her chest, her voice muffled in his shirt. "All the animals do. Why wouldn't they?"

He laughed, the anxiety of the hunt for the gray cat fading away. She was so comforting, so sure of what to do next. He loved that about her.

Love.

Ethan had never been in love, but the more the words tumbled around in his brain, the more inevitable they seemed.

"All the animals like me, huh?" A smirk tugged at his lips as he looked down at her and her cheeks flushed.

"Hmm." She gazed up at him, eyes soft. "Maybe a little more than like."

"Yeah?"

"Yeah."

He leaned in close and closed his eyes, breathing her in deep. "I a little more than like them too."

The kiss was slow at first, soft, like it was the first one again. Maybe it was, in a way. The first kiss wrapped up in this new feeling that hung in the air around them. Ethan slid his hands up to her cheeks and deepened the kiss, trying to put all of that tender new emotion into it, since the words wouldn't come. When Brooke responded by wrapping her arms around his neck and holding him even tighter to her, the scent of lavender overwhelming his senses, Ethan knew he was a goner. This woman was it for him. Everything had been leading him to this. All the pain in his past, the disappointment and uncertainty. Here was proof that letting go of control and allowing fate to guide him was the only way to live.

Wanting this would have made it that much easier to have ripped away. It could only have happened when he wasn't trying. He never could have predicted someone like Brooke would come into his life.

She cared without being controlling. She never made him feel like he was lacking, or like his RP was a burden. He could let whatever happened next just happen, knowing she would be there next to him, leading the way to whatever was next. Fate had guided him to Brooke, and now she would guide him into their future.

He pulled out of the kiss, wishing it could last forever but knowing they had to find that wayward cat. The shelter was surprisingly quiet, the dogs almost all asleep, only the soft lapping of one drinking water cutting into the peace that stretched between Ethan and Brooke.

Tucking a strand of her dark hair behind her ear, he let his fingers thread into the waves.

"Your hair isn't straight today."

Pink crept across her face and she looked down. "I didn't have time this morning."

"It looks good. Reminds me of the first time we met."

The flush in her cheeks turned scarlet. "Ethan, you know I never would have yelled like that if not for—"

"It's fine." He wrapped her in his arms again. "All of that led me here, to you."

He could practically feel her eyes roll. "You mean it was meant to happen?"

"Well, Lucky could have escaped at any other time, but it was when you were home to see him go into your garden."

"Is raising puppies something you think the shelter should get involved in?" She looked up at him. "Maybe we could partner with them. What do you think?"

He loved that she was asking his opinion. He loved her.

"Maybe . . . " He played with the ends of her hair as a dog barked in the back. "I've actually been thinking about another fundraising idea."

"Another auction?" Her eyes glinted with a familiar spark. "You definitely wouldn't be participating this time."

Planting a kiss on top of her head, he chuckled. "No, but still something with firefighters."

"Oh?"

"What about a calendar? They could pose with the animals. I could see if the guide-dog charity is interested in the idea too."

"That's a great idea." She beamed up at him. "You have so many of them. Your talents are wasted as a fire inspector."

The words hit him like a punch to the chest. He knew it was supposed to be a compliment, but the uneasy, heavy feeling he'd been carrying around since that last inspection with Jerry flowed through him before he could stop it.

"I might not be one much longer." The week of Thanksgiving didn't feel like the right time to bring up anything with Jerry or Chief Stevens. Better to wait until one of them brought it up first.

She stilled in his arms. "Did you call the doctor?"

With a pang that sucked the air out of his lungs, he realized she thought he meant he'd have to stop because of his RP. Thinking back to their conversation in her car a few days ago, he'd told her he was waiting for a sign about his job . . . then immediately after that he admitted to not being able to see the dice.

That wasn't the reason why he wasn't a good fit for the inspector job, but he couldn't find the words to explain. How could he tell her about the mission Jerry had given him, that it was the reason he'd been so nice to her at the party? Then he'd have to explain that he'd been hoping to use her and the shelter to get to know people in Adamsville. It had all seemed to make sense at the time, the universe guiding his actions like it always did, but the words disappeared before they could reach his mouth.

Would Brooke see it as fate, or think he was selfish and manipulative?

Yet blaming his RP was the last thing he wanted to do, especially when it wasn't true in this case. Reminding her of how much his life would change when they were just at the beginning of something couldn't possibly be the way to go.

"I haven't had a chance to call yet."

Her lips twisted to the side, and she stepped out of his arms. "Do you"—she inhaled deeply—"want me to call for you?"

His stomach dropped. Moment ago, he'd been ready to let her lead them into this new life together. Now that she was actually offering to take control of the part of his life he'd never have control over, he wasn't so sure it was what he wanted.

When did wanting things ever turn out well?

He reached out his hands and took hers, giving them a squeeze. "I've got it. Thanks for offering."

She squeezed back. "I'm here for you."

The air in his lungs turned to bricks. Wanting her to be there could only lead to one outcome: she wouldn't always be. Nothing he did or said would change that. At this point, he knew there was no way he'd ever stop wanting her, so what was there really to say other than . . .

"Whatever's going to happen will happen."

Brooke's eyes dimmed at his words, but before he could ask her what was wrong, a pitiful meow echoed in the hallway.

"Sounds like we've found Cloudy." Chuckling under her breath, she pulled her hands out of his and rolled her eyes. "I'll go get him."

She walked into the hallway, taking a little piece of his heart with him that he knew he'd never get back.

TWENTY-FIVE

BROOKE

Brooke's hands were shaking as she organized the ingredients for a magic potion.

Not a smoothie. This one had to be magic.

This was the cure-all potion, the recipe that Gran refused to drink when she was sick. The one Brooke had made countless times and the old woman hadn't even looked at. Heart heavy in her chest, Brooke dropped everything into the blender and pushed the button.

It was Wednesday afternoon, the last day Ethan would be volunteering before he left to see his sister for Thanksgiving. They were driving to the shelter together, but the jittery dance of her nerves had less to do with seeing him in a few minutes and more to do with the concoction she was pouring into two glasses on the counter.

Whatever's going to happen will happen.

If he'd said anything other than the echo of Gran's almost final words to Brooke—not just once, but twice—it wouldn't feel so urgent. It couldn't be just a coincidence. Ethan needed her help now, before something worse happened.

Though just a few months ago Brooke still doubted the

smoothies were doing anything, the proof was now too strong to ignore. There was the mood booster she'd had a few weeks after he started volunteering at the shelter. It had been a wretched day from the moment she'd opened her eyes, but by the end of her shift, and the end of her smoothie, things seemed so much brighter, so much more hopeful. There was the beauty booster she'd made before the auction. He'd barely looked at anybody else all night. Even while talking with Krista, his eyes had kept sliding to her.

There was no denying that the one she'd made him when he was sick had worked wonders. In less than two days, he'd been feeling completely better. It just wouldn't have been possible otherwise.

She'd had her doubts at first, with the rosebud tea. Even if it hadn't made him fall madly in love with her the way she'd imagined while giggling about it with Krista and Aisha in middle school, it had definitely done something. There was no way he'd have come to talk to her at the party if he hadn't accidentally drunk it. Now here she was, weeks later, halfway in love with him.

Love. That's why she was doing this. Seeing someone she loved go through something like this for the second time in as many years was too much for Brooke's heart to handle.

Faced with his worsening condition's impact on his inspector job and how resistant he was to doing anything about it, this felt like the only option for her to help. He wouldn't talk about it. He wouldn't call his doctor and hadn't wanted Brooke to either.

He definitely wasn't going to ask her for a magic potion, because he didn't know it was a possibility.

A little spilled, and she ducked automatically to grab a cleaning spray from under the sink. The neatly folded gloves and the memories of Gran threatened to overwhelm her. She closed her eyes and breathed in three slow breaths, but they were too shallow to do much to calm her racing pulse.

That's how Ethan found her—eyes closed, hands over her heart, nearly hyperventilating—when he walked into the kitchen.

"Hey."

She heard his voice behind her and then his arms were around her. The reassuring pressure of them, of his breath on her neck and the strong, physical quality of his presence did what her pointless breathing exercises hadn't. Her pulse slowed and her tense muscles relaxed.

"It's her gloves." Tears prickled the back of her throat, making the words scratchy.

A kiss on her head was the perfect answer she hadn't known she needed. His arms tightened around her in silence for another few minutes.

When the world felt like it was done spinning under her feet, she turned and smiled at him.

"I made us smoothies."

His eyes lit up, and he kissed the tip of nose. "You didn't have to do that."

Oh, but she did. Otherwise, who knew what came next? This was how she could stop the worst from happening. Gran hadn't let her help, and now she was gone. Ethan had only just come into Brooke's life, and she wasn't in the least bit prepared to let him go so soon.

With trembling hands, she wiped up the spill, then handed him a glass. He smiled as he took it, and her eyes tracked his movements as drank two big gulps, then set it back on the counter. She let out the breath she'd been holding in a whoosh of air.

"Brooke, what's in this?" Ethan looked at her, his voice calm, with an edge to it that made her arms prickle with goosebumps.

She turned back to the spotless counter and wiped it down.

"It's just what I made you the other day when you were sick." The lie tasted like ash in her mouth. She cleared her throat. "And a few extra things."

"Like?"

Brooke kept her eyes on the cloth in her hands, concentrating on the slow, circular motions that had always been so hypnotic when Gran did them. "Just some different herbs from the garden."

"And what do they do?"

"They don't do anything, Ethan, it's just a smoothie." The lie tasted bitter on her tongue.

"What did your Gran think they do?"

It took two slow inhales before she could lift her eyes to his, the cloudy gray darker and more intense than she'd even seen them. "It's her cure-all potion."

His entire body stilled, the muscles in his neck going tight. "This is about what I told you on Saturday, isn't it?"

"And yesterday. You said you might lose your inspector job." Her voice was as weak as her argument. Because there was no argument. "I just thought you might need a boost, that's all."

"You thought you could cure me."

"Of course not." But that wasn't true. She wasn't one hundred percent certain it worked, but she also knew these smoothies were something special. So what did that make her? A believer? A half-hearted skeptic? It should be black and white, but she was stuck in the middle gray area, a place of uncertainty when all she craved was knowing what was going to happen, what was coming.

"Brooke."

"I mean, maybe? Just for like, a second?" She didn't know what she was saying. The words came pouring out of her, trying to make excuses for what she'd done. "I—I figured it couldn't hurt."

"You thought trying to cure my incurable disease with a smoothie wouldn't hurt?" He ran a hand through his hair, the lines on his face so tight it looked painful. "Is this what it's going to be like? You'll just spend the rest of our lives hoping I'll magically get better?"

"No! I don't believe in magic. Not the way you do."

He dropped his hands and glared at her. "There's a big differ-ence between accepting the hand life deals me and trying to cure my vision loss with plants."

Her heart hammered in her chest and her mouth went dry. It had all seemed so logical this morning. It had made sense, but now nothing did. "You just seemed so upset. I wanted to help."

"You help when I ask for it. You don't force it on me."

"But the other one worked."

"The smoothie?" His incredulity echoed in the kitchen. "I took antibiotics, that's how I got better."

"Not just that one . . ." She swallowed. "There was the tea. At the Halloween party."

"What?" He went completely still. "What are you talking about?"

Was she really going to tell him everything? That's not what she'd planned on doing today. Nothing with Ethan ever seemed to go according to plan.

"You remember you grabbed a pitcher from the fridge with purple water that tasted funny? That was, um, a love potion."

He didn't say a word, her pulse pounding so hard in her ears she wouldn't have heard him anyway, even if he had said something. She kept talking, the words tumbling out of her.

"I didn't mean for you to drink it. You grabbed the wrong thing by mistake. But you were so nice to me afterward and then you offered to bring me the inspection reports and then volunteered at the shelter . . . that's the reason why. It's why you care about me, or at least, why you did at first."

He didn't say anything.

Panic gripped her chest, pulling it tight and making the next words squeak out of her. "So, you see? The smoothies definitely do something."

It was irrefutable. He couldn't deny it, not when he believed in fate and the universe sending him what he needed. Now he'd understand why she thought, just for one ridiculous moment, why the cure-all smoothie might do something for him.

"That's really what you believe?" His voice was low now, almost a whisper.

"Well, yeah. What other reason could there be? We hated each other, then it all changed in an instant."

The look on his face was unreadable. Her heart was in her throat. She couldn't say anything else.

"I was nice to you because I needed to be for my job."

Now it was her body that stilled, her lungs empty of air and her muscles frozen in place. "What?"

He rubbed a hand across his mouth. "Jerry told me to get more involved in the community. He said it was important to get to know people in town, and he seemed impressed by your family's name that day at the shelter. He was upset he wasn't invited to your Halloween party. All he cares about is status and making the right people happy. You were one of those people."

The room tilted, and she held out her hand to brace herself against the counter. Had her heart stopped beating? "So you didn't want this."

Didn't want *her*.

"Of course I didn't want this." He threw up his hands and began pacing around the kitchen. "I didn't want any of this. I never wanted to quit a job that I've been doing for ten years that I was actually good at. I never wanted to be an inspector and spend my days behind a desk. Then I had to help at the shelter when I didn't really know you and was sure that you're going to say no, all so that my boss who kept changing the requirement for a job I didn't even want wouldn't think I'm completely incompetent."

Now that he was talking, it was like he couldn't stop. Like he wasn't even aware Brooke was there, each new declaration a dagger in her chest. Part of her was furious at him. Part of her thought she deserved it.

Ethan kept going, stalking around the room without looking at her as the words continued to flow.

"I didn't want to start going blind. But that's the reality. Whatever will happen, will happen. I can't change anything, so there's no use in wanting anything to change. I do the best with what I'm given. I've accepted it, and if you can't accept that about me, then I guess this wasn't meant to be either."

"It was never meant to be. It was just the tea." She didn't know if she said it to convince him, or to convince herself. "I didn't mean for it to happen, but it did."

There was a look in his eyes, a flash of pain before his face fell, and his arms dropped limp at his sides.

"Is that what you really think? The love I felt for you was just the tea?" He nodded his head at the glass. "And that's another magic potion?"

She bit her lip, the teeth scraping so hard she tasted blood on the tip of her tongue. The love he *felt* for her. Past tense.

"What else could it be?"

She didn't know anything anymore, other than one thing: He didn't want any of this. He didn't want her. Of course he hadn't wanted to fall in love with her. She'd made him. And she was trying to fix it with yet another smoothie. With a potion. The one that Gran had never wanted to take. The one that she'd made so many times, but the old woman had never even looked at. Because she'd wanted to leave her. Because Gran had never really wanted her. No one ever did.

He ran a hand over his mouth, over the lips that she fell asleep dreaming about, and shook his head. "I guess we'll never know."

And then Ethan walked out the door.

TWENTY-SIX
ETHAN

The drive, at least, was sunny and clear. It was easy, so much easier than anything else had been over the past few days. He was alone with his music, driving his truck, like this was just another typical Thanksgiving for him.

Except when had Thanksgiving ever been typical?

More often than not, either Ethan or his sister were working on the holiday. The number of times they'd actually spent the day together as adults could be counted on one hand. Two Thanksgivings in a row did make it feel a little more like a tradition, and less like coincidence they both had it off.

A year ago, everything had been different. He'd still been a firefighter. He'd had Lucky with him. He'd just gotten his diagnosis and spent the whole drive building up his courage to tell his sister.

This year was like the start of a country song. Driving on the highway, going blind, with no girl and no dog in a truck.

What would Rachel think about Brooke trying to "cure" him? Less than a day had passed, and Ethan's heart hurt like it had been stepped on. Just the memory of her face twisted with confusion and uncertainty made his blood heat. He gripped the steering wheel and let the anger wash away the pain.

He thought that she'd really seen him, really understood what he needed. The careful planning that was so reassuring to him, the logical way she approached things, all of it now felt like a lie. There weren't words for how torn up he still was about it.

Rachel would have to be on his side. She was, after all, a doctor. Reasonable and analytical, the way Brooke had always been, until she started rambling about magic potions and love tea. It was one thing for her grandmother to believe it, and for Brooke to indulge the old woman who'd raised her. Letting it guide her own life, though, and make her offer him a cure was something else entirely.

He checked the map on his phone. Two more hours to go. Hopefully by the time he got to Rachel's house, his anger would have burned out, or they'd be in for a miserable Thanksgiving.

His sister greeted him like she always did—with a hug and the exact question he didn't want to answer.

"So how was Friendsgiving?"

Luckily for his sister, the anger had burned out about fifty miles from her house.

"It was fun." Ethan plopped onto the couch and took in the stark beige of his sister's utilitarian apartment just a few blocks from the hospital where she worked. Other than a few knickknacks and pieces of furniture, nothing Rachel owned was older than a year or two. It was the complete opposite of Brooke's home full of warmth and history.

Pushing aside the memory of the hours he'd spent on her infinitely more comfortable couch, he leaned forward to grab a handful of peanuts. The crunching made it easier to hide the distress in his voice. As far as Rachel knew, Brooke had kissed him goodbye that morning and was looking forward to seeing him tomorrow night when he got home. "We played Monopoly."

"You lost, didn't you?" Rachel smirked. "Was it as embarrassing as last year? Did you cry?"

Ethan snorted and choked on a peanut. It took a few rough

punches to his diaphragm, but he got it dislodged before Rachel could get out of her seat and perform a perfect the Heimlich. "No crying, but I did lose. It was fun."

"Yes, you said that already." Rachel tilted her head, her gray eyes, the same color as Ethan's—and their dad's—fixed on his face. "What happened?"

"Nothing major." He sighed and leaned back against the couch, about to tell Rachel the same thing he'd told Brooke in the car on Saturday night. It was the reason she'd made him that smoothie, the reason she thought he needed magic to solve all his problems. Opening up to her had turned out to be a mistake, but at least he could trust his sister. "I couldn't keep track of the dice that well. Whenever they rolled too far out of my field of vision, they just kind of disappeared."

Rachel gave no outward sign of reaction. This was her doctor face, the one that made her seem impassive, like her heart was made of stone. But a quick peek down at her hands revealed they were twisted together, clenched between her knees. "That sounds like the normal progression of this kind of disease."

The words were meant to be sterile, void of emotion, to keep it clinical for Ethan. Rachel had been great about staying unemotional about all of this. Nothing could change it, so no point in getting upset about it. That's what he'd told her last year.

Except he'd gotten emotional about it with Brooke. He'd yelled at her. That made it three times in total, and this time was the worst by far. All the worries and setbacks of the past year had just flowed out of him, onto her, like she was a punching bag for all of his anxiety and stress. It wasn't fair to Brooke, but it really wasn't fair to Rachel to keep all of that hidden when she was the only one he could talk to about it now.

"It's scary as hell, is what it is." Ethan put his head in his hands and took one long, shaky inhale. "Everything has been stable for a year. The doctor even said last week there's been no change in my field of vision and then boom, all of a sudden . . . no dice."

With his eyes pressed into his palms, he couldn't see his sister, but he hoped she'd at least chuckle at his weak attempt at a joke. Instead, he heard the deep intake of breath that she let out slowly. Calmly.

"Ethan, you should really talk to someone about all of this."

"I'm talking to you now. You're a doctor."

"That's not what I mean. There are groups and forums and—"

"And what good will they do?"

He stood up, his belly hot and swirling. He paced the small space between the couch and the fireplace, burning brightly with the flames he'd put there not a half hour before. Something he still knew how to do, something he still understood better than anything, but what good did it do him? What would he be now, a professional fire-lighter?

"Nothing will change what's going to happen to me. There's no point in fighting it."

"Talking about it doesn't mean you're fighting it." Rachel was using her calm doctor voice when he clearly wanted to get into a shouting match with his sister. It was infuriating. "It just means you're dealing with it."

"I am dealing with it. I found another job I can keep doing for longer than firefighting." Except he was pretty sure he would quit long before Jerry got anywhere close to offering him the position. He just needed a sign that it was the right time.

"I stopped driving at night." To the detriment of his social life. The shelter had given him a reason to talk to his former crew again, and now he didn't even have that anymore. "I'm rolling with it. That's all I can do."

"This is a huge change, Ethan. No one expects you to adapt instantly."

"It's been a year. Longer, even." He was standing behind the couch now, facing her, his hands gripping the back of it. "I've adapted."

"Clearly not, or you wouldn't be standing here yelling at me."

Rachel folded her arms over her chest, her glare a familiar one from long-ago summers when he'd been the one to come home at two a.m. and she'd point-blank refused to lie to their parents about it. She was holding him accountable, which was the last thing he wanted right now.

Even if somewhere, in the back of his fire-fueled brain, he knew that's exactly what he needed.

"I'm not yelling," he yelled. "I'm just talking loudly. This is my voice. It's loud sometimes."

He held her gaze for a beat, then another. The corner of her lip ticked up. He felt the tickle of a chortle make its way up his throat and into his nose.

Then they both burst out laughing.

It wasn't a regular laugh, but a giant, gasping guffaw that hurt his belly and his chest the longer it went on. The bellowing laughs were so hard they brought tears to his eyes.

Then there were just the tears.

He leaned his head on the edge of the couch and let the tears flow, the sobs racking his body and heaving chest. He couldn't remember the last time he'd cried, let alone a complete sob-fest so incredibly powerful he thought his legs might collapse.

Actually, no, he could remember the last time. He just didn't want to.

Beside him, Rachel stood, silent, not touching him, but close enough so that he knew she was there.

"Everything's changed." The words were hoarse, his throat dry and cracking like the logs in the fireplace. "And I didn't want it to."

"I know." She rubbed his back, the same slow, smooth motion she used to do when he was sick as a kid. He wondered if Brooke would have done the same if he had let her in.

Because he hadn't really let her in, had he? He'd kept all of this hidden, all the sad, angry, ugly feelings that he didn't let himself feel. The feelings that he told himself were pointless in a world where everything was decided for him and he just had to go along with whatever came his way. Then everything had exploded out of him and onto Brooke.

He let out a ragged breath. "You know I roll with whatever the universe sends my way. I don't waste my time wanting anything. But I don't want this."

Rachel stayed quiet and kept rubbing his back.

"I can't change it, but I can't stop not wanting it."

"So do something about it."

He stood up, her hand falling away. "I just said—"

"I don't mean about the RP. Of course you can't change that." She brushed her hair back from her face and looked so much like their mom in that moment his heart almost stopped. "But you can change how you're handling it. If you want to feel more in control, you can find out more about it. It won't change anything, but burying your head in the sand clearly isn't working."

She was making a lot of good points, and he wasn't interested in any of them.

"It didn't work with mom and dad fifteen years ago, did it?" Rachel asked.

It was a rhetorical question, but Ethan shot back a response anyway. "I got through that."

"Not on your own."

He let out a frustrated huff and started pacing again, like the movement would keep her logic from sinking into him. Those first years after their parents died had been rough. He'd been unable to stop looking into all the ways their accident could have been avoided. Then, he ran into a friend from high school who was planning on attending a training camp for the firefighters' physical test.

"How do you know it's what you want to do?" Ethan had asked him.

"I don't. But sometimes you've just got to trust the universe has something in store for you."

It was perfect timing, the perfect physical distraction. Moving his body, using it for a purpose, made everything make sense again.

From there, it was like everything just lined up. He studied for the tests with his friend, who hadn't made it, but Ethan had. The next few years of his life were like they'd been all smoothed over for him. The work was hard, but it kept his mind and body busy, and he didn't have to think about the past.

Until one day, out of nowhere, he panicked. It was a routine call, nothing serious, no fatalities, yet he froze for a few seconds, unsure what to do and unable to get his hands and feet to do what they'd been trained to do. When he realized it was because it was the same intersection of his parents' accident, he'd mentioned it to a teammate, who talked to him a few days later.

And then they kept talking.

"Talking about the tough shifts you had helped, even though it didn't change anything," Rachel said from her side of the couch, reading his mind the way she somehow always managed to.

Talking *had* helped. He knew it helped. Everyone at the fire and the police station, all first responders, knew that's what you did when things got tough.

So why didn't he want to talk about his RP with anyone?

Because this was his own body betraying him. There was no accident he could have prevented, no safety drill he could have prepared that would have kept him safe. This was all in his genes, something he couldn't control. It was the universe that had handed him this fate, and only the universe could change things.

He ran his fingers through his hair. "I know you get it, you're a doctor, but it's not the same."

"Well, I can't force you to do anything." Rachel stood up and started collecting the snacks from the coffee table. "All I'm doing is trying to help."

"You sound like Brooke." He shook his head. "At least you didn't make me some magic potion to cure me."

Rachel froze halfway into the kitchen, and turned, her eyebrows lifted high. "I'm sorry, your girlfriend did what now?"

"Ex-girlfriend." Ethan groaned and put his head in his hands, then flopped back onto the couch.

With a clatter, Rachel put everything back onto the coffee table and sat next to him. When Ethan lowered his hands, her eagle-eye gaze was fixed on him. He groaned again and tried to hide, but she pried his hands away from his face.

"Oh no you don't. You don't get to hide after dropping bombshells like that."

The tugging on his arms turned into a mock wrestling match, with Rachel at full strength and Ethan holding back to about half. When that didn't distract her fully, he tried a tickle fight, but Rachel knew all of his weaknesses.

Eventually, she got the entire story out of him, in fits and starts in between the tickle fight that turned into a pillow fight that devolved into throwing peanuts at each other. By the time he was finished catching her up, it was much too late to start cooking the dinner Rachel had planned. They sat across from each other at the dining room table she'd kept from their childhood home when they sold it, eating microwaved frozen meals.

"These are good." Ethan chewed the meat a few more times before he was able to get any down his throat. "I mean, compared to eating nothing."

She threw a balled-up napkin at him. "Thanks. Next time, just tell me everything right away, and we can eat real food."

"There's nothing you can do. What's done is done." With a swallow that took more effort than he was used to, the meat finally made its way into his stomach.

"That's absolutely not true and you know it." Rachel pushed her plate away. "You like Brooke. And it sounds like she likes you. More than likes you."

He more than liked her too. He was in love with her, had been for weeks. Even now, after everything she'd done.

"Funny way of showing it."

Rachel sighed. "I'm not defending what she did, but I don't think it means what you think it does."

"Which is?"

"That she thinks you're broken."

Ethan shifted in his seat, then pushed away his own plate, not hungry anymore.

"Why wouldn't she think that? I am."

"I assure you, you're not, but I won't waste my breath repeating myself. Please refer to our earlier conversation regarding your need to talk to someone about all this."

That got the younger-brother eye roll that it deserved.

"I don't know what to do." He crossed his arms and leaned back in his chair, tracing the underside of the table where he'd carved his name when he was a kid.

Rachel's voice was soft as her eyes tracked his movements. "That's okay."

"Something always comes along." It was an often-repeated phrase, but this time, a tremor of fear that it wasn't entirely true wove its way through the words. Of course Rachel picked up on it.

"I think you might have to be a little more of an active participant in your destiny this time." She raised an eyebrow.

He pouted.

Rachel clicked her tongue. "You both said a lot of things you probably didn't mean."

He pouted more.

"I thought you'd been an adult for fifteen years." She raised an eyebrow. "This is an awful lot of pouting for an adult."

"If I keep doing it, will you tell me what I need to do?"

"You already know what you need to do."

"Apologize?" He guessed, flashing a hopeful smile at his sister.

All he got was the glare that told him she wouldn't be giving him the answer this time.

"Once you figure out what you want, you'll figure out how to get it."

"I want to stop eating this gross frozen meal and go see if there's a takeout place open."

Rachel threw another napkin ball at him and laughed. "Fine. But you're paying."

As they headed to Rachel's car, her words sank deep into Ethan's chest.

Figure out what he wanted. Like it was that simple.

Like that had ever worked out well for Ethan.

TWENTY-SEVEN
BROOKE

If Brooke had to give a reason for why she'd gone to Aisha's house rather than Krista's, she'd have to say it was because of her carpet.

"You have a very comfortable floor," Brooke said from her starfish position on the bright-purple-and-pink shag rug.

"I always thought so," said Aisha from next to her. She was running her hands through the shag and humming under her breath. It was very soothing. Brooke tried to do the same but her fingers got caught in a tangle, and as hard as she tried to think of a song to hum, her brain filled with Ethan instead, which made the tears spring back into the corners of her eyes.

Next to her, Aisha shifted to her elbow and put her head in her hand so she could look at Brooke. "How was the soup kitchen?"

"Fine." Brooke sniffed. After spending the morning at the shelter, the afternoon had been something familiar. "Everyone said they missed me last year. No one mentioned Gran, but they all had that look in their eye."

"Ah yes. The look." Aisha made her eyes bug out, and Brooke managed a weak chuckle through her tears.

This was the real reason why she'd come here and not Krista's.

The carpet was just a bonus. Even though both of her friends had gotten home from their respective families' Thanksgiving dinners an hour ago, Brooke had needed Aisha's softer, gentler comfort. She wasn't ready for the plotting and planning and logic that Krista would give. That could wait until tomorrow.

Tonight she would starfish on Aisha's rug and let her friend make her laugh.

"It wasn't too hard to be there without her?" Aisha plopped back on the floor next to her, letting the question float up into the air between them. The words hung there, glowing as green as the ceiling above them, each one a little star like the stickers Aisha had stuck up there.

Brooke shook her head, the shag tickling her cheeks as she did so. "She was always in the back helping cook rather than upfront. It didn't feel that different. I could just pretend that's where she was."

Aisha didn't say anything, and the silence was like a balm, soothing away the sharp edges of the pain. Which pain, Brooke wasn't sure. Gran, Ethan, the loss of the life she'd had a year ago. All of it.

"I really messed up with Ethan."

"You wanna talk about it?"

Brooke hadn't shared details yet about his diagnosis, so she wasn't sure what to say that wouldn't be a lie. "I made him a smoothie."

"And he didn't like it?"

"I made him the cure-all smoothie."

Aisha sucked in a breath. She knew what that one meant. What Brooke had tried to do with Gran.

"Why would he get mad about that?"

"He has a condition." Brooke ran her hands through the shag of the carpet. It wasn't her place to talk about it, even now. Especially now. "It's something congenital, not fatal, but it's going to change his life one day."

"And yours?"

"I wasn't thinking about me." The words didn't feel quite right. "I mean, I was, but not because of that."

"So why'd you make it for him?"

There was so much patience and curiosity in her voice, with no trace of judgment. If Aisha had asked in any other tone, Brooke wouldn't have been able to answer quite as honestly.

"He seemed so frustrated about it, but he wasn't doing anything to make things easier for himself. He just accepts things as they come, lets fate or whatever decide for him."

"So? We all do that sometimes."

"Not like this. I just—" Brooke shifted, the shag underneath rubbing at her waist where her shirt had ridden up. "I just didn't want to lose him."

"Like Gran."

"Exactly." The anger flared in Brooke's chest. "She never read any of the articles I found for her, never wanted to ask the doctor for more information. She just accepted it. Then, after eighty years of drinking every concoction under the sun, why would she not want to try the one that would help heal her?"

Aisha was silent for a few long, infuriating moments. "Maybe she knew it wouldn't work?"

"Or maybe she didn't really want to stay with me."

"Hey." Aisha was on her elbow again, this time her hand reaching out to rub Brooke's shoulder. "That's not what happened."

"Well, how do you explain it then?" The tears had started trickling down Brooke's cheeks at some point. Her tongue darted out to keep them from running down her chin, the salty bitterness a familiar taste of loss. "She convinced all of us that these were magic. That she was magic. Then, when I actually needed a miracle, she didn't even want to try."

"I don't know why, Brooke, but it wasn't because she didn't love you."

"If she really loved me, she'd have done everything she could to stay."

"Is that really how you're going to judge things? Everything that happened before that, over thirty years of putting you first, don't count?"

"No." Brooke crossed her arms over her chest, ruining her starfish shape and frankly making the floor a lot less comfortable. "Yes."

Aisha put her hand back on her shoulder and squeezed. "I thought it was Krista's job to be stubborn."

"It's my turn this week."

There was another long silence, less comfortable than before, filled with all the things Brooke could feel waiting to burst out of Aisha.

Brooke sighed. "Go ahead and say whatever it is."

"It's just . . . you've never talked to anyone about Gran and your mom and everything, have you?"

"I talk to you and Krista all the time."

"You know what I mean."

Of course Brooke knew what she meant. In the darkest moments of her grief over the past year, Brooke had searched countless forums and online articles, and not a single one had said that therapy would make it worse.

But how could she explain to someone who hadn't grown up beside her exactly what these drinks meant to her? That they were just smoothies but also magical? The logical side of her brain was fighting so hard to win, to understand and plan for everything, and it had never added up. Then when she gave into the magical side of things, that didn't work either. With Ethan, it had made things even worse. How could talking to someone who knew nothing about it help make it make sense?

"Moms are complicated." Aisha's hand found hers in the tangle of the shag and gripped it tight. Her own relationship with her mother went beyond complicated to almost Shakespearean levels of drama. "Gran raised you. It's like you've lost two mothers. That's a lot for one person to deal with, even with two amazing best friends. Talking to someone—a professional someone—would probably help."

A smile lifted the corners of Brooke's lips as a few tears trickled from her eyes.

"I'll think about it."

"Good." With a squeeze of Brooke's hand and kiss on the cheek, Aisha sat up. "Now, I hope you're hungry. My aunt sent me home with three entire pies."

Brooke laughed. "That's the reason I came to see you instead of Krista."

When her stomach growled so loudly it woke her up, Brooke dragged herself off Aisha's floor the next morning, surprised at how energetic she felt considering where she'd slept. It really was a very comfortable floor. After a brief stop at the shelter to check on things, she headed home, trying not to think about how the place was running so much smoother thanks to Ethan and his tweaks to the filing and scheduling.

The best way to not think about something, in Brooke's experience, was to clean.

Unfortunately, as she walked about her spotless house, she realized that was all she'd been doing all week.

Her hand went to the bracelet at her wrist, and inspiration struck. When was the last time she'd cleaned all of her jewelry? Relief flooded her chest to have a project that would keep her from planting herself in front of the side window in the hopes of a glimpse of Ethan.

He's at his sister's, anyway, she reminded herself as she ran up the stairs to her bedroom. *Probably telling her all about what a terrible person I am.*

For the first time in a long time, Brooke considered an apology.

No. She shook her head as she sat down at her vanity and pulled the jewelry chest toward her. Gran wouldn't have apologized. She would have found a way to show she was sorry and not wasted her breath on words.

Brooke had messed up. Now it was up to her to figure out how to fix it. She carefully lined up the bottle of jewelry cleaner and a few clothes on her vanity. The familiar, rhythmic motions helped calm her swirling thoughts as she went through her options.

Never talk to Ethan again? That sounded awful, but if that's what he wanted, she could accept it.

Talk to Jerry? If Brooke's unintentional snub had made Ethan's life more difficult, maybe there was a way for her to fix it. But that felt like even more of an overstep than the cure-all potion.

Proclaim her love in some public, grand-gesturey way? For shy, introverted Ethan, that would be an absolute nightmare.

Frustrated and feeling stuck, she shoved the jewelry box away. Something shifted inside, and a flash of white caught her eye.

Tucked into a corner of her jewelry chest was a letter in an envelope with "Brooke" on the front in Gran's handwriting. Brooke stared at it, not quite sure what was happening. It was under a necklace that Gran had given her when she graduated from college. Citrine and hematite, for protection and joy.

Brooke had never worn it.

There was no way for Gran to have known when she would be cleaning out her jewelry chest, but she would have known it would happen eventually. Because no one knew her better than Gran.

The envelope was small, half the size of a regular letter, and thick, like the paper inside had been folded over multiple times to make it fit. The corners of Brooke's lips turned up, thinking of the wrinkled, spotted hands of Gran pushing down to make the seams as flat as possible. She always did that, put too big of a piece of paper into an envelope, no matter the size.

There was nothing to do but read it. Looking at it wouldn't

change anything, wouldn't make the old woman come back to life and read it to Brooke herself. If these were the last words Gran had ever written to her, she wanted to cherish them for as long as possible.

She opened the envelope, and five pieces of paper covered in the tiny, cramped script fell out. The first one was a recipe for a smoothie. The second was tea. The third was soup. Heart pounding, Brooke threw down the stack of papers.

More magic potions. Brooke ran her hands through her hair and held back a scream. Why bother hiding them here, when she had notebooks full of them in the kitchen?

If Brooke had been hoping for some kind of wisdom, some last words of explanation for those final painful months, then she shouldn't be surprised to find pages full of recipes instead of explanations. Whenever Brooke had come to her with serious questions, with a need for advice, she'd gotten food. It was the answer for everything, except when it had mattered the most. Then it had been pills and doctor's offices, and Gran had ignored the research Brooke had shown her on what diet could do for her condition. The one time Brooke had wanted to believe in Gran's magic, and it hadn't made a difference.

She stood up, leaving the papers scattered on the ground, then her eyes snagged on a word on the last page.

Her name.

Brooke.

The spidery handwriting was uneven, like the hand that had written it wasn't as steady as it used to be.

Choking back a sob, Brooke fell to the floor and picked up the letter, wishing for a moment she was back on Aisha's cozy shag rug, as the cool hardwood beneath her hips grew instantly uncomfortable.

Brooke,

I know you'll be upset with me when the time comes. I know I've taught you never to apologize, to own your choices. It's what kept me and you safe after your mom left. I didn't want you apologizing for her mistakes your entire life.

But I need to tell you that I'm sorry.

I'm sorry you had me instead of your mother. I'm sorry I couldn't stay with you longer. I'm sorry I won't see you get married or have children, if that's what you end up doing. I'm sorry I won't see you fall in love, which I know you will, one day, if you can let yourself trust enough for it to happen. You are so worthy of love, and I know it'll be scary when it happens, but trust that it can be real.

I'm sorry I didn't drink all those cure-all potions you made for me. The end is coming for me no matter what, and I don't want your belief in magic to die with me.

Because I am dying, sweetheart. I'm an old woman, and it's not fair that I have to leave you when you should have had a mother or father with you for decades more. I did the best I could with the time I had with you, and I wouldn't trade it for anything in the world. Not even to have your mother back.

I'm <u>not</u> sorry for loving you more than she did. But I hope you can forgive her one day, wherever she is. Not for her sake, but for yours. Letting go of that pain and loss will bring more magic and love into your life than you can even imagine. No rosebud tea necessary.

Krista and Aisha will take care of you, I know they will. I hope you keep making my recipes for them. But most of all, I hope you know that you are special and loved and deserve all the happiness in the world that is waiting for you.

I'm sorry I didn't say it enough when I was alive, so I've written it down for you to keep with you, wherever you go. Love forever,

Gran

Brooke let the pages fall into her lap and leaned against her dresser, feeling more uncertain than she ever had about what her next steps were.

But also feeling more sure than she had in years.

It was Tuesday, which meant it was his regular shift at the shelter. Or it should be, but he'd heard nothing from Brooke in a week, so maybe he wasn't on the volunteer roster anymore.

Ethan hesitated, hand on his car door as he sat in the shelter's parking lot, waiting for a sign if he should go or not.

No, he needed to decide for himself what he wanted to do.

He'd been flexing the muscle over the past few days, and it had been going . . . well, it had been going. It wasn't like he could change a decade of thinking one way in just a few days.

He opened the door and stepped outside, the late November air whipping at his hair, still not sure if he should go into the shelter or not. But at least it felt more like action than inaction.

Calling a therapist yesterday also felt like action.

Telling Chief Stevens and Jerry this morning that he didn't think he'd be the right person for the inspector job had felt less like action and more like voluntarily launching himself out of a three-story building without being able to see the jumping cushion at the bottom. They'd both been concerned, but agreed it didn't seem to be the right fit for Ethan. Thanking Jerry for everything he'd taught him had been awkward, but when had

Ethan not been awkward as an inspector? That was kind of the point.

Maybe that was enough for one week. Too many decisions might be tempting fate to get revenge somehow. He turned and opened his car door again.

"Ethan."

Everything inside of him stilled. The sound of Brooke's voice floated over to him, settling into all the nooks and crannies he'd blocked off for the past week, all the lavender-scented parts of his soul that still longed for her.

Because he did want her. He just hadn't figured out what to do about it yet.

Maybe the universe was still watching out for him.

He closed the door and turned around, then leaned against the car when his knees threatened to crumble at the sight of her.

It was her hair. Instead of straight and smooth, those unruly, messy waves were back. The shadows under her eyes were deep, and the blue irises were lined in red. She was dressed in leggings and a sweatshirt—one of his he'd left at the shelter, he realized with a stab to his chest. It was the least put together he'd ever seen her.

She was so beautiful it hurt.

Now to see if she was going to hurt him even more.

"Ethan?" She sounded uncertain, like she was afraid he might yell at her.

"Hi." The sun was bright in his eyes, and he rubbed them.

She shifted from one foot to another. "Hi."

There was a pause that turned into a long stretch of silence, broken only by the muffled sounds of animals from inside the shelter. Brooke didn't move. Ethan started to wonder if he was dreaming.

He shifted against his car. "Did you still need to me to—"

"I'm sorry."

She blurted out the words like she was allergic to them, then took a long, slow inhale and a few steps closer to him.

"I'm sorry, Ethan. I shouldn't have made the smoothie, even if I didn't really think it would work. It was wrong and insensitive, and I hurt you and I'm sorry."

Okay, now he knew he was dreaming. All he could do was stare at this version of Brooke standing in front of him, looking and acting exactly the way he'd hoped she would.

It was a sign.

No, it's Brooke. Deciding she wanted something and then doing it. Like he should be doing, but his body didn't want to leave the safety of his car quite yet. He pressed his back into it even harder, the door handle digging into his kidney.

She tucked a dark wave behind her ear and took a step back. "Um, okay, that's all I wanted to say. You don't have to work today. I've got your shift covered from now on." Her gaze on the ground, she started to turn away.

"I want to be here."

"You do?" Her eyes widened, and her hands shoved into the pockets of the hoodie. His hoodie. Holy smokes, she looked so good in his clothes. "I mean, you don't have to if you don't want to."

"I want to." Now it was his turn to take a step toward her. Then another, and another, his body going where he wanted to be, which was closer to her. "I'm sorry too."

He was now just a few feet away from her, close enough to smell the lavender.

"Why?" She bit her lip, and he had to squeeze his hands into fists to stop from tugging at it. There was so much he wanted to do, but he wasn't sure she wanted him to. Apologizing didn't mean she wanted to be with him. "You didn't do anything wrong."

"I didn't share as much as I could have. About everything I've been feeling about my RP. About other things. My parents. How bad it really was at work."

She raised an eyebrow but didn't say anything. Like always, she seemed to know what he needed, and the silence made it easier for him to keep going.

"Everything else up until then was so considerate, so caring. More than anyone's ever taken care of me, and I didn't—I don't like feeling useless. If you'd have known what I'd been feeling, then I know you wouldn't have made a smoothie."

She was shaking her head, like she didn't want to hear what he was saying. "I never should have anyway. I did it from a place of love, but I was still wrong. I'm sorry."

Love. His heart leaped at the word.

"You like saying you're sorry, huh?" He couldn't keep the edge of teasing out of his voice and the corners of his lips curved up.

"Absolutely not." She huffed out a chuckle, then closed the distance between them. "But I'll try to say it more. For you. Just for you." She scrunched up her nose. "Never to Krista."

The smile spread across his face. "Never."

They were almost chest to chest now, their bodies straining toward each other like they couldn't be controlled.

"Brooke, do you still want me to volunteer at the shelter?" The words held only the smallest quiver of uncertainty.

"I want more than that."

His heart pounded in his ears. "Oh?"

She smiled widely, her eyes shining brightly as she licked her lips. "I want you to work there. I think you'd be a great office manager."

The rightness of that idea settled into his chest, like it had always been there, waiting for him to notice. It was what he wanted. He could see that now.

But he still wanted more.

"Is that all you want?" He swallowed hard. "Because I want you, Brooke. I think I've wanted you from that first moment I saw you. I shouldn't have waited for some stupid sign from the universe. I should have gone for it right away."

She raised an eyebrow again, and her lips turned up.

"Well, maybe not right away. You were yelling pretty loudly that day."

Her hand reached out for his and she looked down as their fingers laced together, then bit her lip again. But she didn't say anything. So he asked her instead of waiting for it to happen.

"You didn't answer my question." He traced his thumb along hers. "Is that all you want? For me to work at the shelter?"

Slowly, so slowly Ethan thought he might be imagining it, she lifted up onto her toes and brought her lips close to his. Her breath was hot on his lips, and he closed his eyes, reveling in the overwhelming sensation of her that, up until a few minutes ago, he thought he'd never feel again.

Her words were a whisper against his mouth, the promise of more etched into every single one. "I want you to beat Krista at next year's Friendsgiving."

A laugh burst out of him and the sun shone bright on his face as she laughed, too, the blue of her eyes the same as the sky above them. If this was a dream, he never wanted it to end.

He bumped his nose into hers, the smell of lavender surrounding him. "Maybe there's a lucky potion you can make that'll give me the upper hand?"

"Uh-huh." She nodded and their lips brushed, just for a moment. "You'll win next year for sure. And the one after that, and the one after that, and the one after—"

He crushed his mouth to hers, promising her all the Friendsgivings until the end of time, and everything else they both would ever want.

EPILOGUE

Cloudy was missing, but Brooke knew exactly where to find him.

She opened up the cabinet under the sink and found him asleep in the bucket, the cleaning gloves squashed beneath him.

"I found him!" Brooke extracted the grumpy feline from the bucket and carried him into the living room, where Aisha and Krista were sitting on the couch, the TV pulled into the middle of the room for movie night.

The cat let out a very grumpy meow when Brooke set him next to Aisha, but he was purring within seconds.

"Thank you for finding him for me." Aisha cooed, and Cloudy preened in response, then curled up next to her, leaving no room for Brooke on the couch. "I didn't see him last time I was here."

"He likes to sleep in tiny, enclosed places." Brooke sat down on the chair and threw her legs over the arm. "Maybe he missed his cage at the shelter."

"It's been like six months though." Remote in one hand with a peach and pomegranate smoothie in the other, Krista was flipping through the movie options. Technically they were supposed to rotate who got to pick, but somehow it always seemed to be her turn.

"Six months, three weeks, and two days since I adopted him."

Krista shot her a bemused smile.

"Where's Ethan with the nuggets?" Aisha asked, still scratching under Cloudy's chin.

"I'm here."

The sound of his voice always sent a little shiver up Brooke's spine. Then, just like he always did on movie nights, Ethan stopped to kiss Brooke before setting the food down on the coffee table.

It had been exactly two months and two days since he'd moved in. Though he'd been attending movie nights for longer than that, only missing them when he met up with his former firefighter colleagues for a drink, getting a ride with one of them so she didn't have to interrupt the movie.

"It's about time." Krista dropped the remote to grab a bag, and Ethan snatched it up while she was divvying up the nuggets onto the plates Brooke had set out. Krista pointed at him. "Don't even think about it, Mercer. I've already picked *Escape To New York.*"

"We've watched that twice this month already." He navigated to a different movie app.

"It's in honor of Hayden Carmichael's upcoming wedding." Krista grabbed the remote back. "Unless Aisha wants something else? You're the one with the big news this week."

Pink streaked across Aisha's cheeks, and she concentrated on ensuring Cloudy got all the attention he hadn't on her last visit. "It's just going full-time. It should have happened ages ago. I just didn't have enough courage to ask until Cody brought it up in front of my boss."

"Next step, asking him out." Krista turned her attention back to the screen. "But first, what movie do you want tonight?"

"I like *Escape To New York.*"

Ethan groaned and moved to stand behind Brooke's chair, his hands resting on her shoulders. "Doesn't he have like fifty other movies? Can't we watch one that was made in this decade?"

"No," Aisha and Krista said in unison.

Laughing under her breath, Brooke's chest squeezed tight, the unbearable happiness of watching the now-familiar bickering between the people she loved most pooling in her stomach.

Just like it always did.

He rolled his eyes, then looked down at her, smiled, and bent to give her another kiss.

"I love you," she whispered against his mouth.

He inhaled and closed his eyes, like he was savoring the scent of lavender for the first time. Like he'd never get enough of it. Never get enough of her.

"I love you too."

Brooke felt his words wrap around her heart and sink into the core of her bones.

No magic potion needed.

AUTHOR'S NOTE

Whenever I read a romance novel, I always wonder what's real and what's not.

Yes, I realize the entire point of fiction is that it's made up. But there are always hints of real places, people, and events tucked in between the imaginary dialogue uttered by inexplicably buff and beautiful characters.

Here's a short and incomplete list of what's real and what's not in this book:

- Adamsville, SC: not a real place. I don't think it's possible for a real town to have an aquarium AND only one fire station AND a local newspaper... but no animal shelter. That's the fun of fiction!
- Magic potions: I'll let you decide for yourself ;-)
- Extremely clingy cats who chew through bags of kibble to gorge themselves: very real. I have two of them.
- The law firm of Mendoza, St. Claire, and Forcett: not real, but if you're a fan of The Good Place, these three are probably not the lawyers you want representing you!

- Retinitis pigmentosa (RP): this is a real disease. I spent a lot of time researching in order to portray RP as accurately as possible, but some errors may have slipped in. In reading first-person experiences, I learned how varied the progression of the disease can be. Like any other serious medical diagnosis, everyone's reaction to it will be as individual and unique as they are. Ethan's choices and what his HEA looked like are his alone, and do not represent what everyone living with RP may want or need (though as a romance writer, I truly wish for everyone to get their HEA, whatever that looks like for them!)

WHO'S HAYDEN CARMICHAEL?

Escape To New York and its star, Hayden Carmichael, are featured in another sweet romance I've written, Man Of My Dreams.

Keep reading for a sneak peek!

Chapter 1

You dream it, and I'll make it happen . . .

The familiar words, spoken so close to her ear, pulled Bree out of a deep sleep. Looking around the room, her heart pounded in her chest.

Where was she?

Instead of familiar venetian blinds and small windows, there were large panes of glass covered in frothy pink curtains that let in an enormous amount of light. Too much light for this time of day.

A few blinks cleared the fog, and she flopped back into the unfamiliar bed. The scent of mothballs invaded her nose.

She was in Aunt Agatha's New York City apartment. Bree's apartment now.

Bree wiped away the tear that trickled down her cheek and sat up again. Her laptop was still open on the bed, where she'd fallen asleep watching *Escape to New York*. The voice that had woken her up was Hayden Carmichael's during one of her favorite, swooniest parts in the movie.

The superstar's first big hit was almost twenty years old, but it was what had planted the seed of moving to the city in her middle school brain. That seed had grown over the years into a dream, a massive bundle of desire like one of those gigantic topiary house-plants that took over an entire bookshelf with its tendrils and twists.

With a yawn, she closed her laptop with the movie still play-ing, then stretched slowly as she looked around the room. She'd barely taken it all in last night when she'd arrived, exhausted after two delayed flights and a very expensive cab ride she was sure should have cost at least half as much as she'd been charged. Between her Minnesota accent and her wide-eyed exclamation of joy at seeing the Statue of Liberty, the cab driver had assumed she was a tourist.

Except thanks to Agatha, Bree's first trip to New York wasn't as a tourist, but as a resident. A grin spread across her face. This was the first day of the life she'd always dreamed of.

Sleep still clung to the edges of Bree's eyes, and she rubbed them while stifling another yawn. She needed coffee. Immediately. Then she'd head out into the city.

Though dulled by her exhaustion, excitement was making its way through her system. She wrapped herself in her worn terry cloth robe and slipped on the new sheep's wool slippers she'd splurged on at the airport.

She stood up, and her shins banged into the night table. She turned, banged her knee on the bed, then tripped over her suitcases that were still piled in a heap, wedged in between the bed and the wall.

The smile slipped from her face as she half climbed, half

limped out into the hallway. The bedroom had seemed enormous last night in her half-conscious state of mind, but in the morning light, it was tiny.

Stumbling over creaking floorboards, she walked five steps into the kitchen. It was just as small, and even worse . . .

"Where's the coffee?" she asked the empty room.

Bree hadn't gone without some form of caffeine in her body within minutes of waking for over fifteen years. One of the perks of being a barista for as long as she had was that she knew how to make a good cup, no matter what she had on hand. Instant, whole beans, whatever kind of milk was available. Big cups, small cups, no cups. She could make anything work.

No coffee at all, however, made it impossible to even get started. A frantic search through the cupboards and drawers confirmed that, unless she wanted to make her morning cup out of mouse droppings and dead roaches, she was out of luck.

Did Birdbrain Bree forget to bring any food to an apartment that's been empty for forty years?

The mocking voices echoed in her ears as Bree took a few steadying breaths. She reminded herself that her forgetfulness was what Aunt Agatha had loved most about her. It was even in the letter accompanying the surprising announcement from Agatha's lawyer that she'd left Bree a Manhattan apartment in her will.

To my darling Bree, with a heart full of dreams and her head in the clouds, I hope this leads you to your happily ever after.

"No coffee." She closed a dusty cupboard and tightened the belt on her robe. Sunlight and the sound of honking horns filtered in through the kitchen window. "That's fine. Plenty of coffee in New York."

If her best friend, Leigh, were here, she'd look up the closest and best-rated café in the area. Bree was much happier to wander around and see what she could find. It always yielded the most interesting results. Bree trusted fate way more than Google for these kinds of things.

Before she could let fate do her thing, however, she had to get dressed. Leggings and a tank top might have been okay for a quick run to the store back home, but this was New York City. She could be anyone she wanted to be here. It was her chance to reinvent herself.

She dragged one of her suitcases into the living room, bumping into the couch and the coffee table. Heat was starting to pool under her arms. She took a quick sniff. Did she have time for a shower?

No, coffee was more important. Whatever she pulled out first, she'd wear. She'd only brought her favorite clothes with her and sold the rest, along with her car. With a little luck, she'd have enough funds for a few months before she'd need to worry about finding a job.

As if to make up for the lack of coffee, the most perfect sundress fell right into her hands the second she opened her suitcase. A smile lifted the corners of her mouth, her shoulders dropped, and her body relaxed. It would be okay. This was the perfect dress for what would be the most perfect first day of her new life.

Ten minutes later, she was putting on a pair of strappy sandals when she heard a thump from the hallway. A stream of curses followed. It sounded like an old woman. Like Aunt Agatha. Bree's shoes clicked as she went to the door and peered out the peephole.

It *was* an old woman, cursing up a storm. Her papery-thin white skin was deeply lined. She'd dropped what looked like an entire library's worth of books and was bending slowly to pick them up, one by one, to replace them in her overturned shopping caddy.

Bree didn't even hesitate. This was clearly someone meant to be in Bree's life.

After opening the door, Bree stuck her head out into the hallway. "Hi there, looks like you could use some help."

The old woman turned to look at her and raised an eyebrow. "Ya think?" She turned back to her books.

A real New Yorker, Bree thought with an excited quiver in her stomach. The old woman was a bundle of mismatched clothing. Green knitted leggings peeked out from below a long purple skirt. A light-gray puffy jacket was zipped up tight. It seemed like an odd combination for mid-May, but older people were often colder than others.

Bree stepped into the hallway and bent to pick up a few books. It wasn't that easy with the sundress, which turned out to be shorter than she'd remembered, and the sandals were hard to balance on. This was more of an outfit to be seen in than to help people in.

The woman didn't say anything but did grunt a bit when Bree managed to totter over and place a few books into her caddy.

"I just moved in."

Another grunt.

"It was owned by my aunt." Bree tucked the hair that had escaped her braid behind her ear. "Well, not really my aunt, but someone I knew my whole life who taught dance in my town, and I would go there after school and—"

She clammed up when the old woman paused and peered closely at Bree. Without a word, she went back to the books. There were only a few left now, and it took Bree a single unsteady swoop of her arms to gather them up and dump them on top of the rest.

It was a staggering amount of books, really, and Bree wasn't sure how the old woman planned on getting them all downstairs. They were only on the second floor, but there were at least twenty stairs. Last night they'd felt like a million, lugging her suitcases behind her at midnight.

"Do you need some help down the stairs?"

With a silent eye roll at Bree, the old woman pulled her cart down the other end of the hall, toward a gilded doorway Bree hadn't noticed. Smiling smugly, the old woman opened the door and stepped into an elevator. The clanking of the machinery was earsplitting, but it still would have been preferable to banging her suitcases up the stairs last night.

Hypnotized by the slowly fading elevator noises, Bree shook her head.

The old woman hadn't talked to her at all. Not even a hello, never mind about asking her name. Back home, that would have been the height of rudeness.

New York is home now. The smile slipped back onto her face.

Brushing off her skirt, Bree turned back to her door to retrieve her keys and phone before heading out into the city.

The handle wouldn't turn.

With her pulse pounding in her ears and sweat on her palms, she tried to open the door again, knowing before she even touched it what the outcome would be.

She was locked out.

A familiar flutter made its way up her chest. This was clearly a sign to explore, to discover the city in the spontaneous way she knew would lead to amazing things the way things like this always did.

Thanks to her restless spirit and taste for adventure, Bree had traveled all over the country, where she'd met endlessly fascinating people, collecting their stories while waiting for her own to start. Now it finally was, and she wasn't about to let getting locked out of her minuscule apartment ruin her perfect first day.

The elevator clanged from the back of the hallway, drawing her eye. If all her neighbors were like the old woman, Bree would have better luck getting someone in the street to help her call the building's super.

Without wasting another moment, she walked down the stairs and out the door to see what her new city had in store for her.

The tree-dappled street her apartment building was on led to a wide avenue with a familiar name. Seeing the "Broadway" street sign brought to mind theater marquees and neon lights, but here it was all bright awnings and graffitied trucks. The beep of car horns mingled with the chatter of pedestrians. Words in languages other than English mingled with the unfamiliar and delicious smells that wafted out food carts and open doors.

Dodging people and telephone poles, she weaved in and out of the crowd, taking in every new sight, every new sound. The buzz of far-off construction floated on top of everything.

"Holy cow." Bree had never seen so many people before. It was almost enough to make her remember that she was phone-less and wallet-less.

It was also chillier than she'd expected, but she was from Minnesota. All the shivering her body insisted on was because of her excitement, not the cold.

At least now the old lady's warm clothes made sense. Bree's floaty sundress gave her about as much protection from the biting wind as tissue paper. Several people she walked past gave her slightly raised eyebrows beneath their hoods and hats protecting them against the unseasonably cold May weather.

Ignore them. Just like she did back home whenever her unusual outfits clashed with everyone's small-town sensibilities. Minnesota Bree was flighty and flaky and forgetful. "Birdbrain Bree," as her family liked to call her with a chuckle. She, of course, always laughed along, clinging to whatever unique identity they wanted to pin on her. It was better than not being thought of at all.

New York Bree would be different. She shook back her hair and puffed out her chest, determined to walk in the confident, catwalk stride like people in the movies as they moved along busy New York sidewalks.

Holding each person's eye gave her a small thrill, a sense that despite the rocky start, her dream New York life—her dream New York self—was totally possible. Nothing bad happened when she made eye contact with people, except she almost ran into a few others going the opposite way. Even so, no one shouted at her, and a few people even smiled.

Smiled! Sure, they could have been laughing at her poor wardrobe planning, but through her optimistic eyes, they were all smiles of welcome.

After a few blocks, however, an unfamiliar, uncomfortable heaviness settled in her chest. Her stomach gave a growl loud enough that a dog barked at her from the backpack he was being carried in.

Her eyes flitted from one storefront to another. A gym, a shipping store, clothing for dogs, shoes for humans, a grocery store that took up half a block . . . She should go into one and explain her situation, but which one? It must happen all the time, people losing their phone.

If things got very desperate, she could always go to a police station. Someone in this teeming mass must know if there was a police station inside one of these white-stoned buildings. Someone would help her.

Her attention shifted back to the people streaming past her on the sidewalk. Everyone looked so serious, on their way to work or school, sipping from to-go cups of coffee that Bree tried not to salivate over. Back home, she'd have known at least half the faces and they'd have all gladly helped her.

Except some of the people streaming by did look familiar. Not in a super famous way, more like in a social media influencer way. Like they were all professionally good looking and were paid a lot of money to look that perfect all the time.

Hayden Carmichael lives in New York. The cold left her body, and heat crept up her neck. It was just like the movie she'd been watching last night. A girl, new to the city, bumps into him. He spills his drink all over her new dress . . .

Bree shook her head. The lack of coffee was making her light-headed. It was a city of eight million people. Even if he did live in her neighborhood, which she had no way of knowing, that only narrowed things down by a few million. Out here on the sidewalk, Bree had literally never seen so many people in her entire life.

Except, suddenly, there he was, walking toward her.

The shock of it made her stumble. Shivering as she straightened, she blinked and focused her gaze on him, trying to ignore the pounding of her heart in her ears.

Dressed in gym shorts and a hoodie, Hayden Carmichael's short hair was wet like he'd just showered. His eyes were partially blocked behind round glasses, but there was no mistaking that face, that scruff, those cheekbones. That perfect pout of a mouth that was tugged down in a concentrated frown instead of the wide grin he was usually photographed with, no matter what he was doing.

Bree stopped for a moment, stumbling again when someone plowed into her from behind and cursed at her. Afraid to take her eyes off him, she let her head swivel, looking back. Her heart almost stopped when his head turned, he looked back at her, and their eyes locked.

Was Hayden Carmichael *staring at her?*

A gasp got caught in her throat. This was absolutely the most perfect day.

Letting out her breath in a sigh, Bree picked up her pace, nearly skipping in delight.

I can't wait to tell Leigh what happened. She'd never believe it. Bree turned her head to look in front of her again, just in time to see a door swing open and to run smack into it.

Everything went black.

Chapter 2

Aiden was used to the stares. Through no fault of his own, his face was famous, even if he wasn't. Most days, in the midst of his familiar routine—gym, clients, animal shelter, studying—he didn't even notice the stares.

Did he occasionally stare back? Of course. New York was full of beautiful people. If they wanted to look at him, he'd enjoy returning the favor.

Things never went past looking, however. It took people all of two minutes with him to realize he wasn't the movie star they thought he was. When women gave him the googly heart-eyes the way this one was, he would hold their gaze for a moment, let them wonder, then go on with his day.

Today, however, he looked again.

There was an aura of pure sweetness radiating from her, like she was a fairy who'd stepped out of an enchanted forest and had no idea how she'd ended up in New York. Her long, dark hair and bright-blue eyes hinted at both mischief and warmth. She was impossibly beautiful and improbably dressed.

When Aiden turned his head for another look, a frown tugged at his lips. Was she shivering? Had she not checked the weather before leaving the house in that tiny dress?

Their eyes met again, and time slowed, Aiden's heart beating a staccato rhythm he hadn't felt since those early days in the city a decade ago. His heart stopped entirely when her face smashed into a door neither of them had noticed.

A curse flew out of his mouth that earned him a few more stares.

Before the woman's head had even hit the pavement, Aiden was at her side.

His hand found her pulse the way he'd been trained to do, and he was careful not to touch her or move her in case anything had been hurt that he couldn't see. His stomach gave a lurch when he considered just what kind of injuries she might have.

She was lying on the sidewalk like an extra in a superhero movie who'd been tossed to the side by the bad guy. Without hesitation, he stripped off his hoodie and laid it over her, thankful he'd been on his way to the gym and not on his way home, so it smelled like fabric softener, not sweat.

"Is she okay?" someone asked. A crowd had started to gather behind him, but he paid them no attention and focused on handling the situation in front of him.

Taking a deep breath, he went through the mental checklist of what to do when someone hit their head. She was breathing, and there was no blood. Next, he should see if he could wake her up.

"Miss? Can you hear me?"

There was a flutter of eyelids and a sharp intake of breath that had his pulse racing. Her blue irises were edged in black, and they were now looking up at him with that same intense gaze from before she fell.

"I had a dream about you." Her voice was strong, and loud.

There was a tittering of laughter behind him. Aiden ignored them and the drop in his stomach, staying focused on the woman.

"Oh yeah? What was I doing?" Keeping her talking was good. Head injuries were serious things, and he'd seen quite a few in the various jobs he'd had. Though he felt more confident treating animals than humans, he had the treatment steps memorized for both.

She blushed. "I don't remember."

Her blush suggested otherwise, but it also meant she was reacting relatively normally. He checked his watch, quickly updating his schedule for the day. Just a bit longer. Then he'd have to be on his way, or he'd be late. "What's your name?"

"Bree."

"Brie? Like the cheese? Or is that short for something?"

"I'm not cheese." She frowned.

Despite the tension in his chest, he let out a small chuckle at how vehement her answer was, the lilt of a midwestern accent turning the irritated words into a song.

She shifted slightly beneath his hoodie. "It's short for something, but I'm not sure what. Everyone just calls me Bree."

Uh-oh. Memory loss was never a good sign.

"Bridget?" He guessed.

Another frown and his breath hitched. The puckered skin between her eyes was inexplicably adorable.

Her blue eyes blinked up at him, a little too bright. "You look really familiar. Do I know you?"

Aiden hesitated. She did, but not in the way she thought she did. "You've never met me. I would have remembered someone like you."

She flushed again at this, and he cursed his unexpected candor. Unplanned words didn't often leave his mouth. He got back to his head trauma first-aid checklist.

"Does anything hurt?"

"Um . . . my head." She reached up to touch the rising bump on her forehead and winced.

He gently pulled her hand away, ignoring the tingling in his fingers at the feel of her skin on his. "You fell. It'll hurt for a while. Anything else?"

She shook her head, then her face tightened, and she groaned.

"Don't move, just say the words. Are you sure nothing else hurts?"

"No."

"Can you wiggle your fingers and toes?"

"You said not to move."

Aiden's heart thudded at the slight teasing edge to her voice and the small quirk of her lips.

There were murmurs and movement behind them, and Aiden glanced over his shoulder. The crowd was dispersing, apparently convinced he had it under control. One man hung back, however, and squatted down next to them.

"Should she go to a hospital?" His silvery eyebrows drew together. "That fall looked pretty nasty. And she can't remember anything."

"No hospitals." Bree sat up. Aiden's hoodie dropped away, and her dark hair fell down her back in a tangle of wild waves and half-done braids. She shivered.

An attentive ache rushed through him, and Aiden draped his hoodie around her shoulders again. "Why no hospitals?"

Bree looked around and frowned, pulling the hoodie tight against her body. "I don't know."

"That's okay. At least you remember your name."

A corner of her lip turned up. "Only part of it."

Oh hell, she was too cute for her own good. Every protective instinct inside of Aiden was on fire in a way they hadn't been in a long time. Maybe it was the way her hair fanned out around her head, wispy and cloudlike. Or the way her accent brought to mind wholesome images like cornfields and crystal-clear lakes that were incongruous to the dirty, smelly city that surrounded them.

The city that had literally just knocked her on her ass.

"Can you remember where you live?" It was the other man who spoke, and he kneeled next to them on the sidewalk.

Irritation flickered across Aiden's skin. He had this under control. This wasn't the first time he'd had to use the first-aid certification he'd gotten in college.

Did this guy have that? Did this guy keep it updated every year the way Aiden did?

"No. I remember him though." She tilted her head and looked at Aiden, frowning again. "I don't know from where, but I definitely know you somehow."

A familiar dread dropped heavy and low in his abdomen. The older man looked Aiden up and down before recognition lit up his eyes.

"So, are you really a doctor, or do you just play one in the movies?" A smirk spread across the guy's lips.

Aiden sighed. "I'm a personal trainer and I used to be a vet tech, so I know emergency injury procedures."

Unlike you, he added silently.

He turned back to Bree with what he hoped was a calming look. "You probably have a concussion. You should really let a doctor check you out."

"No doctors."

Did he have time to convince her otherwise? A glance at his

watch told him no, though it took effort to calm down the voice screaming in his head to haul her away to a hospital immediately.

"Fine. Can we call someone? Where's your phone?" Aiden looked around, but there was nothing on the ground.

"Someone probably grabbed it when she fell," said the other guy with a shrug.

Aiden ground his fist into the rough sidewalk. Yet another of the many reasons he hated this city. Leave your stuff unattended for two seconds and it gets stolen.

"I don't think I had one," said Bree.

"You don't have a phone?" Aiden tried to keep the shock out of his voice but did a poor job of it.

No last name, no phone, no doctors. Panic was slowly starting to take over, hot stickiness clinging to the blood in his veins. His mind searched for a solution, some plan that made sense in this totally unprecedented situation.

Instead of an enchanted fairy, maybe Bree was a demon sent to torture him. It wouldn't be the first time New York had turned something he thought was good into something terrible.

"Why don't we get you something to eat?" The older man smiled gently and got to his feet. Aiden did the same, relieved to have a next step to follow, and he reached out his hands to help Bree up.

She was unsteady, and his hoodie fell off her slender shoulders. As he bent to pick it up, he got a whiff of flowers and sugar. Her hair, maybe, or her skin. It smelled just like you'd expect a mythical creature wandering around New York without a phone to smell like.

Whatever it was, it went straight to the calming section of his brain. The anxiety took a small step back, and he could think almost clearly.

Aiden coughed, put the hoodie back on her shoulders, and moved away. "Do you know if you have any allergies?"

She scrunched up her face. "No?"

He exchanged a glance with the other man, who raised his eyebrows and named one of the gluten-free, sugar-free, organic, superfood chains that were more and more prevalent in the city these days. "I think there's one on the corner."

Aiden nodded. "No sense giving her an allergic reaction on top of a concussion."

The older man checked his watch. "It seems like you've got this under control, and I need to get to work." He hurried off before Aiden or Bree could say anything.

Aiden bit the inside of his cheek. Of course he'd be left to clean things up on his own. He didn't have time to babysit. This woman was nothing to him, just a stranger he'd happened to be near when she'd hurt herself.

Most people in the city were friendly enough, and Aiden knew if he hadn't stopped, someone else would have. But he hadn't been able to resist. The unshakable sense of duty and discipline that got him to his goals was sometimes very inconvenient.

Standing next to Bree, the phone-less fairy, Aiden found he didn't mind so much right now that he was the one who always took charge of a messy situation.

"Where's that guy going?" She turned her wide eyes to his, as if she couldn't believe someone would just walk off when someone was hurt. "Do you need to go to work too? I'm sorry, I've messed up your whole morning."

She'd messed up a lot more than that, but Aiden couldn't very well say it when she was looking at him like that. Then someone on the street rushed past, bumping into her, and sent her flying into his side.

Without thinking, he wrapped his arms around her, the sugary, floral scent overpowering whatever logical part of his brain had considered leaving her to fend for herself like anyone else would.

"Don't worry about it. I won't leave you on your own."

Read the rest in Man Of My Dreams!

Man
of my
Dreams
DAPHNE JAMES HUFF

ABOUT THE AUTHOR

Daphne James Huff has been writing romance for adult and YA audiences since she was a young adult herself. Her favorite kind of story has a main character who thinks they've got it all figured out until someone barges into their life and messes everything up. She never says no to free cake or cheese, and can usually be found eating both to stay awake after reading all night.

Follow her on Instagram **@daphnejameshuff**